walk
among
birches

walk among birches

A NOVEL

CAROL MCAFEE

SOURCEBOOKS LANDMARK™
AN IMPRINT OF SOURCEBOOKS, INC.®
NAPERVILLE, ILLINOIS

Published by Sourcebooks, Inc.
P.O. Box 4410, Naperville, Illinois 60567-4410
(630) 961-3900
FAX: (630) 961-2168
www.sourcebooks.com

Library of Congress Cataloging-in-Publication Data

McAfee, Carol.
    Walk among Birches / by Carol McAfee.
        p. cm.
1. Psychiatric hospital patients—Fiction. 2. Mentally ill women—Fiction. 3.
Female friendship—Fiction. I. Title.

PS3563.C264 W35 2002
813'54—dc21

                                                          2002003138

        Printed and bound in the United States of America
            MV   10 9 8 7 6 5 4 3 2 1

To Ralph, Kate, Julia
You hold my heart.

NOTE TO THE READER

The book you hold in your hands is fiction but was inspired by real life. In many ways this book is the story of my personal journey through postpartum depression. It is my hope that the book will serve as a lighthouse and give light to those who need it.

ACKNOWLEDGMENTS

To those who gave me the courage to write.

To Wilma, my white-haired friend. You lift me up. You show me that kindness matters.

To Dianne, Beth and Ed, Muffin, Dr. Lois Conn, and the people of Govans Presbyterian Church.

To my editor Hillel Black and my agent Heide Lange.

And to the memory of my mom. I forget so much about you, but I remember you loved books. I hope you would love this one.

walk
among
birches

PART ONE

THE MENTAL WARD

When I see birches bend to left and right
Across the lines of straighter darker trees,
I like to think some boy's been swinging them.
But swinging doesn't bend them down to stay
As ice storms do.

—"Birches," by Robert Frost

CHAPTER 1

Never trust the quiet. Never, in particular, trust the quiet of a psychiatric ward.

All night it has been like this. The ward has fallen eerily silent, as if a fog has stolen over everything, leaving only the isolated beating of our hearts. Since our last round of medications, even the most talkative of us have found nothing to say. We have all retreated to our rooms, each of us wide awake, trembling, lonely, or maybe here I just speak for myself.

I am waiting. Yet, when the first scream comes, I am taken by surprise. I bolt upright in bed, my nightgown clotting behind my knees.

I tilt my head, listen.

In all that coiled up quiet, not one sound.

The second scream is hungry, piercing. The noise corkscrews down to the roots of my hair. My gums tingle. I think: What's going on? Who's screaming? What am I doing in this place where people scream? Whatever is wrong with me must be very wrong that I belong here.

There is no lock on my door. No way I can make myself safe. And right now, this very second, I wish to hell I *had* a lock because in the lull between screams, I hear a commotion in the hall immediately outside my door.

I want to duck under the thin comfort of my hospital blanket. I want to be home, with my husband Will and daughter Sarah, asleep, where I should be. Yet, curiosity impels me across my room and to the door. I seize the cool doorknob and crack open the door just enough to see Pammy, my favorite nurse, hastening past.

I shouldn't follow Pammy. I should stay put. But I venture out in my nightgown and bare feet. I don't know exactly what I think I'm doing, but I have it in my mind that, whatever happens, I want to make sure Pammy is safe.

And for the next few minutes I'm not sure she is.

Pammy runs down the hall while Joe, the head nurse, runs up the hall. Between them wails Florence Coombs, a stocky, cinnamon-skinned Jamaican woman who, until now, has been the very picture of meekness. Now, though, Florence looms huge; grotesque; monstrous. Clad in her eggplant purple muumuu, she begins to whirl like a crazed dancer, a tornado of color amidst the pallid white walls.

A tornado of color and of destruction, too, Florence gives cause for alarm. I wonder what her target will be, what she might break.

There are so many things she *can* break. There is the blood pressure equipment, a doctor's scale, and a cart on wheels that contains red loose-leaf binders, shelved like books. There is a binder on each patient. There is one on me: Janey Nichols, Room 118. Everything you are in this hospital, on this ward, what privileges you have, what foods you are given, and what medications, is in your binder. Everything, that is, of the sorts of things you can write down about a person without it having to do with their feelings or why they get up in the morning at all.

Florence shrieks again, then veers toward the nurses' station. And toward my carnations.

My carnations are from Will. He is that kind of husband. He is, as I am, suffering these days, staggering from the loss of his son, and I suppose he has, from his viewpoint, lost me too, his wife, to the psychiatric ward—at least temporarily. And yet he possesses the fortitude and generosity of heart to send me flowers. The only trouble is, the carnations came in a glass vase, and we aren't permitted glass in our rooms. So I donated my carnations to the nurses, who have placed the flowers where everyone can see them. Everyone, including Florence, who just now fixes on the flowers in her rage.

I know what Florence is going to do even before she does. Anger floods my body and my head spins as Florence lunges toward the vase and snatches it up. The carnations, pink, delicate, and ruffled, seem to me as fragile as I am just now; they are the symbol too of Will and me and all that survives of our love, and so I want to shout at Florence. I want to stop her from doing this thing that will hurt me. But I, after all, can do nothing.

The carnations quiver and bob madly on their green stems and that is all. That is the last thing I see before Florence hurls the vase to the floor, smashing the glass into a hundred finger-pricking shards. Water grenades in all directions, and Will's carnations scatter across the tiles and across my heart in a violent smear of pink.

Suddenly, briefly, it is silent.

The screaming has stopped. Time itself seems to stop. But the seconds tick on, and now lesser sounds make themselves known—the faint hum of the corridor's fluorescent lights, the distant murmur of the TV in the lounge, the rasping of my own breath. I notice these sounds before Florence moves, and the white heat of panic explodes in my brain.

Because she moves toward Pammy.

I have always liked Pammy; she has been, during the course of my illness, invariably kind. She is a decade younger than me, in her thirties, yet she is the wise one between us. She has assured me more than once that our lives have meaning, even though I've lost sight of what that might be.

And so now I am afraid for her, my nurse with the untamed mane of hair and cowboy boots. I am afraid of what Florence might do.

All around me, patients creep to their doors.

Pammy speaks in a soothing voice to Florence, and tries to get Florence to make eye contact. Florence ducks her head and bulls headlong toward Pammy, but Nurse Joe steps in to grab Florence from behind. Florence struggles to wrench free, but Joe's grip is too powerful. He twists Florence's arm back while Pammy, with her steady capable hands, readies the syringe and drives the needle home.

Not long at all before Florence quiets. Her knees sag. She lets Joe support her, then guide her down the hall. Meanwhile, Pammy turns. She still holds the syringe. She looks wasted, but I can tell that she is okay. She is unhurt, and I begin, for the first time, to breathe like my normal self again.

≈≍

They escort Florence to a place we patients know as the Quiet Room, a locked room padded with mats on the floors and walls. Then they assemble us for a brief meeting, which Joe leads. People talk for awhile, gradually the electricity spins out of the air, and the ward returns to what passes for normal around here. I notice lots of yawns. Patients begin to drift back to their rooms.

I'm about to head back to my own cell when Pammy catches my eye. In the crush of patients, she is several arm lengths away. Normally, I'd be happy to talk to Pammy, but at the moment I see she means business. She mouths: We need to talk. Talk? I think to myself, alarmed. In the wake of Florence's outburst, Pammy has a million things to do. Since when did I become a priority? What can't wait? I pretend I haven't seen Pammy, though I perfectly well have. I melt into the departing crowd, retreat to the sanctuary of my room, and lean my back against the door when it closes.

I am wondering, does it show, how bad I feel? Does grief show on a person, like mumps or chicken pox?

There is a knock on my door, a rat-ta-tat-tat, and Delphina, the patient from next door, pokes her head in. Delphina is a heavy woman with fleecy orange hair and skin as dark as a Hershey's kiss. "Pammy comin'. She say to tell you."

"Shucks," I say. "Foiled again."

"She say you avoidin' her."

"Not avoiding exactly. More like just trying not to be with her in the same place at the same time."

Delphina tilts her head, studies me. She's not well educated; she doesn't have a high school education, but she knows people. She knows me. She knows I always joke around when I hurt the worst, something Dr. Gard, my psychiatrist, hasn't even begun to figure out. "Florence, she scare you, dint she?"

"Me?" I tense. "Nah."

"You look like she done spooked your bones."

"She did, a little," I admit.

"Thank the Lord we ain't all that crazy."

"Yeah," I say. I know what Delphina means. She means that what happened tonight with Florence was unusual. This is a short-term unit for patients with treatable conditions. Most of us have never been in a psych ward before and won't be again. In my two weeks here I'd say the atmosphere is more like a college dorm than *Cuckoo's Nest*. The place is pretty routine: cooking, arts and crafts, group therapy. Generally our biggest excitement is to watch Nurse Joe, with his taxicab blond hair and braided biceps, swing down the hall.

"That why nights you can't sleep?" Delphina wants to know.

"What?"

"You too jumpy?"

"Sort of. I mean, that's part of it."

"What the other part?"

I hesitate, bite my lip.

"Cause you be too sad?"

"Oh, everybody's sad around here," I say.

"Yeah, but everybody ain't loss their baby."

Delphina's words stun me. I have said nothing about this. Not to anyone. Who else in the ward knows? Everybody? I don't like everybody knowing. "Hey," I snap, "why don't you mind your own goddamn business!"

"Sor-ree, girl," she says.

There is a moment of tense silence between us.

Delphina sags a little as she stands there beside me. I have hurt her when she has done nothing except try and be my friend.

"Delph," I say softly. I reach out and touch Delphina's arm just as Pammy appears at my door. Maybe I want to include Delphina in something, make us friends again, or maybe I want to make Pammy think I'm in good spirits. Either way, I end up greeting my nurse with a grin, "Come on in and join the party! You're a little late, though. Delph and I just polished off the champagne."

"Mmn, mmn, good bubbly, too." Delphina laughs. "Sweet."

"Oh?" Pammy says.

"And that dee-licious wedding cake," Delphina winks at me. "Too bad they none of that left neither."

Pammy strides further into the room. "So, who got married?"

"Uh, we did, didn't we, Delphina?" I say.

"Yes, indeedy. We's gay," Delphina says.

"Geez," Pammy says. "All this and you didn't invite me."

"Well," I demur, "the cake wasn't really all that good. It was coconut."

"I likes coconut," Delphina says. Then she looks at me. She knows that Pammy needs to talk to me alone. Pammy, who has come here not for fun after all, Pammy who is after the truth. "Well, see y'all later," Delphina says, and then she's gone.

Pammy scrapes up a chair beside my bed.

Watching her I take a deep shaky breath.

The nurses here don't wear uniforms, and tonight Pammy is dressed in her usual jeans and cowboy boots. She tosses back her hair, which is as brown and dull as baking potatoes, hair so plain it provides a fascinating contrast to her face, not plain at all, her features mobile and animated, her eyes enormous and blue.

Pammy meets my gaze, then gestures toward my bed, "Have a seat."

"Sure," I say. I sit gingerly on the edge of my mattress. I am toying with my wedding ring. I slide the ring up and down my finger. It is a silver ring with a diamond in the middle. The diamond feels hard and sharp.

Pammy knows I am nervous. "I'm not the Spanish Inquisition, you know."

"Good," I say. "Because I don't remember a lick of high school Spanish. Except, oddly, I can say the Spanish equivalent to *Pepe, hurry up. Come into the house, we're having supper.*"

"Well, that's handy," Pammy says.

"Especially if your name's Pepe," I say.

Pammy's smile vanishes. She gives me a frankly assessing look, "As your assigned nurse, I must say I have some concerns."

I abandon the ring on my finger. "Con—uh—concerns?"

"Yes. You're scheduled for discharge Friday, but I wonder if that's not premature."

"No, I'm ready!"

Pammy stares at me.

"Sorry," I say. "Go on."

"Well, let's look at the facts. While you're pleasant to be around and are clearly trying to make yourself part of things around here, it's obvious to me that you're suffering, Janey. You don't eat. Don't sleep. Will told me you seem sad all the time."

I frown at Pammy. How can I tell her that I am eating, that I am feeling great, when in fact I am not? She sees my untouched meal trays. She comes into my room to talk, or reads the reports of the other nurses; they all know I spend my nights huddled in the chair by the window, peering out at the darkness. They think I can't sleep because my body won't let me, but this is only partly true. I won't let my body sleep, either. Whenever I lay down I feel so empty. I miss the bloom of pregnancy, that fullness. Maybe that's why, whenever I do lie down these days, I curl up on my side and draw my knees up to my chest; maybe I'm trying to fill the cavity where the baby used to be.

"Whatchya thinkin'?" Pammy asks.

I'm thinking how I wouldn't mind being left alone, thank you very much, but I can't say this. It would be antisocial and maladjusted, so I say nothing. I bow my head. "People think I'm crazy."

"How's that?"

I shrug. "They figure, you're in the loony bin, you're loony."

Pammy shakes her head. "Janey, you're not loony. This is an entry-level psych ward. We're a sand lot gang, not the major leagues. Most patients here, like you, suffer from mood disorders. You're perfectly lucid, mentally coherent, no one doubts that..."

Pammy keeps on talking, but I stop listening. I feel my throat tighten with yearning, for what I don't know. My heart thuds, my breath comes shallow and fast. I don't know where to look. I don't want to meet Pammy's gaze because my eyes look scared to death about what is happening to me, and why I am here in a psychiatric ward. Finally, I settle for staring at Pammy's blue jeans. I realize that she's worn the denim clear through in the right knee. It's just one big raggedy slit. I glimpse, through the slit, the pale yellow bone that is Pammy's kneecap, and I get all choked up.

"You mean," I finally dare to look at her, "nobody here thinks I'm crazy?"

"You're not crazy."

"I'm here because of a mood disorder."

"That's right."

"Because I'm depressed."

I expect Pammy to say *That's right* again, but she surprises me. "Oh, it's gone way beyond that, don't you think?"

"Beyond what?" I stiffen.

"Janey, you're so busy trying to hide it, but you can't."

"Hide what?"

"You're suicidal."

⚮

Suicidal.

The word hangs in the air between us. I'm not touching it.

"Janey," Pammy prompts me, "do you have a response to that?"

"Not really," I say. I shove my feelings down and down inside me, like someone hastily thrusting wrinkled clothes into the darkness of a duffle bag. I'm not going to think about the reason for my admittance, about the pills. "Listen," I say, "it's late."

"Yes, it is," Pammy says. She looks at me and her eyes fill with sympathy. Maybe she lost a child once herself. Or, maybe she suffered another loss, a parent or best friend, someone so valuable she knew she would never, from that day forward, be the same. "Oh, by the way," she adds, "Dr. Gard's going on vacation for the week. Dr. Silverberg's filling in."

"Yeah? Who's he?"

"It's a she."

"Oh."

"She's terrific. Formal, reserved, but you'll like her. They say she works magic."

"Really?" I try to make my voice hopeful, upbeat. But what if the magical Dr. Silverberg can't straighten me out? So far Dr. Gard, with his abstracted air and cool manner, hasn't had much luck.

I don't know what Pammy would have said next, or if she would have pressured me to talk more about my feelings. Happily, she is called away on the intercom.

"I gotta go," Pammy says. She gets up from her chair and moves to the door, which is a relief to me. But, she lingers, "Promise me you'll eat more. You're positively gaunt."

"I'll get something down," I say dismissively. Still, Pammy doesn't go, she just stands there at my door. Tension thrums between us. You would never know that we had shared things, that she had told me about her farm in Monkton with its sagging hayloft, its horse and chickens. Along with being a gentleman farmer, her husband is a sailor, of all things.

"Can I fix you something?" she presses. "A bagel?"

"Not now," I say.

"But you'll eat?"

"Sure, yeah, sure," I say, though I won't meet her steady gaze. I know she is worried about me. I'm worried, too. I look down at the floor, and when I look up again she is gone.

Alone in my room, I stand at my window and press my forehead against the cool of the glass. Outside it is dark as charcoal. The moon doesn't help much, obscured as it is by clouds. All I can see is the hard rubble of earth from which only the boldest of daffodils have dared sprout. Even these close up tight when night falls, slamming their green leafy doors soon after the sun sinks low on the horizon and a chill sneaks over the raw, patchy grass. It is April in Baltimore, a city known for its pleasant springtimes. Not this year. This year winter just won't let go.

I grind my forehead into the cool spot in the window. I breathe in and out. The ward, I notice, is quiet. Not the coiled-up quiet from before but restful. I think everyone must be sleeping except me, but then I hear Mr. Kramer. He moans *help me, help me*, for the first time tonight; it is a plaintive sound, like the loons calling to one another across the lake through a misty rain.

I know about lakes and I know about loons. We own a cabin in the Adirondacks that we share with Ruth Weber, my white-haired neighbor who used to be my mother's best friend and is now mine. The cabin in the Adirondacks is part of my soul. I have gone there every year of my life.

Harsh country, those Adirondacks. Historically, in winter, even the Indians couldn't make a go of it. The tribe that lived there, the Algonquins, couldn't scare up enough food to live on, so their blood enemies, the Iroquois, called them bark-eaters. A slur. Meaning you can't hunt, you're forced to gnaw bark from the trees. That's what Adirondacks means. It comes from the Iroquois *ratirontacks,* which means bark-eaters.

I have been in the Adirondacks in winter myself. In winter the cold is ruthless and unforgiving of even the slightest mistake. The birches form slick pods of ice on their branches; the lake freezes over and you can go snowshoeing, if you dare. In spring, the ice starts to break up. This, too, is a dangerous time. The more moderate spring temperatures warm the shoreline and the air; your numb toes and fingers rejoice; they are in no danger from the cold. The ice, however, is a different story. The ice has become your biggest enemy, your worst nightmare. The ice will play tricks on you. The depth of the ice has little to do with its strength. In winter, two inches of clear strong ice will support one fisherman and all his gear. In spring, should you be unlucky, should you chance upon ice rotted underneath, dark and honeycombed on top, twelve inches may not be enough.

If you break through the ice and do not panic and are prepared—you have some car keys with you, or an ice pick, or something sharp to gain purchase on the ice—you may live. If you are not so lucky, if you thrash around and lose the oxygen trapped in air bubbles in your layers of clothes, if you're wearing wool that soaks up that cold water and urges you down into the black swirling abyss, hypothermia and shock will take you fast. You will try to live; you will do your best; you will give it everything you have, but that water is just so cold. It is cold enough to make you forget your name, or why it is you bother to struggle at all. Your last thoughts, most likely, will be peaceful. You will see the white blaze of birch trees arching high toward the sun, and the last thing you will feel, ironically, is warm, and the warmth will sing in your veins.

Help me, Mr. Kramer cries again. I know a nurse will get to him soon. The nurses are, for the most part, kind to Mr. Kramer, but the pain Mr. Kramer feels comes from deep inside and no one can really help him. I lift my forehead from the window. I still feel the cool of the glass even though my forehead's no longer pressing against anything. Maybe I'm still thinking about thawing ice. Falling through. Black water. How cold beyond cold it can be.

There is an irritating, jangling sound close by. My room phone ringing. Ringing not three feet away, on my desk.

I snatch up the receiver, praying for Will. Only Will can ease me back into the present. Because, the truth is, I am still feeling the sting of the cold. I am still travelling inside my head.

"Hello?" I say, warily.

"Hey," Will says. "Is this Janey's Pizza Parlor?"

"Yes." I grin. "This is Aunt Chovy speaking. May I take your order?"

"I want a large pizza with sausage and pepperoni, and, yeah, toss on a few mushrooms."

"No problem," I say. "And where shall I deliver?"

"To a lonely guy who misses his wife."

"Aw," I say. There is a long pause between us.

Finally Will says, "I called because I just wanted to hear your voice."

"Me too," I say. "I mean, I like hearing your voice, too." And it's true. Will's nightly phone call is something I very much look forward to. Sometimes hearing his voice and replaying it in my head is what carries me through until morning. I have always loved my husband's voice. It's like an airline pilot's, or a young commanding officer's. You would follow that voice anywhere because the owner of that voice would not lead you anyplace that was not safe, or if he did, he would take whatever was coming first, to try and spare you.

Will is saying, "...but I bet you've forgotten all about me. I'm not a heartthrob like that stud muffin, what's his name? The head nurse."

"Joe."

"Yeah, Joe."

"Well, he may be cute, but he isn't you, Will. He didn't marry me, and he didn't give me Sarah."

At the mention of our daughter's name, there is silence between us. I have reminded us of our other child, the one we no longer have.

Will, gamely, tries to salvage something between us, to keep us both afloat. "Did you get the flowers I sent? The carnations?"

"Yes, thank you. I love them."

"They on your windowsill?"

"Not exactly."

"I figured they'd jazz up your room a little, keep Ruth's geraniums company. Exchange knock-knock jokes. You know." He pauses. "What do you mean, not exactly?"

"Well," I say, and then I immediately want to kick myself. Let him think I can take solace from his flowers. I turn to Ruth's potted geraniums on my sill. Their red petals are startlingly vibrant, but they are not kept company by an arrangement of carnations.

"I thought you said you got them."

"I did, but they came in a glass vase, and we can't have glass in our rooms. You know, suicide risk and all that. So, they put them out at the nurses' station, and everything was fine until Florence got a hold of them."

"Florence?"

"A patient here. She went a little crazy."

"Well, she's in the right place."

"No, I mean, really, Will. She smashed the vase."

"She hurt anybody? I mean, you're okay, right?"

"I'm okay."

He must hear from my voice, which he knows so well, that I am not okay, after all. "Did you...witness this? The vase smashing and all."

"Yes. The thing is, I knew it was going to happen. But I couldn't stop her."

"No. It's good, Janey. I'm glad you didn't try to intervene." He pauses. "So then what happened?"

"They sedated her. The rest of us, we're back in our rooms."

He sighs. "I wish you were here, back at home. You don't need this."

"So, smuggle me in a saw in a cake. Or, a spoon, so I can tunnel my way out. No, seriously, Will, it's okay. Your flowers were beautiful, but there will be other flowers."

"I'll send roses next time. With giant thorns."

"Yeah," I smile. "Good idea."

Silence falls between us.

Then Will adds, "Maybe I shouldn't've sent flowers in the first place." His voice, at first, sounds merely regretful, but then it cracks, and he reveals himself to be what he indeed is: a man in torment. And so now, in addition to feeling sad about the flowers, I feel concern for my husband. I am depressed, my mind isn't half what it normally is, but even I know the guilt he feels isn't about those carnations. "Look, Will, don't feel bad about it. It's not your..." *Fault*, I mean to say. But the lump in my throat is just too big, or maybe I don't want Will to feel all that much better after all.

"I know what you're thinking," he says.

"What?"

"You're mad at me."

"I'm not."

"Admit it. Do me the honor."

"But I'm not mad!" My heart hammers fast and loud.

"Oh, yeah? Why won't you look me in the eye, Janey?"

"Well, that's kind of hard to do over the phone."

"And you won't talk."

"We're talking now, aren't we?"

"Just listen, okay? I'm sorry I wasn't thrilled about the pregnancy. Not 100 percent. Not at first. But I warmed up to the idea. I wanted this baby too, and then when we lost him...it's like you blame me. But, Janey, don't you think I feel bad enough without you putting that on me? Without you—"

"I don't—"

"Oh, yes you do! But, I'm not that powerful. I didn't make what happened happen."

"I never said you—"

"Oh, be honest, Janes. You'll never forgive me. Never."

"How do you know what I can and can't forgive?"

"I *know* you."

"No, you don't... you don't know everything!" I shout, clutching the receiver. I'd better stop now, put a muzzle on it. I stand shivering at my window and take deep sucking breaths to calm down while I peer out into the night. Close by I make out a cluster of pine trees, their spiky silhouettes black against a gray mop of sky. This spring is so depressing. I mean, I think it would be depressing even if I weren't depressed. I don't want to say anything to Will for a minute, not until I'm sure I won't utter something sarcastic or just plain mean. I try to even myself out and remember some good times when Will and I didn't yell at each other over the phone. What comes to me is a time before this past winter, when we went to the Miranda Christmas Tree Farm—Will, Sarah, and I.

I was four months pregnant at the time.

❦

We jump onto the hay wagon as Luke Pederson fires up the tractor. The ride is bumpy. My camera swings on its strap and our Shelty, Toby, holds his ears pressed close to his head as the wagon bounces out into the fields, past the apple orchard, and to the stand of Douglas firs where Luke leaves us. It is a warm day, for November on the cusp of December. In the sun you need a jacket but no gloves. Once in awhile the wind ruffles your hair so you feel like a pirate on a crow's nest leaning into the wind, or like an adventurer.

Sarah, her fiery red hair bobbing in a ponytail, darts in and out among the pointed trees, searching for fat pine cones. Will surveys the landscape, drinking in the fresh air, which I drink in right along with him. You can still smell apples even though they are all down by now; the air is redolent with the sweet scent of their decay as their rotting skins mix with the humus of the ground. Will looks at me, then begins to hike purposefully up the tallest hill with Toby close on his heels. When I see man and dog headed up that slope, I feel my chest grow tight with so much happiness it is like pain, because clearly these two are meant for each other. They are so much alike. Toby is an undemonstrative loyal dog and my husband is equally under- stated, a quiet man, full of kindness. There is an unapologetic gentleness and femininity about Will; he loves to cook and garden; he has more women friends than men. I can't speak for Toby's cooking and gardening skills—he keeps these well hidden—but he is as gentle a soul as my husband. Will told me once, "If I were a dog, I'd be Toby," and the thing was I didn't laugh; I knew just what he meant.

And so the sight of them, our handsome dog and my handsome, long- legged husband with his roundish face and silky black hair, makes me pause for an instant and squint like I am looking into the sun when in truth I am looking at something much brighter, for just then Sarah bounds into the picture, and I am looking at everything I love most. Everything but my friend Ruth, I should say; she's part of our family, too. But, anyway, there is that forgiving sun shining down on us, there is that country air with its haunting autumnal scent of apples fallen and rotting on the ground, and I feel suffused with joy at all life has to offer. My lumberjack boots crunch on the tawny carpet of pine needles as Will gives me a hand up the last steep slope.

"Janey," he says. "What about this tree? This one here?" He stands by his choice, a medium-sized Douglas fir as proudly as if he'd grown it himself.

"Mmmm," I say, considering. Not too tall, or too fat, not too spindly on top, "I like it."

"And your opinion, madam?" Will turns to Sarah.

Sarah approaches the tree, and reaches to explore its soft needles. "I think it's a keeper, Dad."

So, it is decided.

I want to memorialize our tree as it is before we chop it down, so I set my camera on automatic shoot and it snaps a picture of the three of us, or four of us, if you count the dog: Will has his arm looped around Sarah; Sarah is holding Toby's collar while Toby strains to be free; he's keen on chasing a squirrel; and I'm standing happily, with my hand on the fir's knotted trunk and my pregnant belly poking out from beneath my navy pea-coat that I can no longer button at the waist.

I feel sad when Will saws through the last outpost of trunk and our fir thuds to the ground. The woodsy smell of sawdust fills my lungs. I know we'll cherish our tree, water it every day to keep its needles soft, and hang our ornaments and our tiny white-bulbed lights from its branches. And I know our tree will be much admired by the neighborhood when we hold our yearly Christmas party, an informal neighborhood get-together during which we fortify ourselves with oven-warmed casseroles and biscuits, and then brave the chilly night to go caroling at the nursing home up the street.

"Look at Toby sniff the needles, Mom," Sarah says. "He likes the tree, too."

Sarah takes my hand as we head toward the rumble of the red tractor, Luke coming back to retrieve us. I don't comment on how sticky Sarah's fingers are—truly they are gooey with pine sap. Holding my hand is something Sarah doesn't do much lately, and I don't want to do anything to disturb the curl of her fingers in mine.

Back at the weathered picnic tables by the souvenir shop, we drink mugs of hot mulled cider and warm our hands. Helen Pederson, Luke's wife, is a gray-haired woman with calloused palms. She's in charge of the Christmas wreaths each year, and each year her nimble fingers get punctured by the wires she uses to fasten the pine garlands together. Helen is patient with

Sarah and lets her design her own wreath. Sarah ponders each decision mightily because that is Sarah's way: should she tie a styrofoam teddy bear with trumpet onto her wreath, or a Santa Claus with striped candy cane? What color ribbon, tartan plaid or plain red? And what size pine cone? Sarah finishes with her creation long after Will and I have the tree baled in white netting, long after our hot cider is gone and the heat from the lingering sun strikes feebly on our cheeks. Sarah is so happy. She parades her wreath to the van. We wave good-bye to the Pedersons and bump down the rutted country road. Sarah begins to sing. Not Christmas carols, but something she learned in music—an Irish ballad that makes Will smile into his rearview mirror and then at me, beside him. For a brief instant, he reaches for my hand and squeezes it, then he devotes himself to driving again. But that instant when we touched was enough. The van is filled with our love. There is Sarah, the miracle we created together. And now there is another miracle on the way, the humble bulge beneath my peacoat. I place my hand on the swell of my abdomen and think how lucky our unborn son is, to join this family. I had a lonely childhood myself, with largely absent parents, and for a brief moment I wish I am my unborn son, coming into a world where he is so much wanted, where every year growing up, he will have a Christmas tree farm to come to and a blue spruce or a Douglas fir on a cold sunny hillside just waiting to be found.

❦

I turn sharply from my hospital window.

"Will," I say now, in a low voice, into the phone.

"What?" he says.

I want to say, *I forgive you,* but I can't. Will's right. I blame him. I hold him accountable, despite all the good times, like the day we chose our Christmas tree. "Uh, just nothing, I guess. We should hang up. It's late."

"Wait a second," he says. "You got awfully quiet there. What're you thinking?"

"And, plus you've got your trial tomorrow," I say.

"Janey, you're not gonna open up, are you?"

I wrap the black phone cord around my hand tighter and tighter until my knuckles turn white. I think about the phone cord. You can tell I'm in a low security ward. They would never let you have lengthy phone cords if you were seriously mentally ill.

"Are you?" he repeats.

I say nothing.

"Janey, sweetheart, please?"

I step all the way back from the window. I look at the white cinder block wall and the one drawing I have scotchtaped there. It's Sarah's depiction of a mermaid, a voluptuous creature sheathed in aquamarine scales, with spidery eyelashes and red pouting lips. "Will...I can't."

There is silence on the line. Is that static or do I hear Will's heart break? It's true I am breaking my husband's heart by my silences, but I can't seem to help this. My feelings, these days, are too primitive for words. They are pre-words. They are wolves howling at the moon.

"All right, I'll let you go," Will says, defeated. "I mean, you're right. It is late. I'll come see you tomorrow."

"Good," I say.

"Try and get some sleep."

"Okay," I say.

"I love you, Janey."

What? I think. *Did I hear that right?* I've got the receiver pressed up snug against my ear, the seashell swirl of my pinna is laid back flat against my skull, and I'm leaning into my husband's words, afraid to believe what he's just said. It's been weeks since Will has told me he loved me, mostly because I have made myself so unavailable, so unwilling to hear any endearment that might come from him. I have made myself inaccessible and yet he has found me. I'm stunned; tears well in my eyes.

I'm feeling worse, now, than when I first answered the phone. Worse, because Will has given me exactly what I want, and that is hope. Something to live for, something to climb out of this depression for, and I don't know, frankly, if I'm up for that. I grind the heel of my palm into my forehead, where the beginning rumblings of a headache stir. I breathe in and out, but I don't say anything, not one word. Finally I croak, "Yeah, me too. I love you too, Will." But, I don't say this to Will, I say this to nobody, to an empty worm hole of black silence, since Will has already hung up.

≈⌒

After my talk with Will, I try for about an hour to fall asleep, but it's no good. My heart beats like a savage thing. My ear pulses into my pillow. I visualize myself at our cabin on Windsor Island in the Adirondacks. I am swimming in the cool of the lake, cradled in the cove just down the pine-needled path from the cabin. I float on the water on my back. The sun warms my cheeks. The waves lap me gently...

The vision vanishes. I can't fake it anymore, lying on my back, the soothing motion of the waves, or the healing power of anything remotely like the sun.

I am, suddenly, freezing. I burrow under my blanket, seeking warmth. My toes are cold, my lips. I shiver. Seconds later, I am too hot. My face is flushed, my chest bursts into flames. I thrash upright in bed and hurl my blanket off me, just as there is a soft knocking at my door.

"Er, come in," I say, in what I hope passes for a normal voice. I was cold; now I am burning up. Is my face flushed? Do I appear ill?

Pammy walks in. She is doing a suicide check, but she doesn't make a big deal of it. She doesn't nail me under the glare of a flashlight, like some of the other nurses. In fact, she doesn't carry a flashlight at all. And yet, in the semi-darkness, she can see me well enough. She says, "You look like shit."

"Yeah? Well, you should see the other guy," I say, swallowing around the sharp edges of my throat. Every word I say, it seems, lodges like a knife. I think of loons, how they swallow fish whole, just gobble them down. Their throats are elastic. "I thought you went home."

"Actually, I'm about to," Pammy comes closer, " but I wanted to stop by and see you first."

"I appreciate that," I say.

She appraises me, "You take your meds?"

"Yes."

"But obviously they're not working, because here you are, still awake. I'd give you something else, but that's all Dr. Gard has listed on your chart."

"That's okay," I say. Though it's not okay. I am wondering how I can possibly journey through this endless night.

Pammy is feeling almost as badly as I am, I can tell. When she spots my Sony Walkman on the shelf, she suggests, lamely, "You could try those meditation tapes Ruth gave you."

"Yeah, maybe I will, thanks."

"Your Ruth seems like a wonderful friend to have."

"She is." I swallow dryly. I have so much to be grateful for. Why do I feel like I'm drowning? I lean back on my hands, and my palms press into the mattress. I'm not used to sleeping on a mattress this narrow, but this is not why I can't sleep. I am tired, even though my heart races. My body is at war with itself, and I am tired.

Pammy continues to study me. Another person might feel obligated to say something, to break the silence. Not Pammy. She's used to the silence of wide spaces, out there on that farm of hers in Monkton. I'm not comfortable with silences, though, and so I blurt the first thing that comes to mind, "It's not just Will and Sarah I've deserted, but my first-graders. Antonia Gianelli's a good substitute, but she's young; she's green. I worry about my kids getting enough individual attention."

"You really care about your students, don't you?" Pammy says.

"Well," I say. You wouldn't think, with so many in a class, twenty-three, I'd get to know all of them, but I do. I know which ones skipped breakfast that morning, and which ones sit against the wall at recess longing for a friend.

One of my students, Charlie Moody, has been doing a lot of sitting on walls lately. I know that ever since his parents separated, Charlie has managed to alienate every single one of his pals. Charlie looks like a punk rocker, with his spiky marigold hair and pierced earlobe. One time Charlie wrote a poem about the rain, only it was really about riding in the car with his mother, listening to the dull metronome of the windshield wipers, and feeling lonesome, since nobody talked. The split between Charlie's parents is ugly, or so I've heard. They are fighting over custody. Charlie must feel rent in two, and I am not there to help him.

"I see the wheels in your head turning," Pammy says. "What're you thinking?"

I sigh. "I've let everybody down."

"Everybody?" Pammy says. "Don't take on that kind of guilt; you've got enough to deal with. You just hang in there and that Prozac will kick in soon. Remember, it takes a few weeks for the medicine to take hold. In the meantime—"

"I know," I say. "You want me to get eating."

"Right." She nods. "So eat, okay?"

"I'll do Henry the Eighth and his gout proud."

"That's my girl." Pammy reaches over and touches my arm. I like it that she touches me. I miss the physical contact I have with Will. When Pammy moves toward the door, I feel like crying. "It's late," she says gently. "I've gotta get on home."

"See you," I say. "Say hi to the chickens and horses."

"Actually, we've just got the one horse."

"What's his name?"

"Bones, but he's fat." She laughs. I turn away because I can't bear to watch her go. Tomorrow, when I will see her again, seems a long way off. I listen and hear the scuffing of Pammy's snub-toed cowboy boots as she walks her funky walk down the hall. Then, I hear nothing. The silence stretches all around me, like those terrible seconds that stretched on forever in the examination room when we couldn't find a heartbeat.

Oh, I don't want to think about that. I don't want to go there.

I quickly fumble for Ruth's Walkman, scramble to fit the headphones over my ears, and switch the cassette player to on.

I hate meditation tapes, but I need distraction, and this will suffice.

I let my head loll back against the pillow.

A soothing male voice tells me to close my eyes and imagine I am walking beside a waterfall. I am hearing the sound of the rain. I am skeptical, but I quiet my breathing and listen. I lower my body into this nature fantasy; I imagine damp green moss on the north side of trees, ferns bobbing, toadstools, liverworts, chipmunks darting in and out among the bracken. I hike on. I hear more water than I ever want to hear again—water cascading over a falls, drumming on a roof, ocean surf. And then come the bird calls. Singular calls first: an owl hoots, a mourning dove coos, and I can assimilate this. But, then the birds get chatty and all the bird songs begin to overlap: *sweet peabody, peabody* crashes into *caw caw, chirp,*

chirp. There is the cacaphony of collision, a train wreck of sound. My heart slams into my rib cage. I whip the headphones from my head, and leap up from the bed. So much for Ruth's meditation tape.

I am quite wild by now, and it is only 2 A.M., hours away from the salvation of daybreak. In desperation, I begin to pace. Eight strides to my window, eight to the door. My head whirls with images—Will, Sarah, and I choosing our Christmas tree; the lake at Windsor Island; my first-grade classroom; my students. I stop pacing. The hospital room tilts, and I begin to hyperventilate. Another panic attack, or is it my hormones, the plunge in estrogen since the baby? I peel off my nightgown and let it drop to the floor.

Nude except for my underwear, I perch on the edge of my bed and bury my head in my hands. I think that if I just close my eyes long enough, but no, when I open them again, things are no better. There is not only darkness, but that silence again, mushrooming all around me. Am I going crazy? I mean, for real this time?

I've got to do something. Keep busy. I decide to take a shower. A shower isn't conversation or being with someone who loves you, but at least it's noise. And too, if I'm going insane, at least I'll get there clean.

I draw my robe snugly around me as I navigate the corridor to the communal bathroom. Luckily, I see Lil before she sees me. I have to pass by her room without her noticing me, or she will reel me in, wanting to talk.

Lil, I don't know her last name. I know she's in her room, though, because her door is wide open, and I can see her. She's working on a wooden stool for her granddaughter. She's been working on that stool for as long as I've been here. Sanding the wood with such loving care, and now painting it. Lil's mahogany brow furrows as she dips her brush into a bottle of acrylic red.

I am inches from her room now. I hold my breath.

Every other day Lil has these mysterious treatments. The nurses wheel her away on a white-sheeted gurney, and she doesn't return until several hours later, looking very doped up with a looped IV bandaged to her arm. It took me awhile to realize it's electroshock therapy she's getting. I know lots of people get electroshock, and it works, too, lots of times, but it seems medieval, and it scares me. Whenever I think about all those wires and electrodes, goosebumps prickle along the nape of my neck, and I pray to God, please, don't make me have to do that, please make me well.

I am just outside Lil's door, hurrying past, head down, when, to my horror, just as I am squarely visible, Lil arrests her paintbrush midair to fix her gaze on me. Her face, the color of arable black soil plowed through with wrinkles, full of hard living and truths too painful to put into words, lights up when she sees me.

I duck my head and slip on by, coward that I am. I don't acknowledge her, even with a nod. Her son died, too, only hers was grown-up. His name was Calvin. Her grief for him runs deep, and I can't bear to add it to my own.

In the shower the spray is warm, and I begin to fractionally relax. Still, I shower like a penitent, scrubbing myself until my skin feels raw. I deserve it. My body is not much. My body let me down. My body was unable to carry to term and bring into the world a squalling pink baby.

And so, yes, I hate my body, and yet, paradoxically, I feel a tender compassion toward my arms, my legs, my breasts, my now-shrunken uterus. In brief fleeting moments of illumination, I sense I have done nothing wrong. I would have done anything for my child; I would have traded my life for his, so mostly I am confused. How could my baby die, if I did nothing wrong? It is frightening to consider a universe so random. Where does God fit in? What kind of God is that, a reluctant and tardy member of the audience who slips into his seat when the lights are down, late in the second act?

I rinse thoroughly. The shower thunks as I step quickly into my terrycloth robe. I pad over to the sinks. Above the sinks, the mirror stares at me, so I stare back. I don't like what I see—my stringy auburn hair and those tomato-colored blotches on my face from what I don't know. My medication? My skin is otherwise a sickly, fishbelly white. But my eyes are worst of all. I appear frightened, as, indeed, I am.

Back in my room, I lie down. The shower was a mistake, that much is clear. My skin feels electrified, and thoughts ricochet around in my brain. What's more, my hair is damp, and this makes me grow chilled. They don't have the heat on very high tonight, and with my hair all damp, I start to shiver. I curl up on my side and hug my knees to my chest. I've thrown a sweatshirt on over my nightgown and now I coax its cotton rhubarb sleeves down over my fingers. Lying on my side, I feel as lonely as I've ever been. I am conscious of the weight of my breasts. They are floppy and useless and I hate them. The baby never nursed, so my milk never came in, so now I think: What do I have breasts for? What good are they?

Oh, Jesus.

I glance at the clock. Hours to go until dawn, what shall I do?

I am too tired to pace, too jazzed to sleep.

Will and Sarah, though, I bet they're sleeping. I think of Will in our bed. What a luxury it would be to curl up next to him. And, when morning comes, to talk over coffee. I wonder what happens these days when Will goes off to work, and Sarah goes off to school, and Ruth returns to her home across the street. Does the phone ring in the empty house? Or have our friends, after weeks of being solicitous and well-intentioned, given up on us? They don't know what to say or they're scared of me; maybe they've never known anyone who's depressed before. Depressed, sure, but not this kind of depressed: where your whole body, like some monstrous office building, starts snapping out lights, one floor here, one floor there, in an effort to plunge itself into a Saturday of darkness. I think of my dad in Florida, retired from his busy practice, and of course my mom, I think of her. I always think of her when I'm sick. She's been dead a long time now, but sometimes your mind plays tricks on you, and teases you into believing someone is a phone call away when the truth is they are beyond the furthest reaches of long distance, beyond even the coldest planets and stars.

Down the hall I hear Mr. Kramer lament *help me, help me* again. I think of the tremolo of the loons on Windsor Lake. Songs or madness? Music or a wrenching cry of loneliness? Like the loons of Northern Adirondack lakes, Mr. Kramer is shy and solitary. His pain is primitive, the real thing. I wonder if he has ventured beyond all human language. I wonder if anyone can help him. I wonder if anyone can help *me*. I think about the doctor Pammy mentioned. The magical Dr. Silverberg. I try to imagine what she looks like. Is she old? Fat? Ugly at least? I don't want to talk to someone who has it all together when I so clearly do not.

I flop onto my back and open my eyes and stare up at the ceiling. My thoughts stop slamming around like black balls on a squash court. All that is left standing are walls of white silence. I am trapped in this airless space. Between white walls. Just like I was in the examination room.

I should flee this thought. Fight it. All night I have tried to beat back the memory, but now I am tired. Now, finally, it is time.

᠁᠁

I am lying on the examination table, my legs hiked apart, my heels pressing into the stirrups. Will stands next to me. He has come with me to all of my appointments. "Our little rabbit," he always says, when he hears the rapid thump thump of the baby's heart. But this time when Dr. Lingstrom moves the fetalscope over the stretch marks of my abdomen, we hear nothing, and Will doesn't get to say "our little rabbit."

Frowning, Dr. Lingstrom says calmly but with real concern in her voice, "Let's do a sonogram," and after that comes the nightmare, the labor induced by Pitocin, and so much pain. But, the worst part is that original silence that holds the seeds of all our sadness in it. I lie stiffly on the examination table, feet in the stirrups, drawing inward away from Will, closing down, walling myself off, and doing this all so quickly, I am deep inside myself by the time Will reaches over to take my hand. He cross-stitches his fingers with mine, a feeling I know well, but this time I don't let Will comfort me, or himself; I push him away. I don't want to touch Will or anyone, maybe ever again.

We listen more and more anxiously for the baby's heartbeat, tilting our ears toward the swell of my abdomen, not daring to breathe, just listening, listening to the silence. I feel so cold in my skimpy, blue, flowered hospital gown—the kind you can never remember if it ties in the back or the front?— cold enough so my own heart slows, freezes, stops. The child I have been carrying all this time, loving all this time, will, upon our meeting him and forever after, never kick his legs in jubilation at our approach or turn his smile toward our voices.

Our son has made it thirty-seven weeks and no further.

CHAPTER 2

Dr. Silverberg is not old, or fat, or even ugly. I know because I get my first glimpse of her in the morning. It's breakfast time. Delphina and I are sitting in the little cafeteria when we see her.

"It got to be her," Delphina says. "She the only new face around here."

"True," I say.

We take a good long look at Dr. Silverberg, who is, just this moment, standing behind the nurses' station, poring over patient notes. She is surprisingly tall and elegant, dressed in a skirt and silk blouse the soft shade of plum beneath her unbuttoned white lab coat. She is tall enough, in fact, that she towers over the nurses around her. Her hair is long and black, streaked with gray. She's my age, forty, maybe a few years older.

"She be smart," Delphina observes.

"Why's that?"

"She read fast."

"Maybe she's not retaining anything."

"No, she got a look about her," Delphina says. Then she turns to focus hard on me, "Why you so interested in her, anyway?"

I shrug, "I have a nine o'clock appointment with her."

"Thas' in ten minutes. You be nervous?"

"Why should I be?"

"Why, darlin'? Cause we be like watermelons in this place. Them shrinks split us open and all our juices run out. All that pink, all them black seeds hiding inside ain't hiding no more."

"Well," I say, "in terms of watermelon, I prefer seedless myself."

"That make sense, girl. But seedless you ain't. You got more secrets than anybody."

We watch as Dr. Silverberg strides out the double doors, exiting the ward, off on some errand. I keep half an eye out for her return, but Delphina, I see, has already forgotten her. Delphina hasn't forgotten Sherman, though. Sherman is a white patient she has fallen for. Just now Delphina's eyes flick down the hallway, searching for him, for maybe the hundredth time.

"Sherman up yet?" I ask her.

"Not yet." Delphina sighs. "He still be sleeping with the angels."

The only angels I can see the volatile Sherman with are Hell's Angels, but I don't say this, or anything. Because what can you say in the face of love? I do feel sad, though. Sadder even than the ache in my soul I feel when I see the unbearable glory of crimson leaves spinning headlong towards cold autumn ground, because you can tell, even though Delphina loves Sherman with her whole heart, no way does he love her back.

I pour milk over my oatmeal, which rouses Delphina from her reverie. I'm not going to actually *eat* the oatmeal, but Delphina sure would like to. They have Delphina on a strict diet, which just about kills her, and they have me on a high-calorie diet, which just about kills her, too, since she hates to see all that delicious food go to waste. This morning she wolfed down her slice of dry toast and cottage cheese in the time it took me to spear open my carton of orange juice with a straw. "Mmmm mmm mmm," Delphina murmurs now, with genuine longing, "Honey, what I wouldn't give for some o' what you got."

I sigh with defeat even as Delphina's eyes roam over my untouched feast. Oatmeal, four slices of buttered toast, a chocolate donut, milk, orange juice, and I don't want any of it. "If only we could split our stomachs," I say.

"Girl, now you talkin'."

Outside the ward Delphina and I wouldn't have become friends. We never, probably, would have met. We move, as they say, in different circles. While I've got my white-collar job teaching at a wealthy independent school, Delphina washes dishes at a pancake house on York Road, across from the Rite Aid and Discount Liquors.

Delphina is lots funkier than I am. You can tell this right off from her hair. It's not just orange, it's the shade of one of Sarah's favorite crayons: atomic tangerine. I'm a pretty conservative dresser myself, and I doubt I would dye my hair orange, even in my dreams. My hair is red, auburn, just like my mom's, and maybe that's a connection to her that I don't want to change. Or maybe I'm just a conformist, jealous of Delphina for making her hair as outlandish as she wants. She can reinvent herself; she can be the whole box of Crayola crayons, and there's nothing to stop her.

If outside the ward Delphina and I wouldn't have been friends, in here, where we are stripped down to the bones of our souls, we are.

We have been friends, really, since the day we talked about Scott Joplin in the library outside our rooms.

The library is quiet during the day. During the night people blare the small TV in the corner, but during the day they want to encourage people to read so the TV is kept off. Typically, I love to read, but since my depression, I find I can't concentrate. There is something about my agitated state that makes it impossible for me to follow the intricate weave of words on a page. So, I wasn't *reading* the book on Scott Joplin, I was just flipping through it, when Delphina noticed my choice of subject matter, "You interested in the King o' Ragtime?"

"I play piano. But not lately." I shrugged.

Delphina nodded. "He die of syphilis. And he be poor. His wife run a house o' prostitution to keep the money comin' in."

"I didn't know that."

"Musician friend of Joplin's, Scott Hayden his name, he die in a bad way, too. Of some lung thing. Pulmonary pneumonia, emphysema, somethin' like that. He die in the same hospital he done work as an elevator operator."

"You're kidding. You mean this Hayden guy couldn't live off his music?"

"Umn umn."

"And Joplin couldn't either? Even after 'Maple Leaf Rag'?"

"Oh, Mr. Joplin make some money, but he be the son of a man who useda be a slave, and honey, they's jus so far you can go in white America."

I frown, "How come you know so much about this?"

"Because Scott Joplin be my great great grandaddy."

"He was?"

Delphina laughed. "No, I jus' teasin' you. You white folk think all us black folk related. We just keep on procreatin', like rabbits."

"No, that's not it."

"Then it be this. You figure cause I don't speak good, I be dense in the head."

I stared at the plump black woman across the library table. I hated to admit it, but Delphina was right. I didn't exactly consider her dense, but I dismissed her as intellectually inferior to me. I failed to look at the person beneath the grammar to see that she could teach me things.

Nothing more was said between us, but after that day in the library, I started to listen to Delphina. On her part, she looked out for me. That night when the TV was blaring in the library, Delphina stormed out, snapped off the TV, and sent the offending parties packing. She said they were interrupting my sleep. *My* sleep, like she cared more about me and my sanity than she did about her own.

Reflecting now on that night, how Delphina chased everybody away from the TV, I figure that sharing my breakfast with her is the least I can do. I glance around the cafeteria to make sure no one is looking, and I slip her my chocolate donut.

"Girl, you'se a saint." Delphina gnaws off a hefty chunk of donut and rocks her plump body side to side with pure delight. She's munching away on that donut so contentedly I feel happy for her, but then her whole body tenses. *What's up?* I think. Delphina swallows her remaining donut with a guilty, raggedy gulp as, curious, I turn in my chair to see who has come up behind us.

It is Dr. Silverberg.

She smiles politely to Delphina then addresses me, "Janey Nichols? I'm Dr. Silverberg. Have a minute?"

"Sure," I say. The fact is, I have more than a minute; I have all day.

There is an awkward moment, then Delphina offers, "I's getting ready to go anyway," though she doesn't move. She only stares mournfully at the four slices of buttered toast untouched on my tray.

I quickly shove my plate at her and say, "Don't forget your toast."

Delphina winks at me as she heaves herself to her feet and carries off her tray, leaving us.

Dr. Silverberg, who didn't appear to be observing our transaction, folds her long torso and legs into the vacant chair and says, "Lost your appetite, huh?"

"I guess."

"Looks like Delphina's found hers."

"Right," I say. I wonder if I'm in for a lecture about how we're not supposed to trade food with other patients.

But Dr. Silverberg only says, "Are you able to eat at all?"

"Oh, sure," I say. I take my spoon and again stir my milk around in my oatmeal to show her, see how normal I am? When I see the gooey clumps of oats swimming in the milk, I feel queasy.

Dr. Silverberg says, "What, for instance?"

"What, what?"

"Can you eat."

"Oh. Well, bananas, for one thing. And rice."

"Anything outside the bland family?"

"Well, unfortunately, the bland family pretty much has a lock on this area. Racketeering, bootlegging..."

"I'll keep an eye out for guys with violin cases." She smiles, and I decide in that moment that I like her. Up close, I can tell she's wearing perfume, a scent that somehow evokes spring, honeysuckle in sweet bloom and pitchers of lemonade with lots of sugar in it. I wouldn't call Dr. Silverberg beautiful, but she's attractive in that she makes the most of herself. Some tall people are gentle in their tallness, and this is her. Nonetheless she intimidates; her intelligence hums like an electric field. Oh, and one more thing: she wears a wedding ring; she must love someone, then.

She says to me, "So you've pretty well lost your appetite. How about insomnia. Been sleeping?"

"Not much," I say.

"Tell me, what does that feel like?"

"It feels..." I let my voice trail off. I am not about to tell her, although this is the single worst part about not sleeping: you are so alone. You have to go all night without holding onto the man you love. You can't see his profile in the moonlight, or smell the smell of him, or feel the warmth his body generates beneath the blankets. By the time bleak gray daylight peeks into your room, you have lost all hope. Your heart has splintered into a thousand pieces, like a chunk of rock candy dropped to the floor. You are so lonely you wonder how you can stand it, but here you are, alive, husbandless, another day in your face.

"It feels what?" Dr. Silverberg prompts.

I shrug.

"Hard to put into words?"

"Yes," I say.

Dr. Silverberg studies me a long moment, long enough for me to feel uncomfortable. Does she know how much I know but don't say? I'm afraid she's going to press me for more, but she doesn't. She merely asks, "What has Dr. Gard prescribed for you?"

"To sleep?"

"Yes."

"Restoril. Sometimes it catches hold and I get some sleep, and sometimes it doesn't."

"Are you rested when you sleep?"

"Pardon?"

"Do you feel rested the next day?"

"Uh, well..." I stall.

"It says here," she consults my chart, "you've been having nightmares. Is this true?"

"Well..." I feel trapped. "Yes."

"Tell me, what are your nightmares about?"

"I don't remember."

"No?"

"Sorry," I say. "I don't remember a thing."

Dr. Silverberg looks at me quizzically. Does she know I am lying? Every time I sleep I have the same dream. In fact, that's what I call it: the Dream. Does she know I have memorized every detail of the Dream, and that it keeps coming at me, and it won't stop? I think Dr. Silverberg is maybe waiting for me to say something else, to admit how troubled I am, but she simply consults my chart again, "Let's have you try Xanax tonight."

"Xanax?" I say. "After I take it, will I glow in the dark?"

She smiles. "Xanax may sound scary, but it isn't. Now you know it's not a sleeping pill per se. It's an anti-anxiety medication. But, I think it will work for you."

"Sure, okay."

She jots down something in her notes, then fixes her penetrating gaze on me. This time she's looking at me and she won't stop. Her eyes are blacker than I thought. Pools so black I can't see to the bottom of them. They are truly bewitching eyes; maybe that's why they say she works magic. You look into those eyes, and you fall a little in love with her, whether you want to or not. I wonder if her husband fell in love with her because of her eyes, and I find myself blurting out, "You're married, right? I mean, I see your wedding ring."

"Yes, I'm married."

"Did you keep your maiden name or is Silverberg his last name?"

"Silverberg is my name."

"So you're a feminist, huh?"

She smiles at me. "Maybe. Or, maybe I kept my own name because my husband's name is something dreadful."

"Mmm." I say. "What does he do? Your husband."

"He's a carpenter."

"No, really."

"Really."

"Oh," I say.

"What? You expected that he would be a professional? Something white collar? A doctor? A lawyer?"

"No, no. Nothing like that," I say. Then, "Yes."

She smiles at me. "Now let's get back to you, to our conversation before you artfully steered it away from yourself. Tell me about your family of origin. Your father is...?"

"A doctor."

"He in town?"

"No. He's retired. Florida."

"And your mother?"

"Deceased."

"I'm sorry." Dr. Silverberg studies me, "Did she die of natural causes?"

"Pardon?"

"Natural causes."

"Ah, no. Not exactly. Basically, she had a problem with alcohol."

"Mmmmm," Dr. Silverberg says. "Alcoholism is a terrible disease for all those involved."

I nod. Perspiration beads on my forehead. I don't want to talk anymore about my mother. I don't want any more questions about my family, period. I pray Dr. Silverberg will move on, but she asks, calmly, "Any siblings?"

I hesitate a beat too long, "...No."

"No?"

"No," I say more firmly. If I were hooked up to a lie detector, the needle would be jumping in jagged peaks on the graph, whole mountain ranges of lies, "No brothers. No sisters."

"So, you were an only child?"

"Yes!" My heart pounds in my ears.

"Janey," she says in a soothing voice, "I'm just trying to get my facts straight here."

"Right," I say.

She is watching me carefully.

I hold my breath.

Again, she waits for me to say something, but I don't, and the moment passes.

"Now, Janey," she moves on, "we need to talk more specifically about your depression, if you don't mind."

"Not at all," I say. I try to look open, ready to help her. I think anything has got to be easier than to talk about my family, but here I am quite wrong.

She asks me, unblinking, "Why are you depressed, do you think?"

"Why...?" I swallow dryly, then glance down at my oatmeal that slowly congeals in the bowl. I have only one wish: to disappear. My wish is not granted; I am still here. Finally I say in a low voice, "I'm postpartum. I lost my son. Doesn't it say so on my chart?"

"Yes, it does."

"Well, then, do we really have to talk about this?"

"We really have to talk about this."

"Fine, okay." I think a moment. I'm not sure the words will come, and I'm grateful when they do, "It was my second pregnancy. He died, uh, in utero at thirty-seven weeks. The umbilical cord..."

Dr. Silverberg nods. I appreciate it very much that she says nothing because what is there to say? She glances again at my chart and says, perhaps to remind me that I have not lost everything, "You have a daughter? Eight?"

"Yes. Sarah."

"And she's normal? The birth was—"

"Normal, yes."

"And how about this second pregnancy. Did it seem normal, too?"

"Yes. I mean, right up until the end." I pinch the bridge of my nose. I can feel a headache coming on and there is nothing I can do to stop it.

"Janey? Want a sip of your orange juice? You look ashen."

"No, that's...I'm fine."

"Mmmnn," Dr. Silverberg says. "And then afterwards? Tell me about that."

"You mean," my smile is oddly twisted, "how did I end up here?"

"Yes."

"Well," I say. How *did* I end up here? It has been such a roller coaster, the whole experience. So different than with Sarah, when Will and I returned home to a tower of presents and the hugs of friends, and all their expressions of joy when they peeled back the pink receiving blanket to see the baby girl in my arms. This time around we returned to an empty house; I wasn't cradling any baby in my arms; in fact, I only got to hold my baby that one time, and only then because Dr. Lingstrom knew to ask. I was sitting up in the birthing bed. It was very solemn. She handed my baby to me, swaddled in a blue crocheted blanket. Even though Max did not breathe, I could see he had all his fingers and toes. He had a tuft of hair the color of Popsicle sticks, and eyes so blue you could swim in them. He was, to me, beautiful. I stared a long time at his face. People in the delivery room were sniffling; somebody was handing out tissues. I turned to

Will, but he shook his head no, and I handed our baby back.

"Janey," Dr. Silverberg says, and I can tell this is not the first time. I have been following my own thoughts.

"Sorry," I say. "What was it you asked?"

"I know this must be painful for you, but I need to know your symptoms."

"Symptoms?"

"Yes. We've talked about your lack of appetite and your insomnia."

"Jesus," I stiffen, "isn't that enough?"

She smiles. "That's your body. What about your feelings? Dr. Lingstrom, your obstetrician, was certainly concerned about you."

"Yes."

"What did she do to help you?"

"Gave me Seconal to help me sleep."

"Seconal?" Dr. Silverberg repeats.

"Yes."

"Go on."

But I don't want to go on. I don't want to talk anymore, especially not about the Seconal. I shrug, and say, "I'm tired."

"I bet you are. You've been through an awful lot." Dr. Silverberg is studying me, and for the first time I get a feeling of real warmth from her. "Obviously you're terribly sad. Anyone would be, in your place. You were pregnant nearly full term and you lost your child. You are grieving, as any mother would. But I'm concerned about your suicidality."

There is that word again. First Pammy, and now Dr. Silverberg.

I'm feeling cornered, and so I say nothing.

"Are you feeling suicidal?" she prods gently.

"Oh, no!" I say. "I feel good."

"Mmmn," she says.

I frown, "You don't believe me."

"It's just that most people on suicide watch don't, as a rule, feel spectacularly happy."

"Well, I do. Feel happy. Maybe not spectacularly, but, you know. Happy enough."

"Like you've just won the lottery, eh?"

I wince at her sarcasm. "Well, not exactly. Breakfast this morning *was* a trifle disappointing. No Eggs Benedict."

Now it's her turn to frown.

I clear my throat. "Honestly, Dr. Silverberg, I've been doing beautifully here. All the nurses say so. Pammy and...everybody. I go to all the cognitive therapy sessions, the art workshops, all that."

"I'm sure you're a model patient, but that's not what I asked."

"No, right, of course not." I bow my head. She wants to know if I'm suicidal; she wants to talk about this, and I cannot. It's more than that it may jeopardize my chances to leave on Friday. Essentially I am a private person. I can't talk about my feelings, at least not on command. This is why I like kids and dogs so much. Their world is nonverbal. With kids you can slather peanut butter on a pine cone and roll it in sunflower seeds to feed house finches; you can create a cardboard monster out of a Cocoa Puffs box, an egg carton, and some green paint; you can play on the grass until the sun sets like an orange on a table of white sky; you can feel the wind ruffle your hair and lean your heads close together and watch a ladybug motor over your shoelace and not talk at all.

"In view of your history, Janey, I feel we must discuss this. The night before you were admitted to the hospital, your neighbor Ruth was sufficiently alarmed that she emptied your prescription bottle of Seconal into the toilet. Did Ruth overreact?"

I tense, then I realize I *look* tense, so I deliberately uncoil my body. "Overreact? Uh...."

I twist my wedding ring on my finger. The ring catches glints of light, even though there looks to be no daylight to spare because of the upcoming storm. Outside, the gray sky is darkening rapidly to a purplish black. The clouds remind me of bruises. Within moments the rain will begin again, the dispiriting drizzle that is this spring's signature.

"Janey?" Dr. Silverberg prods.

I keep toying with my wedding ring, "I'm thinking...."

I resist the memory, but my mind flips back, and there I am, back in the bathroom, holding that bottle of pills in my hand. Before my hospitalization I'd taken to roaming the house in the early morning hours, and on this one particular night I was lurking in the bathroom, really feeling blue. As I stood at the sink, I thought I'd take a pill, and then I thought why not two pills or three? Why not empty the whole damn bottle? And while I was considering this, I reached for a plastic cup to fill with water and I tripped over Sarah's footstool, the one she uses to step up to the sink to brush her teeth, and I stubbed my toe. "Shit!" I muttered.

Ruth emerged from the guestroom. By now, Ruth was staying overnight with us. Since she lived across the street anyway, alone, widowed since Cliff died three years ago, painfully, of lymphoma, she insisted it was no problem to stay. But, of course this was a sacrifice, to give up her own space, her privacy. Every morning she had to wake at 6 A.M. at our house to return to her house to let out her three springer spaniels. Not only did Ruth assume Sarah's care, but she also kept watch over me, which seemed necessary. So there Ruth suddenly was, shuffling out in her big-eared bunny slippers that Sarah got her last Christmas. Ruth's silvery white hair was fluffy and wild on one side, and matted on the other side from pressing on her pillow. Her normally youthful face was showing all of its sixty-two years. But, if Ruth looked unkempt, I must have appeared downright eerie. In the butterscotch glow of the bathroom night light I was this very thin, almost emaciated woman huddled over the sink, counting out pills like they were oyster pearls.

"What are you doing?" Ruth asked me.

"Just... I dunno..."

"You want to give me those pills?" she said. Ruth kept her voice even, but she was scared, I could see that. I didn't understand what she had to be scared about. I wasn't scared to die. It felt like the right move. I wasn't any good to anybody anymore. If I weighed our collective needs on an imaginary scale, I figured it wouldn't be such a big loss for Ruth, for Will, or for Sarah. But, for me it would be a great big relief. I wouldn't have to worry about eating or sleeping anymore, and I wouldn't have to act fine in front of Sarah.

"Please." Ruth held out her hand. The yellow of the bathroom light distorted things, and she became translucent, like a wax figure with cords of blue paint for veins.

"All right," I said, and my voice sounded dead, even I could hear it.

"I love you," Ruth said. "I don't want you to hurt yourself," and she brushed past me to flush the pills down the toilet.

With all that flushing going on, it took me a minute to realize Will had joined us. He stood in the hall, in his purple rugby shirt, barefoot, scratching his head. Sleep hung heavily on him and his reactions were delayed, but as soon as he saw me, and saw what Ruth was doing, he cried, "Aw, Janey..."

"What are you thinking?" Dr. Silverberg asks now.

"Me?" Panic flutters inside me. "I'm thinking Ruth was out of line."

"So she did overreact?"

"Yes, definitely. I'd say she definitely did."

"You were in no danger of taking those pills?"

"No."

"Then why were you counting them out into your palm?"

"I..."

"Not only was Ruth concerned, but your husband was, too. William, isn't it?"

"Will. He's a trial attorney." I gnaw on my lip. To avoid Dr. Silverberg's gaze I study my untouched oatmeal again. Around the rim of the bowl the rich fat in the milk has begun to separate out. I look up; I wonder what I can possibly say to prove I'm not lying when in fact I am, and a miracle of sorts happens: I spy Will at the double entrance doors. I don't feel ready to see Will yet today, he usually comes by *after* work, but for now he provides me with the perfect excuse, "Can I go?" I ask Dr. Silverberg. "Are we through? I have a visitor. My husband, actually."

"Fine," Dr. Silverberg says. "See you tomorrow. We'll talk again."

And just like that, I am released. The magical Dr. Silverberg, despite her mesmerizing black eyes, is not so magical after all. She lets me go, and I haven't told her a thing.

Will catches sight of me as I stand up from the table with Dr. Silverberg. We move toward each other, and, before I know it, he's wrapped me up in a hug. It's painful, this hug: it knocks the breath from my lungs. Everything I am, everything I feel, rises up inside me. The splendor and the sadness of the world, that's what Fitzgerald called it, and that's what

I'm feeling now. And so I can't be near Will without remembering last summer and where we were when we conceived our son: upstairs in our cabin in the Adirondacks, overlooking the stillness of the lake, rocking the four-poster bed the morning Ruth took Sarah for a long explore through the woods.

"Hey," Will murmurs into my ear.

"Hey," I say. I can't help it, a tear meanders down my cheek.

Will's voice is thick, "What's wrong?"

I shake my head. That is my only reply, but I let Will tighten his arms around me. I lay my head on Will's shoulder, glad he can't see me. I want to tell him *go home, go home*; it is too much, his being here. But, instead I struggle for control, step back, and ask, "How's Sarah?"

"She keeps complaining of stomachaches."

"She misses me," I say. "She misses our routine."

Will nods. Then he looks toward the cafeteria and where Dr Silverberg and I were sitting when he came in. "Who was that you were talking to?"

"My new doctor. Silverberg. Dr. Gard's on vacation."

"She looks nice."

"Does she?"

"Yes. Something about her eyes. She really focused on you while you two were talking. Her whole body posture was leaning toward you. Not like that Dr. Gard. He always looked bored—" Will interrupts himself. "Janey—what?"

"It's just...she asked me about the baby, Will."

"Ah, sweetheart."

"Yeah," I say. I'm blinking like crazy trying not to cry because, God, once I start, there'll be no stopping me; they'll have to pin back my arms like Florence Coombs, pump up a vein, and shoot me up with something liquid and powerful so I can't feel.

There is a commotion in the hall around us. Group therapy has just let out. "Come on," Will tells me, "let's go to your room. We can talk there."

"Okay," I say.

As we walk down the hall, we pass Delphina. She's with Sherman, and because she's always happy when she's with Sherman she gives me an exuberant grin, "Hey, Skinny Lady!"

I nod back.

Will and I keep walking. Will looks back at Delphina and says to me, "You've made friends."

"Yeah, the psych ward. Great way to network. How to make friends and influence schizophrenics."

"You don't have to be sarcastic."

I study Will's face. "You're right. I don't. I'm sorry."

"How sorry?" Will asks playfully as we reach my room. He flings his arms around me, but I wriggle free. He grabs after my hand, misses. He shrugs, then lets me go, and shoves his hands into the pockets of his business suit. He surveys my room, and I know why: he hopes my room might be different than the last time he was here. If the room is different, maybe his wife will be different. Better. Healed. But no, it is the same. Same white walls, same narrow bed, same desk, same window where a dismal gray rain pelts against the glass. "This is the worst spring we've had in years," he says, staring glumly out the window.

He looks so lonesome, I decide to stand beside him, and so together, shoulders touching, we peer out the window at the rain.

The rain slides down the glass of the window.

Will fixes his gaze on me. His look contains so much yearning, I feel my heart turn over. I want to make Will feel less islanded, so I send a bridge across, even though something tells me I may already be too late, "Will," I say.

"Honey?"

"What you said on the phone. It's true."

"What?"

"That I'm hard to reach lately."

"Well, you've been a little withdrawn."

"I know." I swallow. "I need to be right now. I'm sorry."

When did my withdrawal begin? My quest for inaccessibility? I thought it was when we were in the examination room and couldn't hear the heartbeat, but now I wonder if it didn't happen sooner. I wanted this second child for myself, and I didn't care so terribly much what Will wanted. I convinced him that two kids would be so much better than one.

In our musty cabin, in the big four-poster with the mothball scented canopy, from which, lying on our backs, we could see a cathedral of birches arching whitely, elegantly over the lake, I plotted and planned. When Will moved on top of me, when I synchronized our grunts of pleasure, was I distancing myself from him even then, wanting his sperm more than I wanted him?

I look over at my husband now and wonder if he is attractive. He is to me. A medium tall man with thin black hair and luminous green eyes and the longest sweetest eyelashes you have ever seen. Lately Will has put on weight, maybe ten pounds. He's supposed to watch his cholesterol, but when he's upset he cheats. He goes to Burger King and McDonald's.

"What are you thinking?" Will asks me.

"About the floor of your Mazda."

"Why?"

"Is it littered with wrappers from Big Macs?

"Absolutely not," he says. "I can assure you."

"Really?"

"Yes, I've moved on to Quarter-Pounders with cheese."

I have to smile.

He shrugs. "When you're not around I miss you."

"Does it help, to eat?"

"Sometimes..." His voice trails off.

I stand at the window and watch the rain dribble down the glass. I know exactly what Will is talking about, since I miss him, too. We have been together for so long that he is a part of me. "You know," I look over to him now, "when I first liked you?"

"No."

"I mean, really liked you. At that dance in the gym. Eleventh grade."

"When Murph came over?"

"Nice guy, but a geek. And you rescued me. You reached over and took my hand to make him think we were together."

"I remember."

"I liked holding your hand, Will."

"I wanted to ask you to dance."

"I kept wishing you would. We were standing by the punch bowl.

Neither of us knew what to do. I tossed popcorn in the air and you caught it in your mouth. And then, I don't know, you drifted off."

"Big mistake." Will smiles.

I smile too, then ask, "Why didn't you?"

"What?"

"Ask me to dance."

"Too self-conscious. My acne. I was afraid that's what everybody saw about me. I should've realized you were different."

"Well..." I say. I am deeply touched, but the fact is, I judged Will far too long by his appearance, as people do, especially people who are young and insecure and in high school.

Will's acne was a source of anguish to him. It even, I think, shaped his personality. Funny, thoughtful, and bright, Will positioned himself not at the center of things, but more at the immediate periphery, someone who watched what went on, but didn't miss much. If Will had been a football star or more conventionally good-looking, I can't imagine him for one second being overlooked, but he was.

At this dance, though, when Will rescued me, I began to see him in a new light. That same night, back home as I lay in bed, I remembered what it felt like to hold his hand. The next week Will asked me to play tennis, and I said sure, and after that we started shooting hoops in my driveway. We played a lot of basketball that spring. Afterwards, we'd sprawl on the lush green backyard grass and sip lemonade with ice cubes so cold that when you sucked on them you shivered clear down to your toes. We talked in the shade of sugar maples. Even on rainy days, when it was clear there would be no basketball that day, Will would walk me home. He understood the secret life of my mom. You never could tell one day to the next. My mom might be curled up in the agony of her own loneliness on her bed with all the blinds drawn, or she might be down in the kitchen, her makeup and lipstick on, happy to see us, baking cookies.

For a long time Will and I didn't make out; we didn't even hold hands again, but we were gone on each other. You might say I was lucky because of that one night, that one dance, because by senior year, everyone, not just me, could see he was a prince. But by then Will knew by heart the way to my house; he knew all the quirks in our orange basketball hoop so he could sink a shot from just about anyplace.

I study Will's face now, as he stands beside me. I reach over and absently trace the faint pockmarks of his cheeks, so faint you hardly notice them. But I can feel them. I can feel with my fingertips the pitted purplish hollows of his skin, so tiny, that nearly proved an obstacle to my knowing him. I grow older everyday, but I'm not sure what is ugly and what is beautiful anymore.

"Whatchya thinking?" Will asks. "I *did* shave this morning."

"Just..." I intend to keep things light, to merely brush my lips over his, but as it is, I hungrily clamp my mouth over his. He kisses me back, and then he pulls me in tight against him, as tight as we can get. I can feel his heart beat inside the frail armor of his ribs. A shudder runs through me.

"Let's...on the bed," I say in a raspy voice.

"What?" He is surprised. "I thought you didn't—"

"I do, though."

Will closes the door, then together we walk to the narrow bed. I am to tell the truth, scared; my heart is all fluttery. I can't speak; I am mute in the face of Will's, and my, need. He pulls me down gently so that we lay on the bed together. He cups my face delicately inside his palms. We are kissing, idly at first, and then the kissing takes on purpose and intensity, heeding a gravity all its own. It is like falling down a hill; maybe Jack and Jill were on to something. I fall and fall, feeling weightless until Will eases his hand inside my sweatshirt, inside my bra, to touch my nipple.

I jerk away.

"What?" he says.

"Nothing." I am breathing fast.

"You don't like me touching you."

"No. It's fine."

"You feel...I dunno...stiff."

"Me?" I say. I don't know what to do. When we first kissed I felt too much; now I feel nothing at all. I am so confused. I place my hand over the zipper of his pin-striped trousers, "Mmm...talk about stiff."

Will's breath caresses my neck, "Could we? I mean, will anyone inter-rupt us? There's no lock on the door."

"Who cares?" I say. I kiss my husband with an urgency I no longer feel. His breath comes out in a moan. I remain unmoved. He keeps kissing me, his eyes closed. My eyes are wide open. I see the white hospital bed, the white sheets, the white walls. I wonder if my face is white, too. Everything white when it should be passion red.

Will and I have been together so long that he knows me. He knows I can't go through with this. He stops kissing me, more resigned than angry, "It's not happening, is it?"

"No," I say.

"When you come home, then."

"I'll wear your favorite satin underpants."

"The green ones?"

"From Victoria's Secret."

We shake on this, and laugh. I don't reflect on how easily Will has let me off the hook or what this might mean. Nothing is expected of me, and so I relax.

We are cuddling each other on the bed, Will facing me and me facing the white cinder block wall across the room. I like this closeness, the feel of Will curled against me, against the seahorse swirl of my spine. "Do you miss it?" I ask him.

"What?"

"Making love."

"I can wait till you're better."

"But do you miss it?"

"Not as much as I would have thought."

"No?"

"What I miss most is holding you. Like we are right now." He pauses, and adds in a strangled voice, "At night. When I'm in bed. I'll have read to Sarah, or Ruth will have, and Sarah will be safely tucked in and sleeping, and Ruth will have said good night and locked the front door behind her, and suddenly it will be just me awake in the house. And I don't know what to do with myself. Sometimes I do paperwork from the office, or I have a glass of wine. But sometimes..."

"What?"

"I just lie there against the pillows. And you know, I listen to the silence, and it feels like I'm the last person on Earth."

"That sounds lonely."

"Mmmn," Will says.

I shift around on the bed so now I'm facing him. I stroke his jawline, then plant a kiss on his forehead. "I'm sorry I'm not home with you. In our big bed. I'm sorry about all of this."

"Don't be," he says. "Hey, you're coming home Friday, right?"

"Right," I say. And then my heart skips a beat, "Which reminds me."

"What?"

"This new doctor I have—"

"Silverberg, yeah?"

"She asked me if I have a brother."

"How'd she know to ask?"

"Well, brother or sister. She wondered if I had any siblings."

"And you told her?"

"No. I figured why get into it?"

"Maybe she can help you."

"Oh, I don't think so."

"Did she ask about your mom, too?"

"Yes."

"What did you say?"

"I mentioned the drinking, but not the whole tragic saga."

"So, you didn't tell her about the Island or the ice—?"

"No, I didn't," I say, "and I'd just as soon leave it that way." I feel panic rising inside me. I bite down hard on my lip.

Will reaches out to hold me. "Hey, I'm here."

"It doesn't help," I tell him, which is not true. It is only true for now, for this moment when I'm feeling overtaken by the blues, "To be close to you."

"Gee, thanks."

"Nothing helps."

In silence and despair, Will buries his face against my skin, presses his noise into the aging, wattled folds of my neck, as if I have something to offer him, still, something precious, my ordinariness perfumed with meaning, like the aromatic red mysteries of a rose.

Delphina is watching me. She is watching my hands.

We are in art therapy. I am working on a ceramic hot plate. I was a little late getting here. I walked Will out to the parking lot, and we said goodbye. Just now I curl my tongue in concentration as I carefully add a new leaf-shaped tile to my design. I haven't glued down any of the little tiles yet. I am being very particular.

"Say, hey, Skinny Lady," Delphina says.

"Hey, what?" I say.

"How many times you gonna push them tiles around?"

"Till I get enough mileage for a free flight."

Sherman, who is sitting beside Delphina, snorts. "What are you making anyway?"

"A trivet."

"A say what?" Delphina asks.

"A trivet. Thing for keeping hot dishes on. You know."

"A trivial trivet," Sherman says.

"And you're both making leather change purses, right?" I say.

"Yeah, me and Sherman," Delphina says, like they're a couple. But, they aren't so much a couple as a study in incongruity—plump lady and scrawny man; black skin and white. I wouldn't say Delphina is passive, but she suffers quietly compared to Sherman, who carries more rage than a volcano. His rage, in fact, is his defining characteristic. Sherman seethes even as he walks barefoot around the ward in jeans and striped dress shirts with their tails hanging out, his hair wildly unkempt like Beethoven's. He plays the piano too, or says he does. I imagine him banging out thunderous chords on rainy days.

"Mine's no change purse," Sherman says, "It's a condom holder."

Delphina bursts out laughing. Sherman laughs, too, and for a moment they hold their laughter high, like a gleaming silver trophy, between them.

Cyndi, our art therapy instructor, blonde and quite pretty, comes over.

"How's it going, table three?" she asks.

"Fine and dandy," Delphina says.

"Life sucks," Sherman says.

"Thanks for sharing," I say.

Delphina laughs. "Sherman, you *is* one big sourpuss."

"Any problems?" Cyndi asks.

"No," we all three say.

Cyndi turns to me, "You want to line those tiles up, and make your final decision about your design, okay? Then we'll glue everything down."

"Right," I say. I don't argue. Cyndi keeps nudging me along. She wants me to finish up this project and move on to another one. But I like my trivet. I like how I feel when I am working on it. It is the one thing I look forward to each day.

"I'll get you the glue," Cyndi says to me.

"No rush," I say.

Cyndi moves on.

Sherman says to Delphina and me, watching Cyndi's backside, "She's a ripe one. Tight ass."

"Sherman, you bad," Delphina says.

Sherman just rolls his eyes. "You know who else has a fine ass is that new doctor."

"Silverberg, you mean?" I say.

"Yeah, she's not bad, especially for a married lady with kids."

"Dr. Silverberg has children?" I say.

Sherman nods. "Two. Her son's older, in college."

"How do you know that?"

"Through the grapevine. The younger one, the daughter, she's got problems."

"What do you mean, problems?" I ask.

But Sherman doesn't answer. "Damn!" he exclaims. He's straddling his chair, tipped dangerously backward on two legs, but now he crashes the chair forward to the floor. The two front legs slam into our table, jostling my trivet and making my blue tiles bounce all over the place. "Stupid needle is stuck!" Sherman cries. Sure enough, his needle is jammed in a hole in the leather. The needle just won't budge.

Delphina laughs, but Sherman is still angry.

He flings down the condom holder, exasperated. "Fuck this! No time to finish it, anyway. Come tomorrow, I'm outta here."

Delphina freezes, her needle poised midair. This is news to her. I know just how she feels. I know from listening for my son's heartbeat. If she moves, just one muscle, or even dares breathe, it will become true: Sherman will be leaving.

"You're being discharged?" I ask Sherman because I know Delphina can't.

"Hell, yes."

"When?"

"Right after breakfast. Soon's I get my papers signed."

"Sherman?" Delphina's voice quivers. Her eyes are wide with shock, with the hurt she hasn't even begun to feel. For a minute I think this is how she must have looked in the helpless seconds before her ex-husband, who used to beat her, smacked her with the backside of his hand, raising bruises and welts.

Sherman smirks, "Yeah, Delphie, didn't I tell you? Don't worry, I'll call you. Every day."

"You shittin' me?" Delphina asks.

"No, for real," Sherman says, looking like Beethoven again, tossing back his mane of black hair as he holds Delphina's earnest, desperate gaze. There is sincerity burning beneath the anger in Sherman's voice, and I believe him. Delphina starts kidding around about condoms again because she believes him, too. I am happy, Delphina is happy, and I don't want to upset this new equilibrium. This isn't the time or place to get back into it. But I am left with questions about Dr. Silverberg—what problems does her daughter have? Big problems? Little problems? I mean, everybody has problems.

After art therapy I place my trivet back on the cabinet shelf and go line up for my afternoon meds. At the dispensing window Joe hands me a paper cup with my Stuartnatal pill. The Stuartnatal pill is huge, yellow, and all but bearded, a Goliath among pills, and there is no way I can force myself to swallow it. Don't they know not to remind me? Stuartnatal pills are for pregnant women, but I am not pregnant. Not anymore.

I palm the Stuartnatal, tuck it into the dark pocket of my jeans, and go to my room, flop face down on my bed, alone at last. My nose is smashed into the valley of my pillow, and I suddenly wonder what it would be like to suffocate. Maybe not so bad. I hate myself.

When the phone in my room rings I think I'll just ignore it, but I get up from the bed and grab the receiver. "Hello?" I say.

"Mommy?" It is Sarah's thin voice.

I pinch the bridge of my nose. "Hi, sweetie. Aren't you supposed to be at school?"

"The nurse sent me home. Here. Ruth wants to talk to you."

"Wait. Honey, are you sick—?"

But Sarah has already clunked down the receiver. I hear Toby's sharp bark. A door slams.

"Janey?" Ruth says.

"Yeah, listen," I say. "What's up? She coming down with a cold?"

"No."

"Fever?"

"She's fine." Ruth pauses. "Full of energy. She just ran outside to play with Toby."

"Then why did Mrs. Dwyer send her home?"

"Sarah keeps running in to see her. She says she needs Band-Aids."

"What's wrong with that? She fell on the playground, maybe."

"No, that's not it," Ruth says.

"But, kids can get pretty banged up at this age."

"Janey, there *are* no cuts."

"What?"

"Sarah would ask for a Band-Aid and the nurse would say *Where?* And when Sarah pointed to the spot that hurt, on her arm or her leg, there would be nothing."

"Nothing?"

"No cuts, no scrapes, nothing."

"Oh."

There is a pause between Ruth and me. Both of us are busy thinking.

Finally I say, "Obviously I'm not doing my job. If I were home instead of here, in the hospital—"

"Don't blame yourself."

"I'm her mother..." I twist the black phone cord around on my hand. The phone cord feels painfully tight, but I deserve it. "What should we do, Ruth?"

"It might help if Sarah came to visit you."

"No, not here!"

"She misses you, Janey."

"I know that! Don't you think I know that?" I snap. "Look," I say in a calmer voice, "let me talk to her, okay? Can you put her back on?"

"Sure," Ruth says.

There is noise, the sound of doors banging, Toby barking, and then, "Mommy?" Sarah says.

"What's going on with the nurse? Mrs. Dwyer."

"She lets me sit on her knee."

"You like that?"

"Uh huh."

"Mmm," I say. I bite my lip. My freckled, coppery-haired Sarah goes to second grade in the same school where I teach. All day she knows I am one floor below her; when she scrapes her chair back on the floor, she and her classmates, I can hear them. On recess duty, my eyes follow her on the playground, and Sarah knows this. Sarah knows I am watching her, or at least nearby, as she darts among the towering oaks to collect acorns to hide from the boys. She tucks the acorns into the folds of her sweater, in an impromptu pouch. How much does she miss me when I am not there to see that lump in her sweater, or the glorious smile she wears, glorious and self-conscious both, now that she has lost her milk teeth and wears glow-in-the-dark retainers each night to bed, now that she is eight?

"Mommy," Sarah says now, "can I come visit you? Ruth says I might."

"Oh, honey."

"Please!"

"I'll be home for good on Friday. That's not long at all."

"But, I want to see where you sleep!"

"It's this cramped little room. It's not much, Sare."

"So, can I? Can I come?"

I would have said no. Certainly I want to say no, but Sarah's thin voice cracks, and not just that, but she says something else. She says, "Mrs. Dwyer is, like, okay, but I really like Mrs. Gianelli."

I am so surprised that I can only react reflexively, "It's *Ms.* Gianelli. She's not married."

"She waves to me when I'm on the playground."

"Oh?"

"She wears your silver whistle, Mommy."

"Well, she should. My class is *her* class now. She has to take charge."

"You mean, you won't be coming back?"

"Not this term. Not until the fall."

"Mommy, it was so cool. Once she even let me blow her whistle."

"She did?"

"Yeah. All the kids came running to line up from recess, and I was the one that made them. You have to come when someone blows the whistle."

"That's right," I say. I am thinking about Antonia Gianelli, with her expertly dyed ash-blonde curls and her fifty pairs of shoes. I have always felt, in the world of personal relationships, of give and take, that she is more a taker than a giver. She has grown up in a privileged world of afflu-ence, and I wonder if teaching, for her, is just something to dabble in, before she moves on to other, more exciting ventures. But I may be wrong. Though she complains constantly, she is not lazy; she is well-prepared with her lesson plans. And, if she lacks a natural touch with the kids in the classroom, she is, still, excusably, green and inexperienced. I may be too hard on her. Will thinks I am. He likes Antonia. With men, particularly, Antonia is charming and flirtatious, and so winningly manipulative that she has you wanting to help her, or to make her laugh. She is, undeniably, pretty. And now, in my absence, this pretty woman has made friends with my daughter. I suppose I am jealous of this; why else would I find the words escaping my lips, words I would not other-wise say, "I tell you what, Sare. You want to come visit me in the hospi-tal, I guess you can."

"Really? Great!" Sarah's voice is plummy with pleasure.

"Not today, though, honey. Tomorrow." And not on the ward either, I think. It's too depressing here. As I told Pammy once, the trouble about being around all these depressed people is it's depressing. "Why don't you and Daddy meet me in the cafeteria?"

"Cafeteria! Cool! You're the best mom in the whole world! Here, Ruth wants you—"

"Bye. Love you," I say, but Sarah is long gone. I hear squeals of delight, then Ruth comes back on the line, "I take it she's coming."

"Tomorrow night. For dinner."

"Good idea," Ruth says. There is a pause. "Listen," she adds.

"What?"

"Maybe this is a good time to bring this up, maybe not. I don't know."

"Bring what up?"

"Windsor Island. We need to open up the cabin for the summer. I was thinking we'd go over Memorial Day. We've got to get the water and electric hooked up, anyway."

"Oh, Ruth," I say, "I don't know."

"What? Too many memories?"

"Something like that."

"But we've had good times, Janey. You love the Island."

Of course she's right. I envision our cabin snuggled deep in the north woods. I have taken many hikes; I have looked up and seen paper birches bending in all their elegance toward the lake, and what can I tell you except that it is there I find my truest home.

Ruth makes plans, "We'll take a sunrise hike. Then we'll sit on the dock hugging our knees and listen on the lake for the loons..."

"Oh, hell," I say, shattering the moment, "if it's loons I want, I can just poke my head out the door and listen for Mr. Kramer."

Ruth sighs.

There is a pause, between us. What I am thinking is this: it was cruel what I said about Mr. Kramer. Whatever he suffers from is not his fault.

"Ruth?" I say.

"What?"

I pinch the bridge of my nose. "I'm just not sure I'm ready."

"Okay," she says.

≈)(≈

After my phone call with Ruth, I go for a walk.

The nurse Gwen lets me out with her key.

"You have campus alone privileges?"

"Yes."

Before me unfold the grounds surrounding the ward. There is a clay tennis court with no net, a concrete basketball court, and a sloping acre of patchy newborn grass bounded by a chain-link fence and the roaring traffic of Northern Parkway. I walk along the sidewalk, head down. It's cold; I should have worn a coat.

I am thinking about Ruth and how much I owe her.

Shortly after Cliff succumbed to lymphoma, I invited her to come read to my first-grade class. I thought I was doing her a favor. Turns out she was doing me one. Ruth used to be a librarian and is a *wonderful* reader. She can do lots of voices, and plus she has a way with kids.

This past February, when I was very pregnant, feeling slothful and fat, Ruth dusted off *Stone Fox* and said she was coming in again. *Stone Fox* is the story of the young boy who tries to save his grandpa's farm by running a dogsled race. He's winning the race, on the road to all that prize money, when his dog Searchlight up and dies on him, dies of an overworked heart.

When Ruth read about Searchlight, no one in the classroom moved, no one even breathed. And when Ruth closed the last page on *Stone Fox*, the February sun slanted in through the window, striking diamonds in her white hair, and my kids, in a circle around her, blinked and blinked, not crying, but blinking an awful lot, while I sat there with my swollen pregnant belly and thought how lucky I was to have a friend like Ruth, who can feel things so deeply she makes you feel them, too.

Of course, in these last few weeks Ruth hasn't been reading to my class. She's pretty much had her hands full taking care of me and my family. From the moment I entered the hospital, Ruth has been the one to oversee Sarah's homework, and to pack her lunchbox with a silly note tucked inside. She has even, on one occasion that I know of, rummaged through the trash to retrieve Sarah's glow-in-the-dark retainers from a clump of congealed spaghetti noodles.

But, it's not just Ruth's reading of *Stone Fox* that makes me love her, or even all her help. It is our shared history. Ruth knew my mother, was friends with her, despite everything. She was there when my mom drank: she *knows*.

I remember the time I was fifteen or so and Ruth came to dinner. Cliff was busy that evening; he played bass in an ensemble, so it was just Ruth and my family.

It was a simple meal. Chicken. Mashed potatoes. Something like that. Everything was going well clear through to dessert, when Mom disappeared through the swinging door into the kitchen. The seconds ticked by, and my father began to fume. When Mom swept back into the dining room with our wedges of cheesecake, it all seemed fine. She wore a big smile, so maybe she hadn't grabbed a quick nip of gin after all from one of her hiding places. And yet it quickly became clear how unsteady she was, how sloppy in her movements. Ruth, who sat next to me, said nothing. Ruth had a sixth sense about my mom, always. She seemed to hear the agonized soul of my mother crying out over the clinking of silverware; she did her best to stick up for her. When Mom spilled her iced tea and everyone could smell the gin she'd laced it with and Dad cried, "Dammit, Clara!" Ruth leapt to her feet and said calmly, "Let's get a sponge to wipe that up."

But, even Ruth couldn't head off the fight that was going to happen that night. The fight happened an hour or two after Ruth left. The dishes were still piled in the sink; it wasn't my night, and besides, I had a trig test the next day. I heard quarreling and went and stood in the upstairs hall. I stood in the shadows when Dad loomed over Mom in bed and wrenched the gin bottle from her hands. She was in her gray satin nightgown, her breasts drooping pendulously, her ruby lipstick smeared. My dad brushed by me in a huff to bury the bottle in the trash downstairs, but Mom didn't see me. She was whimpering. She had the radio on, this country western song she liked, "King of the Road," about this guy smoking and drinking and down on his luck.

I went back to my room and sat down at my desk. I thought of writing in my journal, but that felt stupid so I ended up staring at my wallpaper. There was just this tiny strip that was peeling, but I made the strip bigger by jabbing it back with my pencil eraser.

Not long after that night, after the tense dinner she had at our place,

Ruth started taking me out, just the two of us, about once a week. Sometimes we went out for a hamburger and sometimes we walked around the mall. Ruth gave me the opportunity to talk to her, and after feeling shy the first few times, I did...

⋙⋘

I stop on the sidewalk behind the psych ward and glance up at a purple and menacing sky. I've just decided it's going to rain for sure when, sure enough, I feel tiny pinpricks no bigger than freckles on my wrist and neck. Raindrops pock the sidewalk. I squint up at the clouds as the drizzle intensifies to a rain and then a downpour. It happens quickly, so quickly that, by the time I stumble back inside, my clothes are soaked and cling to me. Gwen muscles shut the sliding glass doors, sealing me inside as a fierce rain slants down. A huge gust of wind topples the branch of an oak tree. The downed branch bounces on the sidewalk, then is still, its naked wet bark glistening, its stunned leaves huddled together like mourners. The world is all gray, all brown. Whatever sun there was, whatever promise of green, is gone.

I head back to my room to change. My sneakers go squish. Inside my socks, my toes shrivel like raisins. I feel an ache in my chest and it is loneliness. I start thinking about the losses in my life. When I reach my room I forget about changing my clothes. I grab my leather wallet from my purse and open the wallet for what I know is tucked in deep in the bottom slot, beneath all my credit cards. It is a photograph. I look at it a long time. My hair drips onto the corner of the photograph and that's when I remember I have just come in out of the rain.

⋙⋘

I leave the photograph, by accident, out on my bed, close to my pillow, and that night Delphina sees it.

She does not see it at first. She is in my room with me.

We're waiting around for our final evening meds, which sometimes they don't get around to giving us until ten-thirty. Delphina is in a funk because Sherman's leaving. She has plunked herself onto my bed, and now she's pawing around the pocket of her ratty bathrobe. To my surprise, she produces a crumpled pack of Newports.

"You've got to be kidding," I say.

Delphina glares at me and strikes a match.

We aren't supposed to smoke in the ward, and we definitely aren't supposed to be packing our own matches. They lock those kinds of things up around here—turpentine, scissors, razor blades—things that might play dangerous in suicidal hands.

Delphina lights her Newport, then shakes out the tiny flame of her match. The stench of sulfur irritates my nose and throat.

"Since when do you smoke?" I say to her.

"Quit. I's starting again, though." Delphina takes a steady drag on her Newport, traps the smoke down deep in her lungs until the nicotine hits, then exhales. The tip of her cigarette glows, orange, a pale echo of the fiery day-glo orange of her hair.

I don't like Delphina smoking; it's not good for her, plus some nurse will smell the smoke and come barging in here and yell at us, and then Delphina will be mad, the nurse will be mad, and I'll feel caught in the middle. Still, I feel bad for Delphina. She is in pain. "You okay?" I say.

Delphina looks crossly at me. I think for a minute she is going to reply, to maybe tell me to mind my own business, but she doesn't, she sucks on her cigarette, and shifts her gaze so she's looking out the window, and that's when we both realize it's snowing. Big white flakes tumbling down from a black sky. When did the rain turn to snow?

"I can't hardly believe my eyes," Delphina says.

"Shit," I say.

Delphina puffs on her cigarette, and studies me. "Never done heard you swear before. Didn't know you had it in you."

"Because I'm too white? Too Junior League?" I am angry about the snow and so sardonic, I could melt the ice outside. "I don't have rhythm either, so shoot me."

Delphina laughs. Then she peers out at the snow again. "You not a Snow Bunny?"

"Let's just say I'm not a big fan of snow and ice."

"Not in April, honey. We none of us is." Delphina sucks down the nicotine from her Newport, exhales.

I am jealous of Delphina smoking. When she smokes she has something to do with her hands. It's funny how I have nothing to do with my hands. I thought my hands would be so busy. Changing diapers. Rocking my baby. Unsnapping my brassiere to breast-feed. Rubbing the sweet dome of my baby's back while he slept...

Delphina taps the ash from her cigarette onto my floor again. With her peripheral vision she catches sight of the small frayed photograph on my pillow. Curious, she leans over and picks it up.

"That be you." She taps at the photograph. "How old you be? Ten? Eleven?"

"Delph, can I have that back?"

"You a cute young thing. Pigtails. Small as a cricket."

"Please?" I say.

Delphina ignores me. She frowns, takes a closer look at the picture. "Who that with you? That little boy?"

"I mean it, Delph. Give. Me. The. Picture. Now."

"Touchy, touchy," she says.

When she hands me back the photograph of my brother, I plunge him deep into the recesses of my wallet, back where he belongs.

That night the Xanax works on me, but I wish it hadn't.

I am lying in bed on my back, my hands laced under my head, looking out at the snow when I fall asleep. It is because of the snow that I have the dream. No, that's not entirely true. I would have the dream anyway.

In the dream we are in the car. I am in the back seat with my little brother. Mom is driving. We are headed for our cabin in the Adirondacks, on Windsor Island, ten long hours north from our home in Baltimore, and we are excited because we are on the last leg of the trip; we are almost there. We have passed through most of the lake hamlets—Blue Mountain Lake, Racquetté Lake, Long Lake—and now we are closing in on Saranac Lake, our destination.

It is late afternoon. On our drive today we have already weathered one big hailstorm, a freaky but not unknown occurrence for March up here in these north woods. But, for the last half-hour there has been no hail; the air is clear, and the late afternoon sky beckons all toward adventure. But now, what looks to be a second storm blows in over the mountains. The sky darkens so suddenly it is like the lights going out in a movie theatre.

The interior of the car turns cold. Mom cranks up the heater. She cranks the radio up, too. It is Neil Diamond. Cracklin' Rosie you make me smile. *Mom likes Neil Diamond. Mom cranks up the volume even more.* Cracklin' Rosie you make me smile.

Mom hands us bubble gum in the backseat, "Almost there, kids," she says. She gives us not one cube of bubble gum each, but two. She takes the remaining one cube for herself. She is snapping her gum when the first of the hail starts to bounce against the windshield. She snaps the wipers on and now they go clack, clack. Mom leans forward and squints through the windshield to see.

A curve, too fast. Mom laughs a little, slows down. When we stopped for lunch she had wine. Too much wine? Has it made her too bold? We are looking for Barlett's Carry, the road that corkscrews around the lake to the footbridge to Windsor Island. Mom cranes her neck forward. She is looking, looking. My brother and I are looking, too.

Another curve. Slow down, Mom.

Mom stomps on the brakes. The tires catch, then slide on a tongue of ice. We careen off the road, toboggan through woods. Bumpy. My little brother flings his toothpick arms around my neck and clings to me.

Panic. We fly through a gauntlet of trees, the branches snap snap snapping. A giant birch looms ahead. Watching with grandfather eyes that see everything. The birch hunches its shoulders and tries to make itself small, but it is a big tree...

༚།༚

I am almost awake, but not quite. I cry out in my sleep as I break the surface of consciousness, thrashing wildly in my blankets, gasping for air. My cry wakes Delphina, or maybe she was awake anyway, I don't know. She comes racing in. She's fast for such a plump woman.

"Wha's wrong, sugar?" she says.

"Nothing," I say.

I'm sitting bolt upright in bed, clammy with sweat. Perhaps I have turned into Mr. Kramer or he has turned into me. Maybe it all starts with a cry deep in your throat, that irreversible descent into depravity. I feel hot and cold both at once.

"Nothing, huh? Girl, you lying to me. You lie like a dead pecker. And, believe me, I knows what a dead pecker is. You should meet Clyde, my ex-husband." Delphina scowls. She's sporting a half-smoked cigarette between two stubby black fingers, and as I watch, she takes one big inhale. "It still snowing," she tells me. "Look it."

I follow her gaze out the window. "Damn," I say.

"Yeah," Delphina nods. She sucks down some more nicotine from her cigarette. A thin, gray ribbon of smoke spirals upward into the air. She taps her ashes on my floor, then inhales again. The Newport comforts her in ways I don't understand. Look at her, eyes closed in rapture, like she was dancing with her lover, dancing with Sherman.

I have never smoked, not even in high school, except to take a few experimental puffs. But I wouldn't mind some comfort. I feel so alone, why not hold onto something, even if it's only a cigarette with tar inside that can blacken your lungs and kill you. "Delph, hand me a smoke, would ya?" I tell her.

CHAPTER 3

At breakfast the next morning Pammy nails me. "You didn't eat. You didn't even fetch your tray."

"I know," I say. "Not hungry."

Delphina says, "I is. Just bring it on. I'll eat whatever she's got."

Pammy frowns. "Look, Janey, they've stopped serving by now. I'll fix you something myself. Eggs, how's that?"

"Oh, no thanks."

"I'll take that as a wildly enthusiastic yes." Pammy gives me a no-nonsense look. "Scrambled? Fried? Or boiled?"

"Scrambled, I guess."

Pammy goes into the little kitchen off the cafeteria some twenty feet away. Delphina and I watch glumly while Pammy cracks two eggs over the skillet. It's technically past breakfast time. In the lull before art therapy the other patients are talking, lounging around, waiting for their morning meds. Delphina and I are the only two in this corner of the cafeteria. Delphina is staring out the window at the snow and I am studying our reflection in the glass.

"Whatchew lookin at?" Delphina snaps.

"Nothing," I say.

Delphina is touchy today. Sherman has been successfully discharged. Delphina walked him to the exit doors and now he's gone.

I frame my chin in my hands. The sleep I managed to get wasn't restful. I feel irritable, cramped, and stiff. Every time I look at the snow outside, I think of tires spinning on ice and that grandfather birch tree that just wouldn't budge. I feel the car fishtail; I feel us careening through the woods all over again. "Delph, you ever have the same dream over and over? You know, that haunts you."

Delphina reflects on this, "Nightmare, you mean? Honey, thas' my *life* we talkin' about. It *all* one big nightmare." She laughs. "Especially now that old Clyde's coming to get me."

"Your ex? Oh, no."

"Umm hmmm. You best believe it. He comin' tomorrow."

"But...you don't have to go with him, right? I mean, he used to hit you. Besides, you're divorced."

"I's also stone broke, honey pie. Landlord done evicted me from my apartment. Ain't got no place else to go."

"You earn a steady income. Your dishwashing job. You could find another place."

"Oh, child," she says, shaking her fleecy orange head at me, "you jus' don't know."

"What don't I know?"

"I can't hold no job more'n a few months. I's a good, hard worker; you can't find nobody work harder'n me. But after awhile I get the thirst again. Pretty soon, I starts coming in late, hungover. I ain't reliable no more." She shakes her head, "Rum and coke," she laments, "be my salvation and my downfall."

"Rum and coke," I repeat.

Delphina looks at me.

I want to say something, to tell her I know about addiction because of my mother. But I'm distracted by Pammy, in the little kitchen. She works fast. In a minute she'll bring over my unwanted eggs. If I'm going to share anything about myself with Delphina, I've got to do it now. But I don't. I look out the window at the snow. I'm still staring at the snow, at the white landscape, and the gray ice that glistens with the dull sheen of Smirnoff's gin, my mom's drink of choice. She liked gin, not for the taste, but because it got her where she wanted to go that much faster. I look from the snow to Delphina and shrug, "I don't drink. I mean, not much anyway."

"So, good. So, you'se perfect, then," Delphina bristles. "You'se perfect in every way."

"I didn't say that!"

"Just cause you don't drink don't mean you ain't got problems."

"I never—"

"I talks about me, but you don't let on about you."

"Excuse me?"

"You don't share nothin'. You be as tight as a virgin."

"Gee, thanks," I say.

Delphina frowns at me.

"Look," I add, "I'm not all that interesting."

Delphina gives me a level gaze, her black face staring down the barrel of my white lie. "It be hard, real hard, to be your friend."

"Why?"

"Cause you puts your heart up high where nobody can reach it."

"Right." I wince. Delphina is so honest, and her words have a rightness to them, like wind in the grass. I can't deny her. I won't even try. "What do you want to know?"

"Who that picture of."

I frown. "What picture?"

"That you hides away in your wallet. Less'n you got more'n one."

"No," I say, "there's just the one."

"Well, who that standing beside you? Little fella you got your arm around?"

I hesitate, then say, in a low voice, "My brother."

"You still rap with him? You know, get along? You look real close, from the picture."

I want to answer her, to explain, but I say nothing. Pammy reappears, plunks down my plate of eggs. It is an act of kindness, and a command.

"Your Grace." Pammy bows.

"Thank you, Your Nothingness." I try and smile, but really, I don't want these eggs.

I turn to the window and once again contemplate the snow, seeking solace from any beauty I can locate there, but of course all I do is stir up more anger, and more confusion. I hate this iron-gray winter that holds us in its shackles. I look from the snow to Delphina who is waiting for my reply. I look at Pammy. My stomach is doing a crazy dance.

"Janey," Pammy urges.

"Skinny Lady?" Delphina is waiting, still, for my answer. She waits with her mouth slightly open. I can see the cheap filling in her upper molar. Delphina wants to know about the little boy in the picture: my brother. Well, what's it to her? She's leaving tomorrow. By tomorrow night, she'll be rolling with her ex-husband or snoring off too much rum, she won't even remember my name.

"Janey," Pammy says again. "Down the hatch."

"Right," I say.

My hand trembles as I raise my fork to my lips. I open my mouth and force down those yellow eggs like a penance. The eggs are too hot and scald the back of my throat. My fork clatters to the table as I scrape back my chair and jump up. "I can't do this, Pammy. Don't make me," I say, though I am looking straight at Delphina when I run from the room.

⁓⌒⁓

The snow outside matches the white of Dr. Silverberg's lab coat.

It is mid-morning. Dr. Silverberg and I sit in the back of the empty cafeteria. Everyone else is in group.

"Second day in a row you've worn that sweatshirt," Dr. Silverberg says to me.

"Oh?" I behold the tawdriness of my old sweatshirt and tug self-consciously on the sleeves. The truth is, I don't see the point in high fashion these days. I don't have the energy.

Dr. Silverberg must suspect I'm a little tense because she adds, "On the other hand, there's something to be said for dressing comfortably."

"Right," I say.

She's noticed what I choose to wear so now I take a studied appraisal of her. She's got on her white lab coat, unbuttoned and open. Her name is sewn on the pocket in red thread: Dr. Marie Silverberg. *Marie,* I think. I realize until now I did not know her first name. Beneath her lab coat Dr. Silverberg has dressed in a tasteful powder blue skirt and jacket. No sweatshirts for this lady. She's too together for that. She arranges the hem of her skirt and recrosses her legs. Her legs are so long that I wonder if she was the tallest person in her class growing up. The one who always had to stand in the back row for photographs.

She looks straight at me, "What're you thinking?"

"That you're tall. Did you ever play sports?"

"Well," she smiles, "when you're as tall as me, tennis or basketball is almost obligatory. But it so happened I liked tennis. Doubles. I played all through college."

"You mean, on the team?"

"Just intramurally. I had to study most of the time. Medical school, and all that."

"So, you like tennis," I repeat.

"Mmmhmm."

"What else?" I say.

"Hiking. Canoeing. And, I love to garden." She looks at me. "You're quite interested in me."

I say nothing.

"What about you?" she pursues. "What do you like?"

"Oh. Swimming."

"Wonderful. What else?"

"The piano..." I shift on the sofa, feeling uncomfortable. I was able to escape Pammy and Delphina, but Dr. Silverberg's going to be more difficult. Just look at her marbled black eyes trained on me, not missing much, not missing anything.

"There's a piano here, but I've never heard you play," she says.

"I haven't."

"Ah," she says.

"What's ah?"

"I'm sorry you don't feel up to playing. That's common for depression. People often don't feel like doing even things they normally enjoy..."

"Well, I guess that's *my* problem," I say and shrug.

Dr. Silverberg looks at me, "Why do you insist on feeling isolated? You think I don't care?"

"It's just...why should you? I'll be gone by the end of the week."

"You afraid I'll forget you?"

"No. Well, okay. Yes."

She pauses, and says softly, "I won't forget you, Janey Nichols."

"You don't have to humor me just because I'm depressed."

"I'm not humoring you. I never forget my patients. Listen, Janey, do you forget your students at school just because the year is over?"

"What?"

"Your students."

"No."

"Well, then."

"Okay," I sigh. "You win. You'll remember me. Lucky me."

"Great!" Dr. Silverberg says, smiling, refusing to take offense. "Since I win, I get to ask you for something."

"You got your eye on that meditation tape Ruth gave me?"

"Pardon?"

"The one with the bird calls? The waterfalls? You can have it."

"No. I want you to tell me what made you run from breakfast this morning. You were talking with Delphina, and then...Pammy said you just sort of shut down."

I swallow. My skin feels cold and clammy. I find it difficult to breathe. I don't want to be here. I want to go back to my room and lay on my back and stare up at the ceiling.

"Janey," she says.

"What?"

"You might find you feel better, if you talk."

"Why?"

"I don't know, really. But people generally do."

"What if I don't?"

"Well, there you'd have me." She smiles.

"Just talk?" I say.

She nods.

I look at her, then I let my eyes travel to the window. Outside, it begins to snow yet again. Like an uninvited relative who plops onto your living room sofa, who just won't take the hint, the April snow settles heavily on the parked cars, on the streets, on the beggared yellow forsythia.

I think again of the hailstorm, long ago, the birch tree, the crash.

"What?" Dr. Silverberg says. "You look like you're in pain."

"No," I say. "I'm just sick of this snow."

"You don't like snow?"

"Not year round, I don't."

The snow keeps falling. I keep staring out the window. The silence between us lengthens. Finally I glance at Dr. Silverberg. I am afraid to look at her straight on, and I know why. Those black eyes of hers remind me of Adirondack water, the water roughening in the lake just before a storm. Honest eyes is what I mean. Honest eyes belonging to an honest person. The thing is, I am an honest person, too.

"Listen," I say to her.

"What?" she says.

"I lied to you."

"Oh?"

"You asked me if I was an only child, and I said yes. But, I'm not. I had a brother once."

"Older or younger?"

"Younger. He died."

"How did he die? Illness?"

"No."

"Accident, then?"

"I guess." *Was* it an accident? Is anything an accident? Or can some things be helped?

Dr. Silverberg is studying me. She can be pretty matter of fact, but at this moment I get a feeling of real warmth from her. "What was his name?"

My chest constricts. My heart flutters inside my ribs. "Max."

"Isn't that the name you chose for your baby?"

"Yes," I say. "Yes, it was."

Dr. Silverberg presses her fingertips together in a steeple. "Look, Janey..." She hesitates a moment, and because she so rarely hesitates, she has my attention, "whatever happened with your brother, whatever unresolved issues linger there, seem to have been triggered by the death of your son. And so you're dealing with not one death but two. I wish there were a quick, slick way to get you through this, but there isn't. You're going to have to feel your grief."

"Yeah, well, *if* I stick around." Too late, I realize I've not only thought this thought but spoken it aloud.

"If?" She tilts her head, then says, "Janey, are you saying you want to kill yourself?"

She says this with such tenderness it rocks me. I stare into her dark Adirondack eyes. Those eyes have tricked me. They have made me fall in love, a little, when I don't want to fall in love at all. I can't be caring about Dr. Silverberg. I want my discharge Friday. I want my freedom. And, after that, well, after that I want to be in control of my own destiny. I speak hastily, my words tripping over each other, all lies, "Honestly, I don't know where that came from. Slip of the tongue. Of course you're right, about feeling my grief. That's good advice. Well..." I stand up from the sofa. "Our time's up. My group is doing cooking now, and I'd hate to miss it."

"Yes, we both know how much you love to eat," she says, and that's when I know I haven't fooled her, not one bit.

⁓⌒⁓

My group is making spaghetti. I remember I used to like spaghetti. Spaghetti, a little red wine, garlic bread. Seems like a long time ago.

The way I'm feeling now I know I won't touch even a single noodle. I think I might just skulk back to my room, but I see Dr. Silverberg is keeping an eye on me, and so I join the group gathered around the stove and the boiling pot of noodles.

"You want to help?" Pammy says to me.

"Linguini fettucini at your service."

"Spread some butter on this garlic bread."

I spread butter on the loaf Pammy hands me, and then I sprinkle on some garlic, which makes my stomach lurch. I squeeze my eyes shut and wait for the nausea to pass. Then I hear my name on the intercom, "Janey Nichols, you have a visitor. Marianne Mullen to see you."

Marianne Mullen? I think. Oh, Jesus.

Marianne Mullen is a fine administrator, principal of the Weybridge Lower School, and my boss. She's the kind of person who likes all her ducks in a row. Nobody has their ducks in a row here, I suppose you could say, by definition. I hope Marianne doesn't run into someone too offbeat on her way to finding me.

I yank off the apron Pammy gave me and hurry toward the entrance doors. Even then I am already too late.

"Janey! Hello!" Marianne exclaims, and her voice is much too hearty. She pumps my hand like she hasn't seen me in decades. And once she's stopped pumping my hand, she won't let go. What's gone wrong? Her face is chalky white. She stands on tiptoe as if poised to flee.

"Marianne?" I say. "What is it?"

"That...man." She casts an anxious glance behind her.

I spot a cadaverously thin man in a formal black suit. His black eyes are sepulchral, hooded. His arms, which he flaps uselessly about him, are like broken raven's wings. You see him you think he is part man, part bird; whatever he is he reminds you of death.

"Oh, " I tell Marianne, "that's Mr. Kramer."

"The poor man keeps asking for help, but no one helps him."

"Well," I say.

"Can't anyone help him?"

"They try," I say.

"But why can't they ease his pain?"

I stare at Marianne. I want to reassure her, I really do, but on the other hand, she only wants pat answers and this, perversely, makes me, suddenly, briefly, hate her. Still, I try to keep my voice even, "They can't ease his pain because they don't know where it comes from."

"What about some sort of medication? You know, to dope him up. Or, perhaps, electroshock."

"It doesn't work for him."

"Oh. I see," Marianne says, although I can tell she doesn't see at all. She comes from a world where if there are questions there are always answers; if there are problems there are always solutions. A man like Mr. Kramer simply cannot exist. Marianne finally relinquishes my hand to take a good hard look at me. I can read her initial disappointment until she abruptly rearranges her face into a false smile. Her smile is of the garden-party variety, as if we've found each other out in the pink of the rhododendrons, nibbling on triangular cucumber sandwiches. "But you, Janey," she enthuses, "look marvelous! Just marvelous!"

Uh oh, I think to myself. I must look worse, even, than I thought. For this I know. I don't look marvelous. My skin is white to the point of translucent, my blue veins show underneath, running like complicated rivers. I have smudged gray moons under my eyes from no sleep. "Let's go to my room," I say, ushering her down the hall.

My room, I realize, is an embarassment. So spartan. Bed, desk, chest of drawers, closet, window. But, I have forgotten about the smell until Marianne sniffs and says, "Cigarettes?"

"Pardon?"

"It smells like cigarettes in here."

"Fancy that," I say lightly, when inside I feel a pang of guilt as I recall my nightly smokes with Delphina.

"You might want to throw open a window, dear."

I frown. I want to be polite. I want to keep my job. But, I hate how Marianne keeps overlooking where we are, and what is really going on here. A mental ward is not a garden party, after all. "The windows," I say in a clipped voice, "don't open."

"No, right. Of course not," she murmurs, chastened.

And so now I feel struck by remorse. Marianne can't help it if she doesn't understand. I didn't understand depression either, or psychiatric wards, or suicide checks. I thought I knew what mental illness was. It was when you were crazy. Since I have become one of the crazy ones, I realize the stereotypes don't fit anymore, they never did. I extend my arm with a courtly flourish, trying to regain the civility I lost, "Would you care to sit on the bed?"

"Certainly," Marianne Mullen says.

Together we sit down. Or, rather, we perch on the edge of my bed, both of us uneasy.

"So," I say, smiling gamely.

"So," she says.

"Here we are."

"Yes, indeed."

"So," I say again.

"So," she says.

I think I'm going to go mad, truly, if we keep this up much longer. I want to ask Marianne why she is here, and what she has come for; in fact, I am going to ask her when she plunges her hand into her briefcase and thrusts a pot-bellied manila envelope at me. "For you, dear. Cards your students made."

I am touched beyond words. "Thank you," I say.

"Open them," she says. "Won't you?"

"Later," I say.

"Of course, yes. You'll want to savor each one," Marianne says. She waits a beat or two.

I ask, "How's Charlie doing?"

"Moody?"

"Yes."

She shakes her head. "He's been sent to my office three times. For throwing erasers, bullying the other students. And, most appalling of all, he skewered your goldfish."

"Lucky? Our class mascot?"

"Afraid so."

"Oh, my," I say.

"And you, dear," Marianne appraises me candidly, "How are you doing? I mean, *really*, between the two of us."

"Between the two of us, just fine, thanks."

"Splendid," she says. "Splendid." But there is just the tiniest catch in her voice.

I tilt my head, as though to catch something she did not say.

"I'm better every day," I add.

"Wonderful," she says.

"Yes, it is."

"I mean, one's health," she says, "one should never take it for granted."

"No."

"But we do, don't we? Take it for granted."

"Yes."

"But in any case, you're better, then?" she repeats.

"Yes. Much."

"Good, good, good," she says, then pauses. During this pause I get the feeling she's about to get to the point. I wait anxiously for her to proceed, meanwhile inhaling the stale odor of the cigarettes Delphina and I have been smoking. Marianne's right, we need to open a window. If we only could.

Marianne clears her throat. "Are you planning to come back to teach in September?"

"September? Oh, definitely," I reply. I scrutinize her carefully.

She nods but says nothing.

"Is there a problem?" I ask. "Is Antonia Gianelli not working out? Do you need me back sooner?"

"No, no, Antonia is competent enough, under the circumstances. She's young, as you know. She hasn't yet found her footing with the kids. But—" Marianne interrupts herself "—Antonia is not what I came here to talk to you about."

Marianne lets her voice trail off. I wait a long time for her to continue. When she doesn't, I ask, "Marianne, what *did* you come here to talk about?"

"Yes, well. It's just that the Board—or I should say, the Board and I—"

"Yes?"

"Feel..." She hesitates.

"Yes?"

"Well, we need to create some sort of policy."

"Policy," I repeat, confused.

"Health policy."

There is an acutely awkward pause. Marianne studies my blank face for several seconds. Then I understand; she's talking about *mental* health. "You mean, because I've been hospitalized."

"Exactly so, my dear."

"What does the Board want me to do?"

"Well, please don't take offense at this, but the Board feels the need to reassess your teaching skills as well as your overall fitness to teach."

"What? Come on, Marianne!"

"I know it sounds a bit much, but what it simply boils down to is this, they want to observe you teach a class or two this spring. And, then, afterwards, ask you some questions."

"To see if I've lost it, you mean. If I still have the stuff."

"Now, Janey, don't get upset. I personally think most highly of you..." Her voice is syrupy with sincerity, and I suddenly don't believe a word she says. Marianne Mullen is gifted in this way, in her slippery ability to persuade. She drums up more alumni contributions and educational grants and scholarship money for Weybridge School than anyone else. This is owing to her inspirational fund-raising speeches, partly because she seduces you with that voice of hers, and partly because she quotes from Abraham Lincoln, or if it's a staggeringly audacious sum of money she wants, John F. Kennedy. She quotes occasionally from Anne Morrow Lindberg, too, at women's clubs, though I doubt the sensitive poet had two hundred dollar-a-plate dinners in mind when she wrote *A Gift from the Sea*.

I stare at Marianne and she stares back.

"I'm not some circus act," I say. "For godsakes."

"Janey..."

"I won't jump through hoops."

Marianne frowns. "Bottom line, Janey?"

I nod. "Bottom line."

"You've got to."

"No."

"That is, if you want your job back."

"Back?" I say. "What do you mean, back? It's still my job, isn't it?"

Marianne waffles, "The Board is concerned..."

"Concerned?"

Her voice is gentle, "Well, you did contemplate suicide, did you not?"

I bow my head. She's got me there. I'm a circus act already. Hey, look at the freak show, the lady who pops pills like M& M's, or wants to, anyway.

"Fine," I say. "Fine." I turn away from Marianne to study intently my moccasins placed side by side on the floor beneath the bed. I am deeply hurt. I understand Marianne's viewpoint and the Board's, but still, why don't they trust me? Don't they know that, come September, I wouldn't attempt to teach if I didn't feel up to it? I would never do that to the kids. It wouldn't be fair to them.

Marianne stands from my bed and coaxes on her coat. I think, perhaps, she is angry. Tomorrow, maybe, I'll wish I'd handled this differently, been more conciliatory, but right now I'm able to meet Marianne's level gaze without crying, without tears streaming down my cheeks, and that is the best I can do.

"You think I'm not in your corner," Marianne says, in such a low voice I have to lean forward to hear. "But between you and me, I think it's a travesty that you have to go through this. I'd take you with one arm tied behind your back. Honestly, Janey, I'll do what I can."

"Uh, well..." I sputter. I am speechless. I always knew Marianne liked my teaching just fine, but I sensed she didn't care for me personally. I never particularly cared for her. I am so much more liberal, always pushing for new curriculum, more field trips, more projects, and the hell with the cost. I am an administrator's nightmare, and yet here Marianne is, in the hour of my need, surprising me utterly. Perhaps I have cared more about her, too, than I realized.

"Thanks," I murmur. "For your support. It means a lot."

I step towards Marianne, expecting the obligatory embrace where we each kiss the air between us, but she pulls me in for a genuine hug and doesn't pretend to kiss me at all.

≈⊃C⊂≈

I walk Marianne to the exit doors where we say good-bye.

Back in my room, I decide to spruce myself up a bit. In one hour I am meeting Will and Sarah in the cafeteria.

I scoot by Lil's room without her seeing me this time. I take my shower. Afterwards I look into the mirror above the sinks.

What despair could Marianne Mullen discern in my face just now when she came to visit? I hope she didn't see what I see now: a middle-aged lady with a sallow complexion who has never seen the sun. Don't gaze too deeply into my darting, frightened eyes because I will scare you. I look like a fringe person, scuttling about on the edge of society, belonging nowhere. I appear to be, at best, marginally employable. Certainly not suitable for the likes of Weybridge School and impressionable first graders.

No, I look good for very little, someone you'd hope to lose in the shadows of the graveyard shift. I could mop floors for you while everyone sleeps, the smells of floor wax and ammonium chloride my only companions.

The cafeteria is a mistake.

I get permission to leave the ward. I could walk to the cafeteria via a labyrinthian indoor route, but I choose instead to walk outside along the snow-encrusted sidewalk on a route that traverses the front of the hospital. The snow, at least, has stopped. But it is cold. My lungs feel brittle enough to snap, and my nostrils pinch together every time I breathe. I am wearing a jacket, but no gloves. I did not expect, in April, to need them. I burrow, chin down, in my jacket and thrust myself forward. My boots make a lonely, crunching sound in the snow.

The main cafeteria, home to the hospital staff and open to the public as well, is crowded, and I am overwhelmed from the moment I step inside, stamping snow from my boots. I make a quick survey of faces, but I find no Will, no Sarah. I feel the first flutterings of panic. To distract myself, I line up for some food.

I inch my tray along the metal track, past endless choices that clamor to be made: blue-plate special? Bread and rolls? Cold cuts? Salad bar? Some fruit, perhaps? Jell-O? Pudding? Soup? I pick vegetable soup only because it's right in front of me. I reach into the barrel of crushed ice and scoop out an orange soda, then grab an apple pie encased in cellophane. Before I know it, the cashier is ringing me up, "Two thirty-five," she says.

"What?" I say blankly. Then I remember: money. She wants cash, only I haven't brought any. I'm so used to simply picking up my tray in the psych ward, or *not* picking it up, as the case may be, I've forgotten that the rest of the world, the rest of the hospital, even, doesn't work that way.

"Two thirty-five," she repeats.

"Right," I say.

My heart thunks in my chest. I have no money at all; I have not even thought to bring my purse. What would I have done if Will hadn't, just that moment, appeared at my elbow?

"How much do you need?" he asks the cashier.

I stand uselessly beside my husband. I feel nothing but shame at how childlike I've become. Will must sense this because, as we head for a vacant table, he says, "So you forgot to pay. No big deal, Janey. Me, I forget to put on matching socks half the time, and there I am in court, standing before the judge, one black sock, one blue."

I look at Will as he puts down my tray. What a kind man. I am lucky to have him.

Behind us, and the table we have chosen, I see Sarah approach. I glimpse the usual startling red of her hair and the willowy beauty of her body, and then my eyes narrow. Her right arm is mummified by an ace bandage. I immediately turn to my husband, "Will?"

"Don't worry," he says. "She's not hurt. Only accessorizing. Like with the Band-Aids she got from the nurse."

I don't know whether to be more concerned or less that Sarah's injury is only imaginary.

At just that moment, our daughter joins us.

"Mommy," she says.

I open my arms and she falls into them. There is a neediness in her, which I can feel clean through me. Her head leans against me, presses into my ribs. It must be hard to be so young and have your mother in the hospital. She must be so scared.

We hug for a long time. Finally, she extricates herself, stands back, and shows me her bandaged arm. "Daddy doesn't believe me, but I broke my wrist."

"Oh?" I say. I look to Will. I don't quite know how we should handle this. Does Sarah think she needs to be injured for us to love her? Is she emulating, after a fashion, her dead brother?

"You don't believe me," she says, her voice cracking.

"Oh, Sare, I—"

"I can tell from your face. You think I'm faking it, just like Daddy! Oh, I'm getting in line for some ice cream!" With that, she stamps off.

Will and I watch her.

"She'll calm down," he says.

"When did *this* start?"

"With the arm? Oh, just before we came."

"Why, do you think? Is she trying to be like Max?"

"Or like you."

"Oh. You mean, I'm damaged, she has to be damaged?"

"That sounds perjorative. But you *are* in a hospital. Maybe she just wants to belong here, too."

We sit down at the table.

Steam from my soup spirals into the air.

"You should eat," Will says, "before it gets cold."

"Right," I say.

I dip my spoon into the soup and raise it my lips. I smell the tomato, the peas, the potatoes. My stomach roils. I put the spoon down.

"Janey," he urges, "you need to keep your weight up."

"I know," I say.

Will looks at me. He looks at Sarah in line. He rakes his fingers through his hair, an anxious gesture, and sighs. He seems old, deflated, and I suddenly realize what a toll my depression has taken on him.

"You okay?" I ask him.

"Sure," he says.

But he appears haggard. And something else. Lonely.

I think back to yesterday in my room when his kisses burned my lips, and I wonder what he's been doing for release. Does he buy one of those magazines I sometimes find stuck in his dresser drawer? Does he do a quick and antiseptic jerking off in the bathroom or, more langorously, in bed? And, more importantly, does he think of me? Or does the airbrushed lady with peroxided blonde hair in black leather and black stiletto heels on the cover of one of those magazines seem more real to him than me? And if not more real, certainly more willing.

"Will," I say. "I'm sorry."

"For what?"

"Yesterday. The room. You were kissing me, and—"

"Oh, that," he says. "Don't worry about it."

I choose my words carefully. "You said you can wait till I'm better. But can you? Are you honestly all right with that?"

His cheeks flush. He pulls at his tie to loosen it.

"Janey...let's not talk about this now."

"Why not? I think we should." I look straight at him. I am steadfast in my gaze. But he won't meet my eyes. He won't acknowledge his own loneliness, sexual or otherwise. Instead, he stands up from the table. His business suit is rumpled; his tie, which he has loosened, still appears to be throttling him. I spot a tiny bloody gouge in his cheek where this morning he nicked himself shaving. But he doesn't want to talk about how overburdened he feels. Perhaps he finds the cafeteria atmosphere nonconducive to the sharing of confidences. Or he feels I'm not well enough to help him with his problems. Or, worse yet, he feels his problems are so catastrophic, they are beyond solving, by anyone. In any case, he's already started after Sarah. "I'm going to rustle up some coffee. Be back."

"Fine," I say, though the fact is, when Will leaves me to get in line, I am not fine. My body turns all quivery. I decide to try some soup again, to boost my blood sugar, but it's no good. I dip my soup spoon into the bowl. I want to force myself to eat, but I am looking down at that soup swimming on my spoon, that greasy clump of potatoes, those oily carrots, and my fingers start trembling so much, I can't even guide the spoon into my mouth. Defeated, I shove the soup bowl away.

"Mom?" Sarah says.

She's inexpertly balancing her parfait glass of ice cream on her plastic tray. Her face is pale with worry.

"Oh, hi, honey!" I say, with false cheer.

She is no dummy. She watched me lose my battle with the soup, and she knows it's not normal. She's not used to seeing me so easily intimidated, on the verge of tears. She wants her old mother back, who could handle a roomful of first graders. I want to tell her, *me too*.

But right now there's nothing be to done except change the subject. I graft enthusiasm onto my voice, "Look at you! You got gummy bears on your ice cream!"

She looks at me, distrustful, but she knows not to call me on this. She lets me clear my tears away and pretends not to notice. "Want some?"

"Uh, no thanks," I say.

She sits and dutifully eats her ice cream. She keeps giving me anxious glances. She notices I'm still not touching my soup.

Will returns, slumps into his chair, and nabs a quick jolt of caffeine from his steaming styrofoam cup. I wish he didn't have to be drinking out of styrofoam. I wish instead he could wrap his hand around the comforting solidity of one of our mugs back home, and while he was at it, wrap his other hand around mine. Thinking this, I reach across the table and lace our fingers together.

He smiles feebly.

Sarah keeps after her vanilla ice cream. Her ace bandage feels too tight around her wrist and so she tugs at it. She can't get it right, though, so she yanks the ace bandage off altogether and leaves it coiled on the table. She returns to her ice cream, wielding her spoon easily, raising and lowering her wrist with no problem, no sign of pain.

"Sare," I say gently, "if you ever want attention, for Daddy and me to hug you or talk with you, you can just ask, okay? You don't have to be hurt."

"I really *did* hurt my hand, Mom!" Scowling, she snatches up the ace bandage and winds it defiantly around her wrist. Her motions are as ruthless as a threshing machine's; if there were something wrong with her wrist, surely she'd cry out.

Whatever's going on with my daughter, I don't understand. I know this, though. I know, because of my own illness, that our minds are worthy of respect, even when they are broken. Our minds work like little soldiers. They march into the fray, they do battle for us, and sometimes they get hurt.

Sarah polishes off her ice cream. She nudges her parfait glass aside and then reaches for Will's tray, for the chocolate pudding he bought along with his coffee. She immediately starts in on the chocolate pudding. Will doesn't bat an eyelash. As far as I know she's had no dinner. "Wait a second," I say. "Two desserts?"

"It's okay," Will says. "I...thought we'd let her have a treat tonight."

"Yes," Sarah says, innocently. "It was our deal."

"Deal?"

"Because I didn't want to come here."

"Oh?" I say. I am so hurt I don't even try to hide it. I can feel my face crumple.

Will shakes his head. "What...uh, she meant to say, was—" He turns, exasperated, to Sarah, "You really could have been more diplomatic."

"What's diplomatic?" she says.

My cheeks are burning, still. I turn from Will to Sarah. "Is this true, Sare? You didn't want to come? I thought, on the phone, that you really did."

"Well, yeah, I did, but...when we actually got here and walked through, like the lobby, I didn't like it."

"Why not?"

"It smells like sick people."

"Oh."

"And besides," Sarah says. "I want to get home. Antonia's coming over."

I am surprised. I picture Antonia with all her prettiness, that tumble of blonde hair. I turn to Will, "She is?"

"Just to drop off a casserole," he says.

"After you leave here?"

"Yes." He is terse. He takes another shot of coffee before he catches the look on my face. "What?" he says.

"Nothing," I say.

There's a sudden commotion as the physicians and nurses from the adjoining table get up and shout their good-byes. I can't tune out the background din, footsteps, laughter, voices. If the hospital smells of sick people, it must smell of me, because I am sick. I can't stop this disturbance in my ears. It feels like I have tinnitus, everything crackling in a silvery way, like tinfoil. I put my hands up to my ears, to block the sound.

"Janey?" Will says.

"Mommy?" Sarah says.

They are both staring at me.

I force myself to change the subject and pretend everything is okay. "So...Sare, tell us about school. You still collecting acorns?"

"Oh, Mom. Acorns are for babies. In science we're doing metaphoric rocks."

"I think that's metamorphic, but great."

"We're looking at all kinds. I like tiger's eye."

"I like that one, too."

"Dad," Sarah says, giving up on her pudding now that she's decided she's full. "Can we go now?"

"Janey?" Will says, deferring to me.

"Fine," I say. The truth is, I want them to be gone. I want to go back to my cell in the ward and curl up in my narrow bed.

"You're sure?" Will asks.

I nod. "Let me walk you out."

Outside, the parking lot is slick with snow. We all stand by the Mazda, our breaths misty in the crisp air, as Will fishes in his pocket for his car keys. Behind him, the wan crepuscular sun quickly descends and the twilight deepens from pink to purple. Will's black hair is tousled, and his face, with those green eyes, looks so beautiful I think I could fall in love with him all over again. Now that my mood has changed, I'm not so keen on being alone, back in the ward. I want to tell him, *Stay a little longer; don't leave.* But, I help Sarah into the back and make sure her seatbelt is done up nice and snug, and I wave to her through the window, through the little porthole she made in the fogged-up glass. I don't look directly at Will. Not once. I'm wondering about Antonia Gianelli and why he didn't tell me about her stopping by, wondering would he have mentioned it, if Sarah hadn't.

≈⊃⊂≈

Delphina offers me a cigarette, "Smoke?"

"Absolutely," I say.

Delphina and I are sitting in my room with the door closed, our legs splayed on the floor, our backs propped up against my bed. A chipped coffee mug serves as our ashtray. Sarah and Will headed off about an hour ago. I stood in the parking lot and waved to them until they drove out of sight. Then I stuck my hands in my pockets and returned to the ward.

Just now, I pop the Newport between my lips, strike a match, and light up. I suck down too much smoke and cough. I try again, and then again. I am not practiced at this. My cigarette is burning down. I flick the ashes off too hard. The fiery ball of tobacco crumbles off and the lit ashes tumble to the floor.

"You done lost your cherry," Delphina says.

"What?" I stomp the lit ashes with the heel of my shoe.

"You calls it losing your cherry when them ashes fall off like that."

"Great," I say. "Not that we're into sexual metaphors or anything."

"No, nuthin like that," Delphina says.

Feeling like the true beginner I am, I light up my cigarette yet again. This time I trap way too much smoke in my lungs. I manage to hold back on the cough, but I turn green; I know I do.

Delphina laughs, "You ain't no natural-born smoker."

"No."

"You one of them goody two shoes?"

"In school? Growing up?" I say. "Yes."

"So, why you smoking now?"

"Trying to be a goody one shoe, I guess."

While Delphina watches, I mount another assault on my cigarette. This time I inhale just the right amount of smoke, and I find myself confiding, "This teacher at school? Antonia Gianelli? I think she's after my husband."

"Say what?" Delphina taps ash from her cigarette into the chipped mug, looks straight at me.

"Yeah." I nod.

"Whoa, girl. You sure 'bout this?"

"Course not!" I mutter, irritably, then take another raggedy drag on the Newport. "It's just...Will and Antonia have always hit it off. Whenever there's a Weybridge function, some kind of school thing, I see them off in a corner talking. Will likes her."

"Ain't no crime."

"You don't understand. She's got this way about her. She's the kind of person who gets you doing things for her and you don't even mind."

"What she look like? She no dog, I take it."

"Oh, no. She's thin and blonde. The kind of blonde, pale and lunar, it cools you off to look at."

"Natural?"

"I've been told the blonde is an expert dye job, but the curls are natural. They must be. They're so corkscrewed. You could never get a permanent to look that good."

"She be an ice princess. Ain't no crime in that neither."

"No."

"What, then?"

I swallow. "I saw them once."

"Doing the dirty?"

"No, nothing like that. It was at this cocktail party. Maybe she had too much to drink. Maybe Will did, though usually he sticks to a glass or two of wine. Anyway, there was this moment."

"The Earth moved?"

"Stop it. No. When I happened to see. She leaned in to him and he leaned back. And the look in her eyes. I don't know....It was like they were in their own world."

"Maybe they just bein' friendly, and the alcohol helped them along."

"Maybe." I shrug.

"You tell her?"

"What?"

"To back off."

"No." I swallow. "No, I mean, it could have been nothing. It could have been...you know, just a moment I exaggerated in my mind or something."

"And Will? You talk to him?"

"No way."

"Why not, girl?"

"Suppose he liked her back?"

"Better to find that out."

"I guess." I take a final drag on my cigarette, then stub it out in the hairline cracks at the bottom of the coffee mug.

"Well, I gots a question for you. Can this princess cook?"

"Oh, you mean the casserole. I don't know."

"Let's hope not, Skinny Lady."

"Yeah, let's hope not."

Maybe I shouldn't feel jealous. Maybe I should feel grateful. Antonia's the only person, except for our closest friends and neighbors, who's thought to bring dinner recently. Still, I wish she'd stayed away.

Delphina. Now, Delphina I feel the opposite about. I want her to stay with me, here in my room, forever. But we're out of cigarettes, and

Delphina's starting to feel blue so she wants to be alone, she says. She extinguishes her Newport, hauls herself to her feet, and slouches back to her room.

Alone, I fetch the photograph of my little brother from my wallet. I know I am obsessing over this. Maybe I think if I just keep staring at the photograph, I can transport myself back in time. I can rearrange history more to my liking. I can keep tragedy at bay.

I am reluctant to fall asleep, but the Xanax Dr. Silverberg has prescribed starts to work on me. I tuck the photograph back in my wallet and lay down on the bed. Before I know it I am back in the Dream.

꽃꽃

I am in the car again, in the backseat with Max. Mom is driving. I see the car ashtray pulled out; inside it is a jumble of Mom's lipstick-smeared cigarette stubs. Cracklin' Rosie *is on the radio.* Cracklin' Rosie you make me smile. *Mom hands out the bubble gum. "Almost there, kids," she says. Max and I pop two pink cubes of bubble gum, each, into our mouths. We are laughing, happy. Then the sky opens, and hailstones pummel the hood of the car, the roof. Mom hunches over the steering wheel and peers out the windshield to see. A curve, too fast. Mom? Mom, slow down. Another curve. Ice. We fishtail. I smell the bubble gum breath of my little brother as he flings his arms around my neck. Mom hits the brakes but the brakes won't catch. The car skids, lifts off the ground, airborne through the woods, toboggan ride. Whee! Max is laughing, but he is holding on tight, too. I can feel the heat rising off his delicate white skin. I see the birch tree. That giant birch that looks almost friendly, the friendly giant too big and clumsy to get out of our way. Max sees the tree too. I feel his long narrow piano-key fingers tighten around my neck; I smell his smell; he's only eight, and so small; is he wearing his seat belt? As I turn to see, I feel the shudder, the whiplash of impact...*

CHAPTER 4

The next day, in art therapy, we blow out Easter eggs. I'm not in much of a mood; I'm still carrying around the vestiges of the Dream. And I'm sad, too, because Delphina's going to be discharged. Clyde's coming for her at six o'clock.

I must say, Delphina and I are quite some pair, because if you think I'm sad, you should see Delphina. I look like a carnival compared to her. She keeps saying she can't wait to go home, but I'm not so sure.

Our art therapist, Cyndi, unlike us, isn't sad in the least. She's all but skipping around handing out white, Grade A, extra-large eggs. She's a regular Easter bunny.

"Janey!" she says. *"Delphina! Come on. Cheer up, you two. This is a fun project, you'll see!"*

One thing about Cyndi is that she talks loudly to us, like we're foreigners, or perhaps mentally retarded. She is *all but shouting!* Maybe somebody told her once that we depressives are hard of hearing. I don't know.

"Thank you, Cyndi!" I holler back, taking my egg.

Delphina starts to giggle. She holds up her Grade A, extra-large, white egg and says, "You know the one about eggs and bacon? The hen she be involved, but the pig he committed."

"No, *we're* committed," I say, smiling wryly.

"That not funny," Delphina says. "We's voluntary patients, free to leave anytime. And I's voluntarily leaving tonight."

"I know," I say. "With Clyde."

Delphina frowns at me. "You don't likes him."

"He used to hit you, Delph."

"He won't no more."

"I hope not," I say.

Delphina doesn't want to think about this anymore, not about Clyde, or her future, which is hazy at best. She redirects her attention to the white egg she palms in her brown hand. "Tell me, girlfrien', how we ever gonna get this yolk out?"

"Easy," I say. "Watch."

I have taught entire classrooms of students how to do this. The key, I think, is patience. I carefully poke two holes in my white egg, then I, equally carefully, blow out the egg's insides with a blue nasal syringe.

"Jesus, girl!" Delphina exclaims. "It be flying all over, like snot! Like some kinda ugly! I ain't never gonna eat no egg again."

I suction with the blue syringe until my egg is flushed out. The egg is dripping wet and sticky, but inside it is hollow. "Ta da! Happy Easter, Delphie! Of course, we still need to dye it, but—"

"No, honey, I needs to diet," Delphina says. She rolls up the sleeves of her sweater over her beefy arms, "Hand me that syringe, girl. My egg, he saying, blow me, baby, blow me..."

I laugh, glad to see Delphina's feeling better. This morning so far she's been more depressed than I've ever seen her. She's been eating a lot, even for her. For breakfast she demolished three cheese danishes. And after breakfast, before lunch, she ordered pizza on the sly and snuck it into her room.

Delphina is all packed up. I know because I saw the jaws of an old battered suitcase open on her bed. We exchanged phone numbers. Delphina gave me the number at the pancake house because Clyde's phone service got cut off due to his failure to pay. We promised to keep in touch, which is the first time, as far as I know, Delphina and I have out and out lied to each other.

Delphina works in silence on her egg. I see her blue mood steal over her again. She makes a face, "What eggs got to do with Easter anyhow?"

"People have been coloring eggs since like the fifteenth century. Eggs symbolize the rebirth of nature from the dead of winter."

"Dead of winter?" Delphina says. "But that be a regular egg, right?"

"What?"

"You talkin' about."

"Right."

"So, what's a blowed out egg? What that stand for?"

"Well..." I study my egg, hollow, its white shell dripping with the last vestiges of yolk. My egg is my heart, scoured out, emptied by losses—my brother, my son, my mother. My egg is her heart, without Sherman, with no place to call home except with a man she should stay the hell away from. "Beats the heck outta me," I say.

Delphina has gone back to pumping the blue syringe. Suddenly her egg's insides blow every which way into the mixing bowl. Delphina starts to laugh, then cry, "Sherman never did call."

"I'm sorry," I say, then pause to add, "If he *does* call here, I'll give him your number at the pancake house, okay?"

Delphina stares at me. She knows that Sherman's not calling—not today, not tomorrow, and so do I. I want to be honest with Delphina and tell her I'm not sure she'll get over Sherman, just as I'm not sure I'll get over what I need to. But, I hope Delphina will keep the faith and not give up, even though *I'm* thinking about giving up; I think about it all the time so hard I sometimes forget how to breathe. But right now Delphina is worse off than me. Life is too much effort just now, or at least art therapy, because she suddenly shoves her egg away and, with a sigh of despair, lays her head down on the table, into the chocolate nest of her folded arms.

Cyndi comes over to see how we're doing.

"*Janey, great job!*" she gushes. "*Delphina, you catching five winks, there? That's fine!*" Cyndi addresses me since Delphina's got her eyes closed and it's clear she doesn't give a damn, "Janey, now listen. I'm going to hand out food coloring next. And once we're done dyeing our eggs, Joe's conducting his aerobics class. *Oh Janey, look at you! I see you've already changed into your gym shorts! Good girl!*"

"*Thank you!*" I say. I am such a hypocrite, pretending I care. I want to make points by going to Joe's exercise class. I want to go home Friday.

"Come on up to the sink, Janey, and I'll get you what you need."

"*Okay!*" I say. I turn back to my friend, "Delph, you coming?"

Delphina reluctantly raises her head from the haven of her arms, "You lookin' like Jane Fonda there, in your cute little gym shorts. I figure you can handle it."

"Okay," I say. "Just try to contain your excitement."

I leave Delphina—for how long? Not long at all, though every second will count. I follow Cyndi to the kitchen sink. My sneaker's undone and I bend over to lace it. Cyndi hands me four tiny bottles of food coloring— red, blue, green, and yellow—and three plastic cups of vinegar. I am juggling all this, trying to catch Delphina's eye and signal to her—come help me—when I realize our table is vacant. Delphina is no longer there.

I figure Delphina went to the bathroom; she'll be back. I return to our table and arrange all the food-coloring bottles and cups of vinegar and water. Still no Delphina. I decide to dye my egg blue. I squeeze two drops of food coloring into the vinegar and lower my egg into the cup with a copper wire spoon. Because my egg is hollow, it floats. When the blue emerges on the white shell of the egg it is the sweet pastel blue of the receiving blanket we got from friends in California. They sent us the blanket before they heard. I don't want to be reminded of the blanket so I quickly grab the green food coloring and squirt in five liberal doses of green. Green seems infinitely safer than blue.

I look around. Delphina is sure taking her sweet time. Still, I'm confident she'll be back. I relax in my chair and let my egg bathe in its green food coloring. That's when I glance out the window to see Delphina heading for the chain-link fence and heavy traffic of Northern Parkway.

I inhale sharply. Where does she think she's going?

I could alert the nurses, but this might get Delphina into trouble. Clearly she's not acting with the classic textbook behavior of a patient ready for discharge.

I cast around, wondering how Delphina got out. I see the sliding glass door slightly ajar. It's supposed to be locked. I glance over to the nurses. Cyndi is helping Lil. Or, better, *She is helping Lil!* Joe is busy, too, carrying a carton of eggs across the room.

I duck out from behind my table, inch my way to the door, and slip out.

The first thing I feel is the cold. God, it's raw. I wish I had pants on and not these ridiculously skimpy gym shorts. The shorts are a flimsy red nylon and leave my legs exposed. Already my thighs prickle with goosebumps.

This is insane, I think. Why am I doing this?

But I start running anyway.

The snow is wet, heavy, slippery. As I head down a slight incline, my sneakers won't grab; I have zero traction. I try not to panic as I take a wild skidding slide in the grass. Mud, snow, and grass smear in an unsightly mess, but I manage to save myself. I'm still going too fast, windmilling out of control, when I slosh into a puddle of melted snow, edged with ice. This time I go down in a crashing alley-oop. Delphina hears me and hazards a backwards glance as I cry out. My legs fly up as though someone has yanked a rug out from under me and I pitch backwards onto my rear end with a thud. I stand up, brushing the snow off me. My naked knees are dripping wet. Like a damp bathing suit, my gym shorts cling to the crack between my buttocks. I feel bruised, shaken, humiliated. Delphina is still watching me. I read amusement on her face; she is gloating. I grit my teeth and take up the chase.

This time as I run I can't help but recall that other time, that other place that was so cold and slippery.

❦

On the way to Windsor Island, the car, the birch tree. Mom is at the wheel. Cracklin' Rosie *is on the radio. A curve, too fast. We fishtail on ice. I smell the bubble gum breath of my little brother as he flings his arms around my neck. Toboggan through the woods. Whee! When we collide with the birch, his arms slip away, and I no longer feel them. After the loud screeching of metal, I hear only silence. Gradually I make out the moan of wind rushing through the shattered glass in the car window. My mother, up front, I hear her moaning too. But there is silence, only silence, next to me in the back seat...*

❦

Delphina has reached the chain-link fence. I wonder what the hell she's doing. Four hundred yards or so from her there is the highway, and all those cars zooming up the hill. Does she want to get herself killed? Delphina is a big woman, and the fence presents a problem. How will she climb over? Delphina glances back at me. She doesn't look so damn cocky. She is panicked now. I am gaining on her. I am maybe one hundred feet away. She grunts, heaves herself over the fence, then lands in an undignified heap. For a moment, she is utterly still. I think she must be winded, then she rolls onto her back, cradling her ankle in pain.

Shit, I think. At least she won't be going anywhere soon.

Knowing I have a chance to catch her, now that she has fallen, I scramble toward the fence. In the final seconds, I don't slow down but hurl myself into the air. I am halfway over, straddling the rusty old fence, when my sneakered toe snags itself in the crisscross of metal and I can go neither forwards nor backwards. I'm stuck. Within seconds my triceps quiver like crazy from supporting my weight. My calves spasm, too. But I can't give up. If I let myself sag, I'll impale my crotch on spikes of rusty metal. Despite the cold, sweat pours down my temples, blurring my eyesight. My legs are being tickled by some kind of green bush. "Delphina, help!" I cry.

Delphina, still wincing, hobbles to her feet and comes over. Once she sees me close up, she starts to laugh.

"What's so funny?" I yell at her.

She keeps laughing. "For such a smart lady, you stupid."

"Great, yeah, terrific. Just get me down."

"Okay, girlfren'." Delphina reaches out her plump black arms to help extricate me from the fence. Once she's got me, her ankle collapses under our joint weight and together we tumble onto our backs in the wet snow.

"You okay?" she asks me.

"Yeah, but don't call me stupid."

"All right, Skinny Lady." She's laughing again. The gold filling on her molar shines dully in the afternoon light. "Except you really *is* stupid if you allergic."

"You're no genius either. Who's that tore up their ankle? Let's not try out for the Olympic pole vault anytime soon, Delph. You've got to learn how to land." I pause. "Allergic to what?"

"You jus' climbed over a mess of poison ivy."

"What?" I snap my head back toward the fence, to the spot where I got stuck. "There? No, that's a blackberry bush."

"Umn umn, honey. Them three green leaves, all in a cluster? With deep red in they stems? That there's the enemy."

"But, wait! It's too early for poison ivy, right? For godsakes, there's snow on the ground."

Delphina looks at me, then she nurses her ankle some more. She slowly peels down her sock, and even from here I can tell her ankle is swollen; it is ballooning up painfully. I'd bet that if I touched it she'd yelp. I still don't know why Delphina ran off like she did but I can guess. She's running away from her dishwashing job at the pancake house, but more than that, she's running away from Clyde. She remembers too late the backside of his hand cracking her jawbone, what that feels like. She remembers the mornings after, counting up her bruises, assessing the damage, feeling so queasy in her stomach that all she will eat that day will be applesauce, even a plump woman like her.

And if she's running *away* from Clyde, is she running *toward* Sherman? Is he somewhere in the white of the sky, in the roar of traffic she hears on Northern Parkway, in the freedom she feels now that we're sitting sprawled in the snow on the other side of the fence? Sherman, who is probably right now banging out desolate chords on his piano and guzzling cheap red table wine. He is not thinking of Delphina, at all, if he ever did.

Delphina says, "Poison ivy, them resins and things, they bad news year round, snow or no snow. If I was you, I'd take me a shower real quick."

And if I were you, I want to say, *I'd forget Sherman, and I'd sure as hell forget Clyde.* But, I don't. I don't say anything.

Delphina starts laughing again.

I think she is laughing at me and my poison ivy.

But then she makes this awful choking sound and starts to cry.

"Delph," I reach out to touch her arm, "what is it?"

She doesn't answer. Her cries become flat-out sobs. I thought Mr. Kramer had a lock on pain, his hysterical cries sounding like a loon's lonely call echoing across the lake, but no. If you heard Delphina cry, you would think the sun had fallen.

"Come on, Delph, talk to me," I plead with her. "Don't hide inside yourself where I can't find you."

But Delphina is past hearing me. Her eyes don't see me, either. She draws her round fat knees in toward her chest, like an autistic child, and starts to rock. She hugs her knees, rocks, and pretty soon she starts singing to herself. Her voice is rich and low, mellifluous. She used to sing in a Baptist choir; I know because she told me. Her singing reminds me of slaves in the cotton fields, and I wonder if anything has really changed. She's black; she's poor; she's got no home. I see tears streaming down her cheeks.

"Delph," I call out to her, "Delphina!" I even shout. Clumsily I try to pull her toward me for an embrace, but she doesn't recognize me.

I feel a hand on my shoulder and turn to see Pammy. "We'll take care of her now," she says to me. "You did a good job to stop her."

"Oh, I don't think she was going out into traffic," I say.

"You don't?"

"No, she just got this way in the last minute or so. She was perfectly coherent. And she wasn't running away."

"Oh, really?" Pammy says. "I would think you of all people would recognize flight when they saw it."

I stare at Pammy. She's right; I know she is. I *have* been running away.

I glance over to Delphina. The head nurse Joe, the good-looking one, is with her, kneeling beside her, but I can tell he's not registering with her. Delphina is wandering in her own world, someplace happy with Sherman where there is no pancake house and no pile of dirty dishes with dried-up maple syrup on them. Two medics, I see, are trotting out a stretcher. They will load Delphina and her sprained ankle onto the stretcher and carry her inside where, sooner or later, Clyde will come to claim her.

I tell Pammy, "He's abusive you know."

"Who? Clyde?"

"He hits her. But she's so depressed, now that she's lost Sherman, she doesn't care."

"Oh, she's not going with Clyde now," Pammy says.

"She's not?"

"No, Janey. She's not ready to go home, obviously. We're sending her on to Sheppard Pratt. A bed there just opened up."

"Sheppard Pratt. But that's for more serious cases, right?"

"Right."

"She was getting better. I know she was!"

"Janey, there are no guarantees."

And that's when I realize this about depression: you don't always get better, you can get worse. If I get worse it's because I can't get over my losses. In life you have to get past losing things because one thing is for sure, if you keep on living you are sure to lose something else.

"Do me a favor?" I say to Pammy.

"What?"

"Help me reach Dr. Silverberg. We don't have an appointment for tomorrow but I want to make one."

"Sure," Pammy says.

I'm sweating hard from all my exertion, and yet I'm beginning to grow chilled. Maybe I'm in shock, too, because I'm suddenly too weak to stand unassisted. Bless Pammy for understanding this. I take one last look at Delphina, so broken, so shattered, I am reminded of that Robert Frost line that always makes me sad, *such heaps of broken glass to sweep away / you'd think the inner dome of heaven had fallen,* as Pammy loops her arm around my waist and together we walk back to the ward.

≈⌒

The first thing I do is strip off my wet things and take a shower. I scrub with my skimpy bar of hospital soap until the bar atrophies to the size of a Wheat Thin. My skin tingles. No signs of poison ivy yet, but then there wouldn't be, not for a few days.

Back in my room, I am toweling my hair dry when Pammy comes in.

"How's Delphina?" I ask her.

"Gone."

"Already? I didn't get a chance to say good-bye."

"Janey, she's not in a place where she would connect with you."

"I know," I say. My thoughts are churning. You never know in life who it will be who will mean everything to you, who will touch your soul. Just as I mean a good deal to Charlie Moody, Delphina means a good deal to me. I try not to feel my sadness, but there it is, a weight inside me, a stone slowly settling to the bottom of a pond, finding its place among other stones, where there is silt and seaweed and wan, filtered sunlight.

Pammy is looking at me. There is tenderness in her eyes, "You liked Delphina, didn't you?"

"I still like her. She didn't *die*."

"No, of course not."

A moment passes between us. "Pammy?" I say.

"Yes?"

"Did you get a hold of Dr. Silverberg?"

"Yes, she can fit you in tomorrow morning."

All afternoon I miss Delphina. The ward just isn't the same without a friend.

In the lounge it's free time before dinner. Tonight is Pizza Night, something that everyone but me, apparently, is looking forward to. I keep eyeing the entrance doors for Will. He said he's coming. I hope he comes before the pizza.

To kill time, I decide to ride the exercise bike. It's an old exercise bike in the corner of the lounge. It's not much. Fat black seat, wide enough to seriously chafe my thighs, but since I don't have anyone to talk to, it will give me something to do.

I work up a good sweat, but when the pizza arrives, Joe calls me over. Reluctantly, I climb off the bike and make myself part of the scene.

Most everyone is ignoring the bleak snow outside and putting on a party mood. Wolfing down pizza, joking, laughing. Every time I look outside, though, I think of Delphina. I think of her slipping in the snow. Then, slipping, in other ways, inside her head.

Joe is growing out his moustache, and people are kidding him about it. "You look like Groucho Marx."

"Yeah, just get him a cigar. The exploding kind."

I leave the table to fetch some apple juice from the refrigerator, and when I sit back down, the topic has switched to ice cream. Not only are the other patients eating food, they are talking about it, too.

"Pistachio, man."

"No way. Plain old vanilla."

"Boring."

"The best, the very best and my personal downfall is Ben and Jerry's Cherry Garcia..."

I don't participate in the conversation until Joe turns to me. He looks good with that blond stubble on his face, but it's wasted on me, I'm so depressed. "What's your favorite, Janey?" he asks.

I feel the group's eyes on me.

I want so much to be normal. I think back to when food meant something. "Chocolate chip?" I venture, but I am guessing. I am relieved when the conversation rolls on, and when, not longer after, Will arrives.

⁓⁀

Will not only arrives, he brings me flowers—a spring bouquet from Eddie's Market: tulips, daffodils, and hyacinths cradled in a cone of fiesta green tissue paper.

"Lovely," I tell him. I press my nose into the flowers, inhale, search for their perfume but can't find any.

Will, who is enjoying my enjoyment of his flowers, suddenly stops smiling. "What'll you put them in?"

"Oh, I'll find something."

Will sighs. Last time he had the carnations delivered in a glass vase. This time we have no vase at all. I know just what he's thinking: this vase business is just like his life right now. He can't win. If he could have one wish in all the world, it would be for things to fall back into place, the way they used to be. He yearns for predictability and routine the way adventurers long for high mountain peaks and thin air. All he wants is for things to be normal. It is a simple wish, and he's not going to get it.

"Come on," I tell him, "let's go back to my room."

"Where's your friend?" he says. "Delphina."

"Gone, actually. To Sheppard Pratt. She got worse."

"Sorry to hear that." Will follows me down the hall into my room.

"Yeah," I say. I toss my new flowers onto the white bedspread, then I turn to my husband, who is standing just inside the door, looking forlorn. Well, I can fix that. I step up to him and curl my fingers like tree roots behind his neck to draw him close, and, opening my mouth, search for his tongue.

We stand there kissing, pressing our bodies into each other, until, abruptly, Will breaks off. "Your breath," he says.

"What?"

"Like cigarettes."

"Oh, sorry."

"Since when have you—"

"Delphina and I have been sneaking smokes."

"Do you think that's a good idea?"

"No, Will, it's a terrible idea. Obviously. Look, I'll brush my teeth, if you like."

"Never mind," he says, distractedly. He runs his fingers through his hair, sits down on the bed. I'm not the only one who's had a rough day, I can tell. While I have been mourning Delphina, Will has been caught up in his own worries.

I sit beside him. "Everything okay with Sarah?"

"Yes. Okay, being a relative term. She hasn't slapped on a cast and put herself in traction yet."

"She'll feel better when I come home."

"Friday, right?"

"Friday." I nod.

"You been eating?"

"Trying."

"Because you look kind of skinny."

I keep hoping for Will to wrap his arm around me, but he shifts his weight and eases further down the bed, a subtle movement on his part, but a rejection nonetheless. With nothing left to do, I study our thighs. I'm in frayed blue jeans and he's in expensive pinstripes. His cologne smells rich and musky, and his fine black hair is blown dry. I realize he is dressed up. This is not office attire he's wearing. He's got on his best silk tie.

"Will," I say, "You going out on the town?"

"Yes." He does not look happy.

"A working dinner, I take it?"

"Yes."

"Which client?"

"You know, Jefferson Pediatric, the dispute about the new hospital wing they built?"

"Sure. So...you're going out with...the architects?"

"And design engineers. Barbara thought it'd be a nice touch."

"Barbara?"

"This is her idea. She's good at this kind of thing."

"Yes, she is," I agree, nodding. Barbara Kirkbridge is Will's up-and-coming associate. I am forever grateful to her. From the moment she joined the firm, she has cut my husband's workload in half. Instead of laboring until ten or eleven at night, Will is now home for dinner. Barbara is bubbly and energetic, dedicated to law and to her career. She worked her way through law school, waitressing nights at the comedy club, serving drinks, poring over her law books between sets. She'd wipe down the tables and close the place up at 2 A.M., catch a few winks, and then hurry off to class—Contracts or Torts or whatever, the next day promptly at eight. She brings that same type of dedication to whatever she does.

She's a swimmer, like me. We belong to the same aquatics club.

I swim recreationally, to unwind from my teaching day. Barbara, though, takes her swimming seriously. She practices with the Masters Swim Team and willingly undergoes punishing workouts. Yet she knows how to have fun, too. I've seen her in the jacuzzi afterwards, flirting with the guys on her team. Sometimes I wonder why she hasn't married yet. Maybe she hasn't found the right man; more likely, she's too committed to law right now to spend the time on a relationship.

I ask Will, "How *is* Barbara these days?"

"Good," he says brusquely. "Fine." He consults his watch. "Listen, we don't have long together. I've booked reservations at the Chaucer Inn."

"Ooh la la," I say.

The Chaucer Inn, off of Falls Road, features white linen tablecloths, soft candlelight, impressive wine lists, and entrees so outrageous the prices aren't even listed in the menus they hand to the women. The fact that the men's menus have the prices and how chauvinistic that is, well, the Chaucer Inn doesn't concern itself with social progress.

"I'm not looking forward to it," Will says. He reaches for my hand, "God, I wish I could stay with you."

"Here? In the ward? Yeah, good food, good wine, who needs it?"

He smiles. "I know it sounds inviting, but it's not all that fun. There's a certain, I dunno, pressure."

"What do you mean?"

"Oh, to be relentlessly pleasant and upbeat."

"Around the clients?"

"Yeah. And I don't feel up to it. You know Barbara and I have been working practically around the clock on this case."

"Not getting much sleep, huh?" I say.

"No."

"I can relate." I try and smile.

"I guess you can." Will thinks a moment, then adds wistfully, "You know what I'd really like to do tonight?"

"What?"

"Barbecue out on the deck with you and Sarah. Hamburgers. Hot dogs. Corn on the cob."

I consider the snow on the ground. "It's a little early in the season for that."

"Actually," he says, "it's warming up. Stuff's starting to melt."

"Wet, then."

"The point is, we'd be together. And there wouldn't be all this pressure."

"You keep saying that. What pressure? Work? Deadlines?"

But Will doesn't answer me. If I had to do it over again, I would urge him to tell me more. As it is, he only sighs and says, "When I'm with you, Janey, my world makes sense. And when I'm not, it doesn't."

"I feel that way about you, too," I say.

For perhaps the first time this evening, Will and I are in accord. I feel comfortable just sitting on the bed with him, holding hands. He says, "So Delphina transferred out? She's the heavy black woman, right?"

"Right. She fell apart, Will."

"Breakdown?"

"Yes." I squeeze his hand, hard. "Honey, it scares me."

"What does?"

"How we can get lost inside our heads."

"Don't *you* get lost," he says. He pulls me in close to him, and there we sit, together on the bed. It doesn't matter, for this one moment, that we are in a psychiatric ward. We could be anywhere. We have fashioned, from humble materials, from nothing but our love, our own shelter between us, a sanctuary, and for just this one moment, it is enough. But the moment ends when Will, in a fit of impatience, yanks back the cuff of his sleeve to check his watch again and I make the mistake of taking it personally.

"I should go," he says.

"Can't you stay one more minute?"

"Actually, no." He looks sheepish.

"What?" I ask.

"It's...just..."

"What?"

"The limousine."

"You have a *limousine?*"

"Yes, and it's waiting."

"Out in the parking lot?"

"Yes."

"Here?"

"Yes."

I wince. The disparity between Will's life and mine makes me feel suddenly, anguishingly, pathetic. "Talk about irony. Talk about being left behind."

"You're not left behind."

"No?" I think about Will and his fancy dinner, and then I think back to last night, to the cafeteria and the supposed dinner we shared there. And thinking of this reminds me of Antonia. I should abandon this line of thinking; this is no time to bring up the subject, but I can't seem to help myself, "So, hey, how was your casserole?"

"Fine."

"Did Antonia stay and eat some?"

"Yes, as a matter of fact."

"What kind of casserole was it, Will? One of those macaroni and cheese jobs? With those little green olives, chopped up? I hate those little green olives..."

"Janey."

"What?"

"Don't."

I shrug. Who am I trying to inflict pain on, Will or me? Because I am hurting myself here. With every word. "Tell me, did this eating of the casserole occur before or after Sarah's bedtime?"

"Dammit!" He rakes his hair with agitated fingers. "Could we just drop it? I'm uptight about this dinner!"

"But you're going, just the same."

"It's my job!"

"So, go. No one's stopping you."

He hesitates.

"Go!"

Finally I have provoked him; finally he's snapped. I've gotten what I most dread, it seems, for now he really is leaving. He rises from the bed and walks to the door. At the threshold, he casts one last glance at me.

I could save us both. I could stop Will from going out that door.

"You want to say something?" he asks me.

"What?"

"You look like you're about to say something."

Hold me, I want to say. *Dance with me a slow dance.*

꙳꙳

Remember the first time you kissed me full on the mouth? On my back porch. I could taste the hot dog and beer on your breath, and I liked it. I liked the feel of your tongue. I had to stand on tiptoe. The moths were fluttering at the porch lightbulb, the cicadas buzzed, and the summer heat slid in a trickle of sweat down the shivery part of my spine. I was stunned at how much passion you, so shy, could put into a kiss. You'd been holding back all night, your whole life, even, just waiting for my doorstep, for the ivory moon beyond the black eaves of the roof, my cherry lips. But tonight if there's a moon you won't notice. Because you're not looking to kiss me.

🐉🐉

"Janey?" he repeats. He is wary but hopeful.

My last chance.

There is the longest pause between us.

Finally I say, "Have a good time," but I don't mean it; this much we both know.

I hear Will's footsteps head down the hall. He is angry with me, with both of us, for not making up. He is angry at his own anger. His stride is quick and purposeful, the scuffing louder than Pammy in her cowboy boots. He doesn't let up in his stride at all, and in a moment, the sounds he makes are absorbed into the life of the ward, by the sponge of hospital noise, specifically by the plaintive, nocturnal cry of Mr. Kramer. *Help me,* Mr. Kramer says, as I sink down on my bed and hunch my shoulders, as if to ward off a blow.

⤚)⤙

Will hasn't been gone ten minutes when my anger falls away. Falls away, and what's left is emptiness.

Oh, why did I fight with him? Why couldn't we make up and be friends? If I wasn't doomed to insomnia already, I am now. Tonight, I will replay our conversation, make it go differently in my head. I will see the parting look on Will's face, and that will be my own peculiar torture.

I hang back in my room, not wishing to socialize. I glance at the manila envelope that Marianne Mullen brought me—the cards from the kids at school. I flip through the cards, not really reading them. I see there is no card from Charlie Moody, and this, on top of everything with Will, makes me frantic with sadness. I think I really will go crazy if I don't get some air, so I go to the lounge and ask Gwen if she can please let me out.

And so Gwen unlocks the sliding glass door to the back patio.

It's the same sliding glass door that Delphina snuck out earlier today.

"Not too cold," Gwen says, stepping out with me.

"No," I say. I peer out into the night. Floodlights illumine the chain-link fence that skirts Northern Parkway, the same chain-link fence I got stuck on. I wonder if I'm going to get poison ivy.

A slight breeze stirs, and I'm not uncomfortable. There is no chill, no bite, in the air. Will was right, what he said about the snow melting. The eaves above us drip.

"Not cold at all, in fact," Gwen says.

"No," I say. "Quite pleasant." I stand next to Gwen and together we look up at the moon.

The moon is beautiful. It isn't always. But it is tonight. Luminous and creamy, it is a swirl of white icing on a chocolate cake of sky. Under this same moon, which he is too busy to notice, Will sits at a table in a fancy restaurant and drinks enough red wine so he can convincingly laugh at other people's jokes. Will isn't thinking about the moon; he isn't standing outside and gazing upwards, but I know he would like to. If he were, we would be doing the same thing at the same time. I turn to Gwen and point, "It's a waxing gibbous."

"What?" she says.

"The moon."

Gwen stares at me.

I know if she were Delphina she would say—*Say what, girl? I'll wax your gibbous, you show off your mouth like that again.*

But Gwen next to me is silent. She's got her hair raked back in a severe bun. Her face is pinched. She's single, or so I've heard. I don't know much else about her except that I don't like her. She is, however, right this moment, the one standing next to me, keeping me from being alone. "Gibbous," I explain. "It's just a term. You know, for a phase in the rotation. Means more than half the moon is illuminated."

"That's good." Gwen nods decisively.

"Why good?"

"The moon reveals itself but chooses to do so slowly."

"Right," I say. I stare at Gwen. I wonder if she knows that I plan to reveal my own secrets, tomorrow, to Dr. Silverberg. No, I decide, Gwen couldn't possibly know this.

Back inside, we discover that medications have already been handed out. Gwen opens the dispensing window specially for me and gives me my Xanax.

Back in my room again I take one last look at the moon. I say a silent prayer and crawl into bed. I think no way can I sleep, but I surprise myself and drop off. Of course I have the Dream again.

❧❧

Max throws his arms around me. He sees the giant white birch, directly in our path, and so do I. We cringe. Endless seconds of anticipation, hearts hammering, then the crash. We slam up against the trunk. I hear the cat-erwauling of automobile metal as the hood contorts itself around the base of the birch. Then there is silence in the woods, muffled by old snow, wise trees.

The first thing I hear again is the moan of wind through my cracked passenger window. I look to Max, to see if he is all right; only, oddly, he is not there.

"Max?" I cry. "Max?"

Nobody answers.

❧❧

I wake up.

The Dream has still got me in its thrall. I feel cold, as though I am still in the Adirondack northwoods, in the backseat of the car, my breath mist-ing in the chill air.

I think of Delphina.

Oh, God, I don't want to end up like her. I don't want to repress my fears until they rise up and subvert my grip on reality. Delphina was scared of Clyde coming, wasn't she? So she retreated to a place inside herself even he couldn't reach her, not even with his fists. But when will the real Delphina venture out again? When will she be back?

I thrust my blanket aside, and sit up in bed. A shudder runs through me.

I glance at my clock. Only 2 A.M. I have the whole night to go. I remind myself that soon I will see Dr. Silverberg. All I have to do is hang on.

≈⊃≈

Finally, late morning, I meet Dr. Silverberg in the back of the cafeteria.

I am so relieved to see her that I want to throw my arms around her. I want to bury my face in her shoulder and sob. As it is, tears spring to my eyes. I avert my face, hoping she will not notice.

But of course, she does. Her eyes are black and velvety; her voice is kind, "You didn't sleep last night."

"Not much."

"Something happened."

"Yes."

"You want to tell me about it?"

"Yes, but can you first give me a hug?"

She smiles at me, a gentle smile. "I know you could use a hug right now. So think of me as hugging you. But in our training we're discouraged from physical contact with our patients."

"Why?"

"Because it's too seductive."

"You're not trying to seduce me. *I'm* the one who asked for the hug."

"I know, but ultimately it will hurt your feelings that I can't always be there for you. And ultimately it's better for you to find your hugs elsewhere, from Will, from Sarah, from Ruth..."

"Who cares about ultimately?" I say. "What about right now?"

"Right now, my heart goes out to you," she says, and I know she means it. Her whole body leans toward me, all the tallness of her, every lanky limb. She positively wills me to be well again, in the same way choir directors wave their hands like beautiful birds, as if the flight of their hands alone could make the music sublime. "Janey, Janey," she sighs. "You look so miserable, like Scrooge after he sees the Ghost of Christmas Future."

"Well," I say. "Maybe I have." My throat tightens. "It's Delphina. She cracked up. And I'm scared."

"Of what?"

"That I'll crack up, too." I remember Delphina in the snow, singing mournfully to herself. I remember glancing into Delphina's room last night;

it was vacant. Early this morning, though, I was surprised. I still think of it as Delphina's room, but there's a new girl in there. Her name is Felicity. Her teeth were silvery with braces and she clutched a teddy bear to her breast, and the thing is, she's too old for teddy bears. She's in high school.

"You think talking will prevent you from cracking up?" Dr. Silverberg asks.

"It's worth a try."

"Good." Dr. Silverberg nods. "You talk. Because I want to listen."

And clearly, she does want to listen.

The trouble is, I don't know where to start. My gaze drifts from the puke green sofa to my left, to the Ping-Pong and billiard tables. There is a Pac-Man machine, too. I remember playing with Delphina. The joystick looked so puny in her meaty hand. I remember her blowing smoke in my face until the nurse told her to please put her cigarette out. I sigh. I look at the floor; I look out the window. The snow has all but melted now. It doesn't look like spring, but it doesn't look like winter, either. Sort of in between. I look at Dr. Silverberg again and this time my eyes stay with her.

"I want to do this for Will and Sarah. And for me. Only I..."

"Don't know where to begin?"

"Right."

"Just talk," she says. "The rest will come."

"Okay," I say. This is so hard. I feel like I'm holding my breath underwater. How long will I last? How long until my lungs burst? "I, uh, keep seeing things. Every time I go to sleep. It's like a dream that keeps coming at me and it won't stop. Except that it really happened."

"What happened?"

"The last day."

"Last day?"

I swallow. My voice thickens, "The day my brother died."

Dr. Silverberg says nothing, but her black eyes fix on me.

"It happened at the Island, years ago. I'd just turned eleven. My little brother was eight. Windsor Island, I should explain. It's located on Saranac Lake in the Adirondacks. You know, New York State. It's really an island, too, accessible only by a small footbridge to the mainland, or, of course, by boat. There are no roads on the island at all, just seven houses with a path through the woods. We've owned the cabin all my life. My family, and Ruth too, I should add. She helps pay expenses so she owns it, too. See, my mom inherited it from her parents and they inherited it from theirs."

"And this is where your brother died?"

I pause, then answer, "Yes."

"Why do you call it the last day?"

"Because it was, in many ways."

"For you?"

"And for my mom."

"Go on."

"It's...too hard."

"Close your eyes; tell me what you see."

I squeeze my eyes shut and envision the Island. It was March. Spring break from school. "My dad arrived on the Island ahead of us," I tell Dr. Silverberg. "He came straight from his medical convention in Boston. It was easier for him to just fly to Saranac Lake and rent a car and plan to meet us right at the cabin. So, it was Mom and me and Max, driving up from Baltimore. We stopped overnight in Syracuse. Next morning we drove on to Utica, then we entered the Adirondack Park. Even though it was March and might have been decent weather, it was pretty miserable. At Long Lake, the skies blackened, the wind picked up, and it started to hail. The hail was noisy, like marbles bouncing off the windshield. Visibility got worse, so Mom turned into this country store and used their phone to call Dad. By now we were only an hour away from the cabin. Dad said to hole up until the weather broke, and then we could barrel on up to the Island. We still had enough daylight left. But something happened."

"What?"

"I mean, on the phone. Between my parents. They got in a fight."

"How do you know?"

"When Mom was talking, her voice got loud and strident, and when she hung up, she wasn't crying but she would've been if these two shopkeeper ladies in green aprons weren't right there behind the counter."

"Go on."

"Max was starving, so we ran across the street, the hailstones hammering on our heads, into this hamburger joint. Max gobbled a ton of french fries and a jumbo hot dog and he was happy. Mom just sat there with a sad look on her face. I suppose we still would have been all right, though, if that man at the bar hadn't sent over a glass of wine."

"Why'd he do that? Was your mother flirting with him?"

"No, no, you've gotta understand my mom was a really beautiful lady. The red hair slayed 'em every time. She was just sitting there. I don't think she noticed anybody in the place except Max and me. But, anyway, she took it."

"The wine."

"Yeah, she raised her glass to the man at the bar in a jaunty kind of salute and then started in drinking. And the thing was, she'd been so good all week, hadn't touched a drop. She wanted to be in fine form for the long drive up. And if she hadn't gotten into that argument with my dad...well..."

"So, she had a few drinks."

"Well, two drinks, I think, which wasn't bad really. But the wine kind of emboldened her and she felt eager to press on."

"With the trip?"

"Yeah. We stepped outside. The hail had let up; the skies were clear. Occasional ice patches marred the roads, and the deepest woods showed snow and the fingers of icicles hanging from branches, but mostly it was perfectly fine driving weather. The cabin was only an hour away. Plus, my mom knew the way. She knew the Adirondacks like she knew the sound of our voices, Max's and mine, even better, because she'd known the cabin longer than she'd known us."

"Was she impaired when she started driving?"

"No, I wouldn't say so. She was happy, tipsy. Feeling no pain. She liked Neil Diamond and she cranked up his voice on the radio. She gave Max and me some bubble gum and we were all chewing away. Singing *Cracklin' Rosie you make me smile*. By the time we reached Saranac Lake, Mom was driving a little faster than usual, but you know, she seemed in control until we hit a patch of ice and hit that birch." I pause, then go on. "It was a fluke, really. Fishtailing on that ice. Had Mom's reactions been better, had she been a little less bold from the wine, would she have been driving a little more cautiously? Could she have avoided the crash? Hard to tell."

"And so that's when your brother died."

Tears come stinging to my eyes. I roughly wipe them away. I speak again and when I do, my voice comes out scratchy and all wrong, like Sarah practicing on her violin. "We told people for years, yeah. That he died in that car crash, hitting that birch tree. It was simpler. But he didn't."

※※

I remember the silence of the woods.

Then the moan of wind coming through the cracks in my window.

Then Mom, moaning up front. Her moan is more emotional anguish than pain, this I can tell. She is all right.

But I'm not hearing anything from the passenger next to me.

"Max?" I cry. "Max?" There is no one beside me.

Trembling, I climb from the car.

My car door creaks on its hinges when I open it. One of my ribs is bruised, and it hurts to breathe.

Mom climbs out of the car too. She looks scared to death and 100 percent sober. She says, "Janey, you okay?" She touches my face.

"Fine, I'm fine," I say. "But where's Max?"

"Here I am!" Max calls, and I turn. At first I am afraid to look; I am afraid he may not be all right. But he is fine. He is all right. He has only the tiniest scratch on his forehead, no bigger than a mosquito bite. In fact, if the truth be told, he looks better than all right. Better than I have ever seen him. He appears radiant, untouched. A glowing white nimbus surrounds him, like light from a bright sun spilling into the gloom of a medieval cathedral. Long locks of black hair, skin pale as any monk's, my little brother the stained glass saint...

※※

"How did he die, then?" Dr. Silverberg asks.

I swallow. I am wearing a cotton turtleneck but it no longer seems warm enough, not by a long shot. I am shivering. My skin feels clammy, and, it seems, I have forgotten how to breathe. My chest rises and falls, lots of effort and not much oxygen. "I killed him," I say.

"Killed him?" Dr. Silverberg repeats.

"Not on purpose. But it was my fault, just the same."

"Was it?" Dr. Silverberg is staring at me intently; her black eyes lock on mine. "You were a child when this happened. Are you sure you're not blaming yourself for something you could not prevent?"

"What do you mean?"

"I mean that there's a world of difference between killing someone and witnessing a tragedy unfold."

"How do you know it wasn't deliberate, on my part?"

"Because I know you," she says softly. Then, "Please. Go on."

"I can't," I say. My throat is one big lump I have to speak around.

"It's okay," she says. "Just take it slow."

"Right." I say.

"You all survived the crash," Dr. Silverberg prompts.

"Yes," I say. Pause. "What happened next, there were no witnesses. No human ones, anyway. But I've always felt the presence of something else, a kind of spirit, that saw everything."

"Spirit?"

"The birch tree. The one we crashed into. That grandfather birch."

I see the expression on Dr. Silverberg's face. She's wondering if I'm crazy after all.

I try to explain. "All these years, after it happened, I had this feeling about the birch, and then when I was researching the Iroquois—Native Americans are part of our first- and second-grade curriculum—it all made sense to me. The Iroquois believed that god is in all things."

"Pantheism."

"Right. What a comforting world view. That God is everywhere you look. In the stars, the moon, the grass, the trees, which brings me back to the birch tree. You know the horizontal black dashes you see on the white bark?"

"Yes."

"Those slashes are actually breathing pores called lenticels. The Iroquois considered those lenticels to be the eyes of the tree. The eyes of God."

"So, what you're saying is, all these years, it feels to you like that birch tree was a witness."

"Exactly."

"To what happened."

"Yes."

"Well, what *did* happen? What did the birch see?"

"Everything."

"Tell me."

"Oh, geez." I take a deep breath. I feel dizzy and shaky. I look straight at Dr. Silverberg, shrug.

"Describe the birch to me. Describe where you were. Take me back with you."

"Back?"

"In time."

"Okay." I squint, concentrating. "Well, this birch towered maybe forty feet. It was on a hill that sloped down to the lake. And to the Island boathouse."

"Boathouse? But the lake was frozen, right?"

"Right."

"So, you couldn't travel by boat."

"Exactly, that was the thing. Our cabin was maybe five minutes across the lake, if you went by motorboat. But with the lake frozen, like it was, the only way you could get to our cabin was by car, along a cumbersome, rutted road called Barlett's Carry. Bartlett's Carry curves and winds for some ten miles before it deposits you clear on the *other* side of the lake. The road literally ends, emptying you out onto a small gravel parking lot. There, you park your car and take the old footbridge onto the Island."

"Footbridge?" Dr. Silverberg interjects. "You're saying there are no roads leading onto the Island?"

"Right."

"And no roads on the Island itself."

I nod. "Just a hiking path through the woods. We're talking rustic here. Windsor Island is only a mile in circumference. There are seven houses on the Island that have been passed down through the generations of the same seven families, and that's it. The rest of the Island is woods. Birch, pine, cedar."

"But back to the boathouse," Dr. Silverberg says. "What good did it do you? The lake was still frozen."

"Right. But in the boathouse is a phone."

"Ah," Dr. Silverberg says. "Go on."

I swallow. "Well, first Mom tried to restart the car. The hood looked like a tree ornament but wasn't so crumpled that it looked hopeless. Mom pumped the gas, but the engine only groaned and made a sick grinding noise and then died altogether; I think she flooded it. Then she got out of the car. She was completely sober now. Hitting that birch really scared her. She hugged Max and me against her chest for a long time. Sunset was closing in fast; it grew darker by the minute, but Mom became very calm. She said, *Kids, you know what? We're not in bad shape. For one thing it's not storming, right? No wind or sleet or hail. And we're all okay, even if the car's not. And best of all, we're really close to the boathouse. We'll call your Dad. He'll hop in his car and drive around the lake to get us.*

"Inspired by Mom's pep talk, the three of us worked our way down the wooded slope toward the boathouse. The boathouse, I should explain, is a green gingerbread structure with a red roof. Running alongside the boathouse is a gray weatherbeaten dock. We stood on this dock as Mom rummaged through her purse for a key that would unlock the boathouse. Once she found the key and turned it, she banged open the wood door and groped her way through cobwebs to the light switch. She flicked the light switch a few times, but the bulb must've been burned out because no friendly welcoming light snapped on. Inside the boathouse was spooky and dark. I could just make out the boats in drydock, up in the rafters. Mom kept the door ajar, so the moonlight spilled in, but it was feeble: *There's no light. You wait out here. Stay put,* Mom told us, and then she reached for the phone on the wall.

"Well, Max and I did just what she told us. We stood on that dock. We could peer *into* the boathouse and make out Mom's faint shape, but you had to really squint to see her. Mom took longer than expected. Max got bored and started hitting the ice off the dock with a stick. He walked to the end of the dock, and I walked right behind him. In the moonlight, the lake looked good and frozen. It had been a long winter.

"Max poked with his stick. He stuck out his leg and thunked the ice with heel of his boot.

❧❧

"Don't even think about it," I told him.

"What?" he said.

"Stepping onto that ice. It might not be safe."

"But it's hard. Frozen solid," Max said. "Maybe we could go ice fishing."

"What do you know about ice fishing?"

"Dad's gonna teach me."

"Not now, he isn't. No fooling around. Mom said stay put. I shouldn't even let you be out this far on the dock."

"I can stand on a stupid dock, can't I? I'm not a baby."

"Nobody said you were a baby."

"Yeah, but you think *it." Max resumed poking his stick at the ice.*

❧❧

"At that moment, Mom stuck her head out the boathouse door and called me over. She was still inside the boathouse, the phone in her hand. I had to walk maybe ten steps to get to her. I was still on the same gray dock Max was, only at the opposite end. *The line's busy,* she said. *But at least your father's there. I'll keep trying.*

"I turned around. I started back toward Max.

"The moon shone bright, but the end of the dock fell in shadow. There were no lights dotting the shoreline this early in the season. I couldn't see Max, but I wasn't concerned. The dock hooks to the right, in a kind of L shape, and I figured he had moved to the end of the L. I wasn't alarmed or scared, in fact, I was thinking about my rib, how much it hurt."

Dr. Silverberg leans forward, "From the crash?"

"Yeah, it hurt, but I didn't tell Mom. She had enough on her mind. But I felt a stabbing pain every time I breathed. I tried to take little shallow breaths, because then it didn't hurt so much.

"Anyhow, I was heading toward the end of the dock, to where it hooks. Now I could see that there was no Max in the shadows. I heard a hissing, cracking sound. Immediately I yelled, *Max!* and scrambled to the edge of the dock. Another noise, like a giant zipper ripping open, and then the sound of Max's plunge into the icy lake.

"*Mom! Help!* I hollered. I started out, slipping and sliding, onto the fragile ice. Mom dropped the phone, which now lay dangling on its hook. She rushed up behind me and snatched me up by the elbow. *Down!* she commanded. *We've got to crawl.*

"We dropped to all fours. Mom grabbed me by the ankles. *You go first. You're lighter than me; you have the best chance,* she said as we ventured out onto the ice. With every forward movement we made, the ice creaked. *We're coming, Max! Hold on!* Mom cried encouragingly. It was clear; Max was panicked. Wildly thrashing at the edges of the ice where he had broken through. The ice kept making this hissing sound and then cracking. Max couldn't grab a hold of it. He kept taking in water. I could hear his choking, desperate gurgling.

"Mom and I formed a human chain. We were spread-eagled on the ice, creeping forward. Now that we were squarely on the ice and it had the task of supporting our weight, I saw how honeycombed the ice was, how rotted underneath. I could see black water rushing below. Ice-cold water. Water that would stop your heart.

"Max was still thrashing around by the time we got close. I saw this as a good sign. If he had that kind of energy, he was probably okay. Subsequently I've learned that the more you struggle, the more air bubbles you lose, and hence you lose valuable buoyancy. Max was wearing cordoroy pants, of all things, which were fast becoming soaked. And what's worse, on his feet were his lumberjack boots. The kind with the thick tractor tread. I hated to think how much they weighed.

"*Max,* I said. I thrust out my hand to him. He was still too far away.

"His eyes were desperate and unfocused in the moonlight. His lips shone a purplish blue.

"*Mom, I can't reach!*

"*Okay, we'll have to move closer.*

"Until now, Mom had kept herself close to the dock, in case the ice underneath us broke through, but now she left the dock clear behind us. We wriggled up on our bellies, our breathing raspy and hollow.

"Up on shore, on the hill, that grandfather birch was watching us. Its thinnest branches were sheathed in ice, knotted like warted witches' claws. There was a sudden gust of wind, and the icicles rattled. And, then, suddenly one of the larger ice-glazed branches snapped and came thundering down, crashing onto the roof of our car. At first I thought it was the ice cracking beneath me. I shuddered, then forced myself to press on, wriggling forward on my belly. All the while I kept my eyes on Max.

"Max, by now, wasn't looking so good. I didn't know the word for it at the time, but it was hypothermia starting to claim him. His teeth chattered. They looked little white tombstones in the darkness.

"Mom, I still can't reach!

"At this, my mother lunged forward, thrusting me forward with her. We were splayed out, vulnerable, on the ominously creaking ice.

"Now, Max, now! I cried. *Give me your hand!*

"Max kicked and scrambled toward us. His body was wracked by chills; he was spluttering, coughing up water. But he made one final brave lunge. I thought I could feel the numbed flesh that was his hand, but maybe I never did, maybe I just felt the cold rush of air when he went under.

"He went under, just like that, just slipped away, into churning black darkness.

"Mom! I cried. *Mom!*

"She let go of my ankles, abandoning all caution, and belly-wriggled up beside me. *Max!* she screamed.

"We waited, shivering, the ice creaking demonically all around us, on our bellies on that ice. Max never resurfaced."

"Oh, my," Dr. Silverberg puts her hand to her mouth.

"Yeah," I say. I tilt my head. "I've learned through the years about the treachery of the ice. I've done some research, you might say."

"Research?"

"Ice changed the whole of my existence. I learned that ice fishermen, well-versed in the heaving and thawing of ice, consider late spring the most dangerous season, and honeycombed ice the most dangerous of all.

Two inches of new uniform ice, making a tight seal on the lake, is very often safe. But honeycombed ice, with its cracks and heaves, with its lack of uniformity, is deceptively weak. And so, for all its thickness, twelve inches of mottled ice may be alarmingly insufficient."

"And you were near the shore, too," Dr. Silverberg adds, perceptively.

"Exactly. Shoreline ice you've got to watch out for. The ground warms the shallow water and begins to melt the ice close to shore. Finally, ice around emergent objects is not to be trusted."

"Emergent objects?"

"Trees, rocks, piers, vegetation—things that stick up from under the ice weaken the ice."

"You mean, like the boathouse dock," Dr. Silverberg says.

I nod. "That dock worked all day to absorb heat from the sun and then transferred that heat to the ice around it, weakening the ability of that ice to support Max's weight when the time came."

"I'm so sorry," Dr. Silverberg says.

But I am lost in my own ruminations. "See, Dr. Silverberg...Max...he didn't really stand a chance. The ice he walked boldly, foolishly onto was refrozen ice. Mottled ice with air pockets. Ice with cracks and crevasses and weaknesses. Ice already changing back into its liquid self, ice halfway back to being water...

"People on shore heard our screams and Mom's weeping. There was a four-star resort nearby, and someone heard us from their cabin. The resort staff wrapped us in Hudson Bay blankets and gave us strong tea by the crackling fire in their lobby while someone got ahold of Dad and he came to get us.

"They searched the lake, as best they could. They didn't find Max's body until after the thaw, some ten days later. The current had carried him quite some distance."

Dr. Silverberg and I sit in silence, now that I'm done talking.

I am all talked out. And so tired. I think I have never been this tired in my life.

At first I think Dr. Silverberg should say something, but then I realize she is silent for a reason, the way you are silent after a prayer or after someone reads a poem or tells you their life has disappointed them, all their dreams come to nothing; you are silent out of respect for them, and silent, too, to let yourself return from where you have been, that quiet place down by the river in your soul.

Finally, though, Dr. Silverberg sighs a little, then looks at her watch. "Janey," she says, "I have a meeting I need to go to, but I can put it off a few minutes. You want to talk some more? Go for a walk or something?"

"Thanks, but I'm kind of bushed."

"How about some coffee or tea? Hot chocolate? I can take you to the hospital cafeteria. How about that?"

"You're being more than kind," I say, "but I think I just want to be alone for a bit, you know, in my room. Ruth and Sarah are stopping by after school, Sarah only had a half-day today, and I want to rest up before they get here."

"Sure," Dr. Silverberg says. "But I want to reassure you; I want to leave you with the knowledge that you did nothing wrong. What happened to your brother, Janey, it was an accident."

"Is an accident a series of events that are in themselves preventable?" I ask. "Because that's what haunts me. The *if onlys*. If only we hadn't hit that birch tree; if only we hadn't tried to phone from the boathouse; if only Max had stayed put on the dock like he was supposed to; if only the ice were stronger. And of course, the thing that really kills me: if only I had stayed with him. By his side. He never would have stepped onto that ice. He never would have broken through. And died. If I had stayed."

"You can't torture yourself like that," Dr. Silverberg says. "That's what I mean. Accidents happen. They happen, and you look back and see what went wrong, but at the time you did the best that you could. *You* did the best you could, Janey. Let yourself off the hook."

"I'll try," I say. I stand up from the sofa, poised to leave.

But Dr. Silverberg won't let me go quite yet, and that's how I know she cares for me, if I didn't already. "Tell you what," she says. "I'm gonna tell Pammy you've had a kind of rough session here, and she'll keep a look out for you. And I'll check in on you later, at the end of the day. We'll talk then. How's that sound?"

"Fine." I nod good-bye to Dr. Silverberg and then I start toward my room. I can't seem to remember how to walk, how to put one foot in front of the other. I feel hollowed out, like I have the flu.

I am alone only briefly. I never get the solitude I crave because, outside my room, I run into Felicity, the girl who took over Delphina's old room. Felicity is still clutching her teddy bear. She is gnawing nervously on her lower lip. She is so nervous, she makes me nervous. She could play the starring role in *A Telltale Heart*.

"Hi, Janey!" she says.

"Felicity." I nod.

She giggles. Her braces glitter. She's got them on both her upper and lower teeth.

"How are you settling in?" I ask her.

"Okay, you know." She giggles again, and that's when I know she is lonely.

"It gets better," I say.

"Like, good to hear. Phew!" she says. "Cause I couldn't sleep a wink last night. I'm like on fire." She giggles again. "But that might be because my boyfriend came by."

"Your boyfriend?"

"Last night. Jimmy Delores. He's a senior."

"In high school? You're in high school, right?"

"Yeah, I'm sixteen."

"Umm," I say.

She giggles again, and leans in confidentially, "We did it in the bathroom. Me and Jimmy."

Did what? I almost ask, but instead I stare at her in near disbelief. She is so young, so giggly and immature; she carries around a teddy bear, for godsakes. Yet she knows more than me. She knows how to be intimate with someone.

"Well," I say. I reflect on Will and my failure. Will and I had our chance the other day, but we didn't do it. No locks. But that wasn't what stopped us. What stopped us was not the locks and keys or the flashlight checks, not the white bed, or the white cinder block walls. It was all the white spaces between us.

"Well, I'm off to play Pac-Man!" Felicity says.

And just as she leaves me, just as I think I will finally be alone, I hear the noise from down the hall, the noise of their approach: Ruth and Sarah. Sarah has her denim backpack slung over one shoulder. She's fairly dancing along the hallway. "Hiya, Mom!" She flings her arms around me. "I brought my rock collection."

"Great, honey."

Ruth gives me the thumbs up while Sarah bounces into my room and without ceremony dumps out her rocks on my bed. "This one here's mica, and this is obsidian..."

"And your tiger's eye. You brought that."

"So smooth. Here, Mom, feel it."

We spend a long time marveling at Sarah's rocks—quartz, jasper, copper, iron, marble, and petrified wood. Sarah talks a blue streak; Ruth and I can't get a word in edgewise. Finally, when Pammy takes Sarah to get a Popsicle from the freezer, Ruth and I have a moment alone.

"What, no bandages?" I say.

"No Band-Aids, either." Ruth smiles. "Oh, by the way, Will is planning to pick you up tomorrow, mid-morning. He has a settlement conference, he said to tell you, but then he's coming right over."

"I'm glad," I say. "I mean, that he's coming. We had a sort of fight last night."

"You had a fight with Daddy?" Sarah joins us. She has been listening.

"Oh, well, not a big one. Nothing to worry about," I say.

"Good," she says. But, she is ready to leave, and makes a move for the door. "Bye Mommy. See you tomorrow."

I walk her and Ruth to the exit. It is incredible to me that tomorrow I will be free to walk out these same doors myself.

They both wave to me. I wave back. The last thing I see is Sarah's knapsack, and, I assume, all the rocks. Back in my room, though, I discover that Sarah has forgotten roughly half her rocks, which remain in a jumble on the bed.

I hear footsteps, and I think it must be Sarah and Ruth, back to retrieve their treasures, and I am glad. I was missing them already. But it's not Ruth, and it's not Sarah.

It's Pammy in her cowboy boots. "Your Sarah's a cutie pie!"

"Thanks," I say.

"Red hair. Freckles. She looks just like you."

"People say that."

"Listen," Pammy leans on my doorjamb, "Dr. Silverberg told me you had a rough session. Productive, but rough."

"Yes," I say.

"In light of that, I wish this could wait, but it can't."

"What can't?"

"Your weigh-in."

"No." I shake my head.

"Yes." Pammy is firm. "We really should check that weight of yours, and, provided you've maintained, we can get started on your discharge papers."

"Provided?" My voice cracks.

"You knew about the weigh-in, Janey."

"I *knew*, but I didn't realize. There's no hard and fast rule about this, is there? About patients gaining or losing weight and their fitness to be discharged?"

"There's no rule, but, Janey, in the last two weeks you've lost, what? Eight, ten pounds. Dr. Silverberg won't be able to, in good conscience, authorize your discharge if you've lost still more weight."

"Oh, I haven't," I assure Pammy, with false bravado.

"Good, let's get to it, then." Pammy smiles at me, but she's picked up on my hostility, and her smile is strained.

"I'll be right along," I say. "I need to, uh, use the bathroom first."

Pammy leaves, but I don't use the bathroom.

I stand beside my bed, bend over Sarah's rocks. I pick up one of the larger ones; it has quite a heft to it. I stand there, feeling that rock in my hand.

I don't hesitate as long as I should, or debate the rightness of my actions. I stuff my blue jean pockets with rocks, not the biggest ones because they'd bulge but some medium-sized. I stuff some more rocks into the waistband of my pants, thinking that it is a good thing Pammy is used to seeing me in my rhubarb sweatshirt. I can pull that sweatshirt over the whole stomach area and no one will be the wiser. Next, I grab a sizeable chunk of limestone. Where to put it? I slip off my moccasin and tuck the limestone up into the toe. I will try not to walk funny. I tuck the feldspar into my other toe.

Now what?

I'm still not packing enough weight. I wonder what to do. I pull up my sweatshirt and take the last big rock—marble—and shove it under my armpit, where its edges dig into my skin. I feel at this point like a sight gag from *I Love Lucy*. Lucy always gets into these ridiculous situations, and then Ricky always laughs his amused tremolo of a laugh at her, forgiving her everything. But in this, I know, I will not be forgiven, should I be found out.

I walk solemnly down the hall. I've got about two pounds of rocks on me, and I've got my fingers crossed.

When I reach Pammy, I smile casually. She waves me onto the doctor's scales. My heart is knocking like the time my dad brought firecrackers back from Canada through customs and he said we only had a pottery bowl to declare; well, inside that pottery bowl were the illegal firecrackers. They didn't conduct a search.

I stand as still as I can on the scales. Pammy nudges the metal bar over to the right, steps back, and says, "One fifteen. You haven't gained back any weight, but at least you haven't lost anymore, thank God."

My toes are scrunched up tight inside my moccasins. I think the circulation in my right toe, the big one, might have stopped. I ask Pammy, "Does this mean I can go home tomorrow?"

"You can go home." Pammy nods, but she's not as pleased as I would have thought.

Sweaty, irritable, I step off the scales, wondering who it is I've cheated with my victory.

Later in the day, just before dinner, we have an art therapy class.

I still haven't talked to Dr. Silverberg, and I wonder if she forgot me. I wonder if she went on home.

"Janey," Cyndi says to me, as blonde and bouncy as ever, even at the close of the day, *"you finally finished your trivet! Congratulations!"*

"Thanks."

"And I hear you're being discharged tomorrow! *How super!"*

"Yes!" I say. "I am!"

I feel like we're caught in a ghastly production of a Noel Coward play, Cyndi and I, only we lack the British accents: *I hear you're being discharged from the military, old chap. Yes, it's this bloody lack of a leg. I keep toppling over...*

Cyndi holds out her palm. There is an egg resting on it. "Do you belong to this egg here?"

"Yes," I say. It's nice to belong, even if it's only to an egg.

Cyndi hands the egg to me. For a moment the two of us regard each other. Cyndi could move on, but she doesn't. She thrusts out her hand, "Janey, it's been a real pleasure!"

"Yeah," I say, "I can't think when I've had more fun."

"Oh, you're the kidder!" She laughs.

I have taken her hand, a mistake, because now she reels me in for a hug. She is a slight girl, Cyndi is. I can feel her bones and my bones glancing against one another. We neither of us have breasts, to speak of. *Where's Delphina when you need her?* I think. Delphina's got some plumpness to her, Delphina whom I never got to hug good-bye.

Cyndi moves on, and I catch my breath after that crushing embrace. And then I do something I still don't understand. I hold my emerald green egg in my palm. I turn my palm upside down. The egg, as you would expect, drops to the floor and breaks. Breaks into so many pieces I can't count them. I glance up, and there is Dr. Silverberg.

I say, "This was my first offense. I was nowhere *near* Humpty Dumpty, I swear."

Dr. Silverberg looks at me, and says nothing. Then she helps me bend over and pick up the eggshells.

Now I am holding the broken and cracked pieces in my hands.

"What's wrong?" Dr. Silverberg says.

I look down at the eggshells. "Honestly?"

"Yes."

"It reminds me of Delphina."

"Delphina," Dr. Silverberg says solemnly. "Yes, she was a good egg."

I grimace.

"Not quite there?" Dr. Silverberg says.

"Let's put it this way. Don't give up your day job."

"But seriously," Dr. Silverberg says.

"Okay," I say. "Seriously. It's...this damn egg soaked itself in green dye yesterday. The whole time I was chasing Delphina through the snow. That's why it's so green."

"Ah," Dr. Silverberg says.

A brief silence falls between us.

Then I level with her, "I thought you weren't coming."

"This evening?"

"Yes. I thought you forgot."

"And how did that make you feel?"

"Not that great really. Not that spectacular."

"What, no jokes?"

"No jokes."

"You actually answered my question about your feelings in a straightforward and honest manner. I see we're making progress."

"Progress? I feel like shit."

"Well, you had quite some session this morning. That'd knock the wind out of anyone."

"Yeah," I say slowly. "You know I read somewhere, Mary Pipher I think it was, she's the one who wrote *Reviving Ophelia*, well, she said, 'That which is unspoken becomes unspeakable.' Well, that was my brother's dying. It remained unspoken and after awhile it became something we couldn't talk about."

Dr. Silverberg nods.

"The thing is," I take a deep breath, "I feel like I just started, you know. Talking. And there's more stuff in there that wants to come out."

"I understand." Dr. Silverberg pulls up a chair. "Janey, do you have plans when you leave here?"

"Like you mean, go out to dinner?"

"No, for therapy."

"Oh."

"Because I think continuing therapy might be very useful to you. I won't say it's imperative, but right now in your life you'd be mighty uncomfortable without it."

"Mmm," I say.

"You know Dr. Gard sees patients outside the hospital. He has a private practice as well as his rounds in the ward."

"Dr. Gard?" I wince. "I don't want to see Dr. Gard."

"Why not?"

"I would like..."

"Yes?"

"To see you."

"Are you sure?"

"God, yes!" I say with such vehemence that she smiles.

"You know psychotherapy's expensive."

"Yes."

"The going rate is $140 an hour."

"Is that with or without a manicure?"

"But your insurance will pick up some of it."

"Okay," I say. "Let's do it."

"Well, hold on a sec. I have to think about my schedule, too. I'm actually not taking on any new patients at this point."

"You're that busy?"

"Well..." she says.

There is a pause between us. Until now we have been talking about me. But now I realize there is another person in this equation. I hadn't considered this. It comes as something of a shock that Dr. Silverberg might not be able to be my therapist. She says, "You realize I'm going to recommend twice a week?"

"Okay," I say. "If you think that's necessary."

"Can you afford that without putting your family into—"

"Yes," I say, "I think so." I look at her, blink hard. Does she know how important she has become in my life? This Dr. Silverberg, first name Marie, who used to play tennis, who married a carpenter, and has two children now, one of whom, the daughter, has something wrong with her.

Something wrong, Sherman said. Does Dr. Silverberg, so tall, so elegant, know that, to me, it matters what she chooses to wear when she wakes up in the morning because I get to see this dress or those shoes? I use absolutely no makeup these days, but I can tell she takes the trouble to apply a little lipstick and some blusher. I bet she flosses her teeth every night, unlike some of us, unlike me.

"Let's see..." she says. She is thinking hard. She is wondering if she can fit me into her already crowded life.

Please, I want to say, but I bite my lip, and say nothing. Only a few seconds have gone by and I am sick with waiting. It matters to me very much if Dr. Silverberg can be my therapist, and I hate her for this. I hate myself that I care. There is Will, there is Sarah, there is Ruth. And now there is Dr. Silverberg, yet another person to tether me to this earth. I would rather be a pink birthday balloon that no child claims; I could bounce on my string to the open window and climb into blue sky and disappear.

"All right," Dr. Silverberg finally says. "I can swing it." She smiles at me. Behind that smile is her belief in me, that I will one day get better, that she can help me get there.

"Good," I say. I take the broken pieces of eggshell and toss them in the trash.

PART TWO

HOME

━━◆◆◆━━

Normal day, let me be aware of the treasure you are.
Let me learn from you, love you, savor you, bless you, before you depart.
Let me not pass you by in quest of some rare and perfect tomorrow.
Let me hold you while I may, for it will not always be so.
One day I shall dig my fingers into the earth, or bury my face in the pillow,
or stretch myself taut, or raise my hands to the sky,
and want more than all the world: your return.

—Mary Jean Irion, *Yes, World*

CHAPTER 5

The next morning I sit with my luggage in my room and wait for Will to pick me up. I've condensed what feels like my life into one heavy tan suitcase and one green knapsack. If you walked past my room just now and saw me waiting here, you might think I look bored, but really I am scared. I wonder if I'm ready to leave this place.

"Knock, knock," says a voice, and I look up, and it is Ruth. "Sorry it's just me," she says. "Will got caught up in chambers. Settlement conference."

"Oh, you'll do just fine." I smile.

I get up from the bed and we embrace. I let go first but Ruth keeps on hugging me. I feel like a well-loved letter tucked safely inside its envelope until she releases me. My shoulders start to shake.

"You okay?" she says.

"Sure."

I grab my suitcase and Ruth takes my knapsack, and together we stop at the nurses' station to sign out. I look around. No one familiar to me is here to say good-bye. Cyndi, our art instructor, is bailing her boyfriend out of jail for DWI. Pammy is sick with the stomach flu. Dr. Silverberg is around somewhere, but not in the immediate vicinity. And, of course, Delphina is in Sheppard Pratt.

The nurse on duty, I don't even know her name, hands me my discharge papers. "So long," she says. "Good luck."

"Right, see you," I say. "Thanks for everything."

It's funny how I end up thanking her instead of the people who really helped me.

Out in the parking lot we heave my luggage into the trunk of Ruth's station wagon. "Forgive the mess." She brushes dog hairs off my seat and tosses a jumble of books into the back. After she starts the engine, she glances at me from behind the wheel, "You're so quiet."

"Am I?"

"Listen, you want to go someplace else first? Get some coffee, or something?"

I consider this for a moment. "No," I say. "I can do this."

The white birch is the first thing I look for when Ruth pulls up at the curb in front of my house. Yes, the tree is the same. It is a young birch, really not much more than a sapling. It bends awkwardly, painfully, toward our house. During its first year it was shaded out by our poplar tree—a fibrous, quick-growing tree that shedded like crazy until we decided to chop it down last year. The birch is dear to me because we transported it to our house by van, its infant branches sticking out an open window all the way from the Adirondacks. Each month the tree grows stronger and more lovely, though now, even though the poplar tree is gone, the birch still bends.

Ruth is watching me. She's wondering why I'm not getting up, why I just sit here, my hand poised on the door handle.

"You want to talk about it?" she says.

"What?"

"Why you're scared to go in."

"No thanks. It's okay," I say. "I'll be okay."

"Hey," she says to encourage me, "it's just a house, right?"

"Right," I say.

Ruth gets out of the car and comes around to open my passenger door, and together we walk up the front steps. On the porch my knees are shaking. Ruth unlocks the front door, and we walk in. My house is both so familiar and so strange. I never realized how rich in color it is, and how spacious and welcoming our family room looks, with its rose brick fireplace, oak post-and-beam ceilings, and broad picture windows.

In the family room I see the table set for one: croissants heaped on a plate, strawberry jam, orange juice.

"Sarah made you breakfast."

"So I see." I can just picture Sarah choosing a brown buttery croissant from the bread bin at the market, clamping it tight between the plastic tongs. She chose, from among the jams, Smucker's strawberry because she knows it's my favorite. Her gesture of love is so sweet, yet so unwanted. I won't be able to taste a bite.

I haven't moved from my spot, I realize; I have been rather uselessly standing on the rug. Meanwhile, Ruth has jogged out to the car and come back lugging my suitcase. Her jaw is clenched with the exertion. The weight of my belongings may be too much for her, at sixty-two. Her face is pale, and I realize with a sharp pain to my chest that she is old; she has grown into the white hair she has owned since she was thirty.

Ruth plunks down my suitcase and straightens up. She still looks pale.

"You okay?" I say to her.

"I may be coming down with a cold."

"Then you should go home and rest."

"That's okay. Besides, I'm under strict orders."

"From Will," I say.

"Exactly." She smiles. But then she scrutinizes me more closely, and her smile fades. She is my good friend; she knows how I feel. "You'd like to be alone, wouldn't you?"

"For awhile. Yes."

She nods. "How about I come back in an hour?"

"Perfect, thanks." I walk her to the door. There is a solemnity to the way we hug good-bye. She knows what waits for me upstairs. After I close the front door, I feel the silence of the house and a shudder runs through me. I'm not quite ready to go up, after all, so I head out onto the backyard deck where Toby greets me. He leaps at my thighs and licks my cheeks. I pet him behind the ears and croon *Good dog, Good dog*, so many times, even *he* knows I'm stalling. I would have kept right on petting him, though, except that he tenses suddenly then scrabbles off the deck to streak along the grass after a squirrel. The squirrel eludes capture, and I go back inside.

At the bottom of the stairs, I shoulder my green knapsack. It sure looks like a long way up, although I know the stairs haven't changed any; it's just me. I climb to the top and stand on the landing. From the upstairs window I gaze down on Toby. He is curled up now and napping in a sunny patch of grass. I swallow dryly. I have delayed this moment as long as I can; there is nothing left for me to do but travel past Sarah's room to the second door on my right, and open it.

In the room, a tangerine slice of sun slants in through the curtainless window to fall on the hardwood floor. The room is completely empty. Either Will or Ruth, or perhaps both of them, removed the furniture.

I walk to the center of the room. I can picture in my mind where we positioned the crib, with its mobile of dancing bears. The bookcase, the rocking chair, the changing table. I try not to picture the infant whose diapers I would have changed. We knew all along we were having a boy, and I was a little nervous about wiping his little penis and scrotum; I was used to the folds of Sarah's vulva, but I believe I would have grown comfortable with our son.

Oh, God, I think, and hug myself.

I suddenly wonder how I would look to a stranger in this moment. Say, to one of the Impressionists. How would they paint me? I am just a woman standing alone in a room, looking, perhaps, a little pensive. I wear blue jeans and a gray herringboned sweater. My eyes are blue. My hair is short and curly, more brown than auburn. My body is thin and angular and I stand tall; I do not double over in a paroxysm of grief. And so if Mary Cassatt painted me, as she painted so many mothers and daughters, mothers and sons, she would not paint the ghost of the boy who might have lived here; she would, with all her intuitive genius, fail to see him; she would say, *What ghost? There is no ghost.* And so Mary Cassatt would capture my thin angularity, the straight line of my lips. She would paint a woman not in torment but in repose.

Here I am standing alone in the room, and suddenly I can't take the silence any longer. I need to be busy. I hasten to my bedroom and begin unpacking my knapsack. My movements are somewhat mechanical, but I am still operating. I remove my Walkman and trivet from the dark cavity of my knapsack. I don't know where to put the trivet; I want to be able to see it, but I don't want to actually *use* it; it might get dirty or break. I finally opt for my bedside table, next to the stack of books I am currently unable to read.

I empty the rest of my knapsack's contents out onto the bed. My toothbrush, toothpaste, hairbrush. I'm shoving my hairbrush back into my drawer when I realize Will's been using the top of our dresser to stash our mail. Next to the pile of unread newspapers there is a stack of bills, among them a bill from the funeral parlor. I could open the bill, but I don't really want to know how much that coffin cost. Maybe that's why Will didn't open the bill, either.

I move toward the bathroom to pop my toothbrush into its porcelain holder by the sink. In the bathroom, I see that Will has bought some new shampoos for his hair, Nioxin, which is supposed to help with baldness. I am surprised at this change. Will doesn't usually care about his appearance that much. And I see a hair dryer, too, plugged into the wall. And a bottle of Jovan musk.

I return to my knapsack, and there I confront my medications. My Xanax and Prozac, both in plastic prescription vials. I decide to put my pills in the medicine chest, well out of reach of Sarah. I take the prescription vials and carry them to the bathroom and make room for them on the glass shelf, and then I stand there staring at them.

It's interesting how in the hospital they doled out my medicine so carefully. Here at home I could gulp down all these pills at once, and there's no one to stop me. I am perfectly alone. Will's not here; Sarah's not here, or Ruth. Goddammit, what am I thinking?

I slam the door to the medicine chest, furious with myself and my warped fantasies. I am so upset I start to tremble, my whole body, just like when you've gone swimming in water too cold and come out with lips that are blue. I try to get myself under control, and stop this shaking, but my body seems to be following its own agenda. I stand there with my arms at my sides; I clench my fists and positively will myself to stop behaving like this, but I squeeze my fists too hard, my jaw clamps with the strain, the pulse in my neck jumps as the blood rushes to my head, and I'm suddenly so dizzy I've got to sit down.

I reel towards the toilet seat, but I don't make it. My legs buckle under me and I slump onto the blue and white tiles. I know I'm about to lose it big time, and I take pride in one last coherent rational housekeeping thought: our bathroom floor could use a cleaning. There is a dollop of shaving cream by the sink where Will was shaving. There is, here and there, some dirt, actual dirt, which Sarah must have tracked in in her sneakers. But I don't really care about the shaving cream and I don't care about the dirt because just now a bubble rises in my throat and a strange keening sound fills the closet-size room, as lonely a sound as I've ever heard, and it's coming from me.

I curl into a ball on the floor. My back presses against the toilet bowl. I cry for a long time, until my throat is raw. It is like a fever breaking, a great sickness that passes, when I fall silent and just lie there.

I smell the strong lime scent of Will's shaving cream on the floor. I feel the softness of the toilet paper when I reach up and rip off a few sheets to give my nose a good blow and wipe my eyes. I stare up at the ceiling and see a fly crawling along, and I wonder what it would be like to view the world upside down. My heartbeat slows. Outside the bathroom window I hear a car rumble by on the street, then Toby's bark. And then, blessedly, it's quiet.

⇒〇⇐

I don't know how long I spend lying there on the bathroom floor. But I hear the front doorbell ring. Ruth. I haul myself up, splash water on my face, and let her in.

"You've been crying," she says.

"Yes."

"Feel any better?"

"Hard to say on account of this pounding headache." I give a little laugh and she laughs, too.

We go into the kitchen and make some tea.

"Ah, wonderful," Ruth says, sipping the tea. "Clears my sinuses."

"Good for your cold." I nod. Together we sit at the oak table in companionable contentment. I feel tired out from crying, but not too bad. Then I feel a maddening itch, on my calf. This itch has annoyed me, on and off, all morning. I hitch up the denim leg of my jeans and scratch away.

Ruth leans over the table to take a look. "Uh oh," she says.

"What?" I take a closer look at my rash. "Not poison ivy?"

"Afraid so."

"Oh, I could just strangle Delphina."

Ruth tilts her head. "But you love her."

I don't say anything. I have never thought of myself as loving Delphina, but I suppose Ruth is right.

Ruth asks, "You got any calamine lotion?"

"Yes, actually." I find the pink lotion and pour it directly onto my rash. The lotion cascades down my leg and floods my sock. My leg is coated with pink scales; I look vaguely reptilian.

"Mmmn...attractive," Ruth says. She pushes her teacup aside and squints at the clock, "Time to fetch Sarah. Come with me, why don't you?"

"To school?" I say stupidly, and my voice cracks. I think of Weybridge and all the people I might run into there. Charlie Moody, and all my first graders. They know Mrs. Nichols as an upbeat, funny, enthusiastic lady who delights in them and their accomplishments, who stays after school to work with the ones the rest of the world might call slow. But there is no one fitting that description at this address. "Oh, Ruth," I say. "I don't think so."

Ruth looks straight at me. "It would mean a lot to Sarah."

I think a long moment. Finally, I say, "Okay. But should I change? Put on a dress?"

"You're fine just the way you are."

Inwardly I brace myself as we take the familiar turn off Charles Street onto the Weybridge campus. I picture Sarah in her second-grade classroom; in just a minute the bell will ring, and then she will come outside and I will get to see her.

Ruth swings her station wagon past the faculty parking lot, where, I see, Antonia Gianelli has parked her spiffy red roadster in my old space. That's okay, I tell myself. She's entitled.

Ruth curbs the car in the pickup lane. Out the passenger window, I idly survey the playground where some students enjoy their final moments of recess. The kids play kickball, climb rope ladders, and chase each other along the blacktop. Mostly they are a happy blur of color, blue flapping jackets and white flying sneakers, brown hair, blond hair, red. But as I follow their antics through my window, I realize, painfully, these are not just any kids, they are *my* kids, the first graders I know and cherish.

I see Erica, for one, shy little Erica whose parents always drop her at Extended Day and are the last ones to pick her up at six o'clock, when the doors close for the night. And, yes, slumped against the wall of the quadrangle, bouncing a green fuzzy tennis ball into his leather mitt, is Charlie Moody, alone. Shall I go to him?

It doesn't take me long to decide. There's something about the way Charlie huddles there that makes me remember just how lonely first grade can be. I tell Ruth, "Be right back," and step out.

Since Charlie is by himself, there is little danger I will be seen, or at least this is what I tell myself. The kickball game is a good three hundred yards away. The swings, the monkey bars, and all that, are farther away still.

My footsteps crunch on pebbles and dirt.

Charlie's hair is wild as dandelions. There is a blonde rat-tail that trails down his neck. His unruly saffron bangs straggle down over his eyes, which blink heavily with disbelief when he sees me.

I am so close to Charlie now that I could touch him. But Charlie shrinks from me and tucks his chin into his chest, letting me know just how angry he is. So I don't touch him at all. It is enough, maybe even too much for him, that I sit down beside him and say warmly, companionably, "Charlie! Good to see you. How ya been?"

He shrugs, "School sucks."

I stare at him. He is so young, only seven, and yet he seems so much older, or maybe it's me, over these last few weeks, grown old.

His voice, a monotone, cracks, "Aren't you gonna tell me I can't say suck?"

"Do you want me to?"

"What do I care?" He scrambles to his feet, frowning down at me with all the derision he can muster, "You're not my teacher anymore! I don't have to talk to you."

To this I don't reply. If I were feeling better, I would know that Charlie is only telling me how much pain he's in—his parents are splitting, they are fighting over who gets to have him, and he is torn apart—but I am not my solidly grounded self; I am ripples of wind on the water, spreading out and out, thinner and thinner, until I disappear. I look at Charlie and he scowls at me while he slouches away. Charlie is much too young to have developed a swagger yet, but this is his intention. He moves away, shuffling his battery-lit black sneakers in the gravel, growing smaller, until his leather mitt seems way too big for his hand.

Feeling disoriented, I turn back toward Ruth and her station wagon. Who am I to think I can work miracles? That I can reconnect with Charlie simply by saying hello?

I head for the station wagon; I want only to retreat, but this doesn't happen.

Erica has always been an observant kid and today proves no exception. She is the first one to spy me, "Mrs. Nichols!" She is a petite thing, Erica, too many freckles on a tiny heart-shaped face, but I can feel the pull of her embrace, and for a moment, slight as she is, she rocks me. Then she steps back to appraise me, "You got skinny."

"Well, yes," I say evenly. "But I was pregnant when you last saw me."

"Your baby died."

I nod. "Yes." There is a long pause between us.

Finally she says, "When are you coming back?"

"Well—" I start to say, but we are interrupted. Above all noises, great and small, one noise prevails: the bell, which rings with all the delicacy of a fire alarm. Summoned by the bell, the kids surge in from the playground to form into class lines. My students catch sight of me and flock over. I am mobbed by my own first graders, "Mrs. Nichols! Mrs. Nichols!"

Their voices are full of joy and make me dizzy.

"Hey, guys!" I greet them, but then my throat constricts and I am rendered mute. I have talked to these kids every day for weeks on end, they know my voice as well as their own mothers'; my words follow them like the aroma from a freshbaked apple pie into their dreams, but just now I can say nothing to them. Maybe nothing is just fine. I am happy to see them and they are happy to see me.

But, then, abruptly, there is an intruder in our midst. Antonia Gianelli, with her unmistakable tumble of ice-blonde hair, appears. I don't know what she's guilty of, possibly nothing, possibly just a cozy moment with my husband that was never repeated, but I find myself wishing cruel things to rain down upon her, an untoward end to her cat, say, or her dog, if she has one waiting for her at home; and, if not, perhaps just the slightest little gouge in the perfect glossy red paint of her sportscar, "Well, Janey!" she enthuses. "What a surprise! Come on in, won't you? Join us!"

Leave my husband alone! I want to tell her. Instead I say, "No thanks, just stopping by."

And so I stand on the pavement and watch my kids file back into the stone building. Some of them turn back around to wave. When Erica slips her tiny hand into Antonia Gianelli's, I feel my heart press down and down, a hot iron on a wrinkled cotton dress. I look for Charlie Moody in the crush of bodies, but I can't find him.

I turn back toward Ruth, wishing I had never left the anonymity of her station wagon, when I hear Sarah's voice. "Mommy!" she cries.

I turn. For a moment I forget that Will might have betrayed me. I have been feeling weightless, insubstantial. And yet I must be more than the wraithlike being I feel I am; I must occupy space on this planet with more than my body; I must communicate some of my soul. I know this because my now breathless and happily panting Sarah, knapsack bouncing against her back, has rushed right up to me; she thinks I'm actually worth rushing for. Child that she is, with confidence sailing on nothing but a buoyant heart, she flings her arms around me, as if, after weeks of disappointment, she's certain to find me there.

We get caught in a drenching downpour just as we arrive home. We pull up in Ruth's station wagon and her three springer spaniels start yelping; in our yard, Toby rushes up to our wooden fence, barking also. Sarah and I join hands and make a mad dash from the interior of Ruth's car, with its flapping windshield wipers, into our house.

Inside, I wrap my arms around Sarah's shivering skinny body.

"Here, let's get you out of those wet clothes."

We towel off Toby's paws after we bring him in, then we put on dry clothes ourselves, and Sarah wanders into the piano room and sits down and plays "Indian Song." She hasn't practiced much since I've been away, two weeks, but I tell her "good job." She stands up from the keyboard, and says, "Mom, now you play."

"Not just now," I say.

"Ragtime, please?"

"I will. Another time," I say. I stand in front of the piano and unfold the cover to the keyboard, plunge those wet and black keys into their silent tomb.

In the kitchen, I fix us hot cocoa and Sarah says, "Let's make something."

"Cupcakes?"

"Um...no."

"How about sugar cookies?"

"That's good. We can make shapes."

So we marshal our ingredients and arrange our mixing bowls and measuring cups on the counter. Butter, sugar, flour, salt, egg, and vanilla extract. We combine the butter and sugar first. The sugar granules make a scritching sound on the bottom of the bowl when Sarah stirs. Next we add the eggs and vanilla. My stomach lurches at the sight of those slippery raw eggs.

A shadow crosses Sarah's face. "Mom?" she says. "You okay?"

"Sure."

"You want me to mix the eggs?"

"Yes, why don't you."

Sarah stands on a stool and takes over for me. Her red hair is smoothed back into a ponytail, held in place by a purple scrunchie. Her mouth is relaxed, slightly open. Sarah favors color blocks, and just now she's on a purple kick—along with that purple scrunchie, she wears a purple sweatshirt, purple sweatpants, and purple socks. Around her neck there is a gold friendship necklace with half a broken heart. The other half is worn by her best friend, Camille.

Sarah is busy with her mixing bowl. I sigh and glance out at the rain. I'm feeling the strain of being home, I guess. I got more used to the hospital ward than I thought. Here, there are so many decisions to be made, and I am tired from making them—do I pick up Sarah from school? Do I play the piano? Do I tell her the sight of those eggs really does make me sick?

"Mom," Sarah looks up from beating the eggs, "are you crazy?"

"What?"

"Camille said you were locked up with crazy people. So are *you* crazy?"

"No, honey."

"Why did Camille say that, then?"

"Well, she's young, like you. She probably doesn't understand. The people in the hospital with me—the other patients—they weren't crazy, Sare. They suffer from mood disorders. They were depressed, mostly. Like me."

"What's depressed?"

"Very sad."

"Oh."

Sarah is busy thinking. What I find most moving about her, as I behold her now, is how the awkwardness of her age holds her hostage; at eight going on nine, she is prepubescent; she is still my baby. She hasn't yet sat at the movies and felt her boyfriend's hand close over hers, hot and moist, as if by accident; and yet, she is not my baby, or anyone's, because in the sharp delineation of her profile, in the planes of her cheekbones, I see no more baby fat but the leaner hollows of maturity. In her eyes I see the remembrance of pain. Sarah is no longer the toddler who so ingenuously stuck fallen rose petals back on a rose thinking she could make the rose whole again. This girl-woman beside me already knows some things, knows that when she falls it may hurt, depending on the landing.

"But Mom," she says now.

"Yes, sweetie?"

"How can you be sad when you have Daddy and me? Don't you love us?"

I stare at my daughter, my only child. I want to tell her that depression is an illness, something that happens to your body, that you can't control. But she won't understand. I can love her and still be sick. "Oh, pumpkin," I say, by way of an answer, and pull her close against me. "You're my girl, aren't you? I'll *always* love you."

Sarah seems content after that. We continue in our baking. Soon flour is everywhere. Flour daubs the counters, dusts the telephone, drops in clumps from the rolling pin. Flour is smeared on Sarah's chin. Flour cakes her waist and streaks her hair.

"Mom," she announces. "Guess what I made."

"Well, let's see..." I examine her cookie. "A giraffe?"

"No, silly. A dinosaur."

"Of course," I say. "That's a T. Rex if I ever saw one."

The rain stops for awhile and then starts again. Will comes home. We order a pizza and Ruth comes over, and we all feast on that and the sugar cookies we baked. Well, by feast I mean that's what they did. I still don't have my appetite back, but at least I was able to get a half-slice of pizza down, and some apple juice. During dinner, Sarah's mood is glowing. For the first time in weeks, she seems herself again. There are no Band-Aids on her knees, no bandages on her wrists.

Now Ruth is gone for the night and we are all upstairs. I pause outside Sarah's room. Will is inside the room, sitting on the edge of Sarah's bed, tucking her in.

Neither of them sees me. But I can see and hear them.

For a moment I am just plain happy. Tonight was just like old times, when we were a family again, under one roof, and nobody was away sick in the hospital. But then I hear Sarah ask her dad, in a lonely voice, "Dad, can I get a pet?"

"What?"

"A puppy?"

"Oh, sweetie. Not right now."

"Or maybe just a gerbil or something. A goldfish?"

"Why, honey?"

"Because it's so quiet around here."

"Quiet?"

"Yeah. With Mom."

"What do you mean?"

"Well, Mommy is trying, but..."

"But what?"

"She's not like she used to be."

"No, she's not."

"Because the baby died. And she's sad."

"That's right."

"Daddy, does God know if we're bad or good?"

"I think so."

"Was the baby bad?"

"Oh, sweetheart, no."

"Then why did he die? God shouldn't have done that."

"Honey, sometimes bad things just happen and nobody did anything wrong."

"You mean," Sarah says, "even if I'm perfect, one day I'm gonna die?" There is grief lacing her voice. She is up against the truth and the truth won't be moved, unlike today's cookie dough she has so easily shaped with her two hands.

Will says gently, "Sweetie, death is part of the circle of life. We all live and one day we die. But you don't have to worry about that. You have years and years ahead of you."

"Really?"

"Really."

"Hey, Daddy?"

"Mmmm?"

"Will you rub my back?"

"Okay."

"No. Scratch with your fingernails."

"Like this?"

"Yeah. Good. You know who else is a good back scratcher? Miss Gianelli."

"She scratched your back when she tucked you into bed?"

"Uhuh."

"The night she brought over the casserole?"

"No, a different night."

"Oh," Will says. Then, "You know, maybe it'd be best not to mention that to your mom."

"Okay. Hey, Dad?"

"Yes?"

"You stopped scratching."

"Oh. Sorry."

Alone in the hallway, I bite my lip, slowly back away from the door, and slip quietly downstairs. On the counter in the kitchen, the bag of flour sags emptily, and no wonder because a fine dusting of flour has settled on every possible surface—on the cutting boards, the rolling pin, the floor, even the telephone. I smell the sweet sickly scent of vanilla extract, and, through the open window above the kitchen sink, I hear a bird call in the rain.

Will finishes tucking Sarah in; I hear his "Goodnight" to her and then his footsteps on the stairs. He is coming to join me and all the while I'm wondering, do I ask him about Antonia? Or do I say nothing at all?

"What?" Will asks me the minute he sees my face. "Something wrong?"

"I...uh..." This is my chance. Sarah is in bed; the house is quiet; we are alone. But I can't do it. I don't tell Will that I overheard him and Sarah talking. And I certainly don't mention that moment, months ago, at the cocktail party, that too-cozy moment between him and my substitute. Has she substituted for me in more ways than one? I can't ask him. I say, lamely, instead, "Want another cookie?" and offer him a sugar cookie from the plate.

He takes one, and nibbles at it. "What's this supposed to be, a giraffe?"

"Dinosaur."

"Mmmmm." He devours the rest of the cookie. I can't look at my husband without thinking of him and Antonia. I wonder if Sarah has seen them hug or kiss. Oh, God...

"Listen," I say. "Will."

"What?"

"I was thinking."

"Yeah?"

I hesitate. I know this is a bad idea, but I'm going ahead with it anyway, my proposition borne out of sheer terror, "Want to break out the green satin underwear?'"

"Really?" he says. In his eyes I see lust, but I also see something else. It may be guilt. It is also, definitely, fatigue. His tie is loosened and his shirt cuffs unbuttoned and rolled up along his forearm. One triangle of white shirt hangs out. The triangle is wrinkled, which seems to sum up his whole day.

For a moment I think Will just might rescue us both, and say, *Let's save this for another time,* but he doesn't. He smiles wanly and jumps into the masquerade right along with me. "Sure, absolutely. Count me in."

Upstairs, Will removes his belt and kicks off his tassel loafers. Meanwhile, I peel off my clothes and cinch my terrycloth robe. When I approach the bed, I let Will unfasten the robe, which opens to reveal my green satin underwear. Will pats the bed, grins, and says, "Janey Nichols, come on down!"

My husband, by now, is clearly interested. Although this is precisely what I want, I'm shamed by my own hypocrisy. I have never felt more unromantic in my life.

Will snaps out the only light in the room, then moves close to nuzzle my neck. His starched white shirt is opened two or three buttons, low enough that I can feel his chest hairs graze my skin when he nuzzles me.

I suddenly feel queasy. "Hon, is Toby back inside?"

"Yes." He plants kisses along my neck.

"Oven off?"

"Yes."

"Front door? Chain on?"

"Yes!" he says, getting impatient. "Everything's fine." Then, "Janey, let's get naked."

Naked? I think. This is all moving much too fast. "Okay, except for my knee socks."

"Your feet cold?"

"No, I got poison ivy."

"Really? Lemme see."

I peel back my sock and Will takes a look. Even in the forgivingly dim moonlight that spills in through the window, the rash is unsightly. I am praying it will dampen Will's ardor, but he opens his arms and says,

"C'mere my little poison ivy queen."

Now we are cleaved together. Will kisses me hard on the lips. My head buzzes. I am hot. Sweat dribbles down my spine. My poison ivy itches like a live thing. I give a little moan that I hope resembles passion.

Encouraged by my response, Will slides his hand down the length of my belly and slips a finger between my legs. I take that as my cue to touch him also. I am out of practice and more than a little clumsy. I fumble under the sheets to take him in my hand and, to my surprise, he is flaccid. "Damn, too cold!" he jerks away as though startled by the chilly touch of my fingers, but that's not it. They are not cold; they are too hot if anything, and he knows it.

Together we lie there in the dark, heads on our pillows, staring up at the ceiling.

I am relieved it has turned out like this, but also frightened.

"Will?" I say.

"What?"

"Want me to do just you?"

There is, from him, only silence. He does not protest, as I wish he would. He acquiesces by closing his eyes as I find him. In the gray room, I see the seductive sweep of his eyelashes. It doesn't take him long. He moves with urgency, then suddenly he's there. I feel him pulsate. I taste the saltiness of him. Afterwards, I lay my head down on the swell of his abdomen, and I smell sex on him, that musty smell of satiation.

He coaxes on his underwear, then climbs back into bed, pulls the sheets up around us, and says, "Sorry you couldn't come."

"It's okay."

"Next time."

"Sure," I say.

He lies next to me, and sighs, "I missed you. I'm glad you're back."

"I'll bet you are."

"I mean, besides that."

We are side by side. He makes room for me to lay my head against his chest. When I do, his chest hairs tickle my ear. "How's it feel, anyway?" he asks. "To be home."

"I miss the hospital, believe it or not. I miss Pammy. And of course Delphina. I even miss Mr. Kramer, bless his poor tormented soul."

"Well, it's a big adjustment for you. I'm proud of you. Sarah seems happy. You're really trying, I can tell."

"Thanks."

"You gonna return some phone calls tomorrow? There's a list by the phone."

"Maybe."

"You can't stay in a cocoon forever, sweetheart."

"I know that."

"I don't mean to be critical, but since your depression, you only hang out with Ruth and me."

"Yeah, too bad I'm not psychotic. I could populate my mind with all sorts of interesting people. Actually, I could *become* all sorts of interesting people. I could be Joan of Arc."

"Janey, please."

"I can't kid around?"

"Not about that."

"Okay."

Will rolls onto his elbow, to face me. He has been relaxed and content in the wake of his climax, but now I feel a change in him, sense the tension coiled inside, "Let's go away."

"What? Where to?"

"The Island. Over Memorial Day."

"Why?"

"It'd be good for us."

"You've been talking to Ruth."

"Sure. And I think she's right. We should go."

"Oh, Will, I dunno. I just got home. Let me think about it."

"Okay," he says. "But don't take too long."

In his words I hear the subtlest of threats. Don't take too long, or what? Why is it so important for him to get away?

I wait to see if he'll say anything else, but he doesn't. I can still feel the tension radiating from him.

"Will?" I say. "You're not falling asleep are you?"

Maybe he can hear it in my voice, my curiosity, my ambivalent desire to uncover the truth, ambivalent because I'm not sure I want to know if there's something going on between him and Antonia or not. Or, maybe my husband is just plain worn out. "Janey," he says. "Sorry. I'm fading here... g' night." He rolls over, abruptly, and gives me his back. I am hurt by how completely he blocks me out. But I am also relieved; I would be lying if I said I wasn't. There will be no confessions, at least for tonight; simple yet effective, look how his shoulders rise up like cliffs, guarding his secrets.

I stare up at the ceiling for a long time, then I get up and go look in on Sarah.

She sleeps with her pink Gund bear tucked under her chin. She has slept with Gundy ever since she was three days old; no other stuffed animal will do. I lean in close to her face. Her breathing is poetry to me, the whisper of wind through apple trees. I used to kid Sarah about stealing my freckles; just now I kiss three new ones I find scattered across her nose.

I think about what Sarah said to her father tonight, *Even if I'm perfect, I'm gonna die?* While she's right, I believe there's more to it than that. I believe that, yes, we are all going to die, but it matters what kind of human beings we are; it matters that we treat one another with kind consideration. I believe in the redemptive power of love. The trouble is, when I think of Antonia Gianelli I don't know what love is anymore; I'm not sure I even *need* to fight for Will, but if I do, I can't say as I'm up to it.

﹆

The next morning I wake up late. I suffered through a fitful night of restless sleep, requiring so much Xanax that when finally sleep came to claim me, it was more a taking than a drifting off. And this morning I am hungover from the sedative, groggy. Antonia was the last person in my thoughts last night, and she is the first this morning. I will run into her later today, but thankfully I don't know this yet. All I know is I have slept longer than I meant to. I can tell because the sun streams in through the window. It is a bright but breezy day. The windows rattle, and the trees outside bow their heads. My own head is throbbing. I wouldn't mind just lying here in bed. Indefinitely. But it's Saturday, and I want to be with Will and Sarah.

Downstairs, though, I learn that Sarah has made other plans.

I come down in my bare feet, knuckling sleep from my eyes, to see Will snatching up his car keys. "I'm driving her to Camille's," he says. "Want to come along?"

"Yeah, Mom, come with us," Sarah says. She looks at me, becomes doubtful. Does she notice the dark circles under my eyes? Does she know how shaky I feel? This is the first morning in a long time that I've woken up outside the security of the hospital.

"No, you go on ahead. I'll see you later."

"Okay," says Will. "Be right back."

So, now they're leaving. "Bye!" Sarah hollers. The front door thunks, and the house reverberates with the sound. I fix myself some coffee. I watch through the window as Will's green Mazda slows at the fire hydrant and rounds the corner. Already I wish I had decided to go with them. I feel lonely down to my bones.

I step with my steaming mug of coffee outdoors onto the deck. It's damp and so windy that the finches have trouble flying and landing on our feeder. Toby barks and comes bounding over to my chair. He loves this breezy weather.

Behind me, our French doors rattle, and the top branches of our oak tree flail in mild panic. A lone brown oak leaf, dangling from a slender branch, twists on its petiole; the leaf has survived the winter, but it may not survive this wind. A squirrel scampers halfway across the drooping black telephone line that leads from our house to the garage. The telephone line bobs and sways treacherously, and so the squirrel stops, crouches down low, and waits out the long vibration until it is safe to move on.

This wind is truly remarkable. Wind, anyway, is a powerful thing. What was silent and taken for granted—doors and windows, the wood planks of our deck—now speaks, and so it shouldn't seem so very strange that my heart, which has been silent, speaks, too. I hear, plainly, unmistakably, the wail of my infant son. The sound seems to be coming from upstairs. From the nursery.

I do not move from my deck chair.

Of course I know it is a phantom cry. But suppose the cry was real? That I really had a son? I would scrape back my chair and run inside, tackling the stairs two by two. Gaining the nursery, I would reach into the crib. How radiant I would be, holding my flaxen-haired son in my arms. He is wrapped in a blue receiving blanket and he wears a woolly hat. The hat is pastels, Easter egg colors. My son looks like Old Man Winter, wizened and weathered every time he screws up his face to cry, but when I comfort him, he relaxes and begins to coo. I lean my cheek against his. How soft his skin feels, how like a cloud. I raise him high into the air, my son, my favorite hymn, and I think: you are the music that makes me dance. But the music ends abruptly with the next gust of wind, which steals all my baby's sounds, even his original cry, burying them in the creak of wood planks beneath my feet.

I sit in my chair and slowly come back to myself. I am a forty-year-old woman, sitting barefoot on her deck on a windy day, holding a mug of coffee. This, nothing more, nothing less.

Inside the house the telephone rings. I consider ignoring it, but then I get up.

"Hello?" I say, into the receiver.

"Skinny Lady, that you?"

"Delphina!" I can tell she's herself again; I can hear it in her voice. "Where are you?"

"I's free, girl. From the dark dungeons o' Sheppard Pratt."

"Hey, I only just got home myself. What'd you do, use your Get Out of Jail card?"

"Thas' right, girlfren. I got out of there right away." There is a pause. "Listen, how you doin'? You been eatin'?"

"Trying to."

"Thas' good. And your meds? You be sleepin'?"

"Enough."

"Thas' fine. Listen, honey, I got a favor to ask. I don't get paid till Friday even though I's back washing dishes. You know, at the pancake house?"

"Sure."

"Anyways, you think you could see me through till Friday? I wouldn't ask, except I's feelin' kinda desperate. The rent's done past due—"

"How much do you need?"

"Fifty dollars. I be sure to pay you back, honest."

"How should I get it to you?"

"Can you come by this morning? I's at my job now."

"At the Pancake House? On York Road, there?"

"Mmm hmm."

"Okay, be down shortly. I've just got to get myself together first."

"Oh, honey, don't we all." She laughs and hangs up.

I jot Will a quick note and tell him I'll be right back, then I head downtown. This is the first time I have driven my minivan since I've been in the hospital. It feels good. I stop by an ATM machine then drive south on York Road, further towards poverty than I usually go. I pass a stone church, the yellow arches of Mickey D's, a discount liquors, a methadone clinic, and then park in the lot of the Pancake House.

The Pancake House, with its peeling gray and white paint, has two shattered window panes. Maybe somebody didn't like their buttermilk pancakes.

I ask the hostess inside where Delphina is. I find her in the back, spraying down plates before she runs them through the washer. The kitchen smells like damp, clotted food. The steam rising up from the dishes stings my eyes.

"Hey, hey, girl!" Delphina doesn't hug me like I thought she might, but in her eyes I see she is happy I am here. She motions for me to follow her. We bang open the back door and go outside. I wish I could say the smell is better out here, but it's not. We face a black dumpster and a rusted Chevy pickup has bulldozed its way to within inches of the overflowing trash.

To our left there is a concrete building with graffiti scrawled on its walls: RATBONE, MCCABE, T-DOG WAS HERE. All around us I hear the rumble of trucks grinding their gears as they toil up York Road. Garrulous black crows wheel in a haze of white sky.

The concrete stoop where we find ourselves is all we've got to sit on, so we sit, propping our backs up against the wall. Delphina hands me a cigarette. For a second our fingers brush against each another. Her fingers are wrinkled, callused, and black. I wonder what my fingers look like to her, and the rest of me, my alien white skin.

I have never seen Delphina in a uniform before. Greasy apron. Pants. Shirt with short sleeves. She keeps her arms close to her belly. I figure she's embarrassed. She's got a real inner tube there around the middle, a bulge of flesh. I bet she keeps her arms close because of that jelly belly.

I take a drag on my Newport and cough.

Delphina takes a few raggedy puffs, blows smoke into the cool morning air. "Oh, my head be singing the blues this morning."

"Hungover?"

"You best believe it."

"You think that's a good idea? To drink?"

"You my mother, Skinny Lady?"

"Sorry."

Delphina inhales greedily on her Newport, sucks that nicotine into her lungs. She's using her left hand to raise and lower the cigarette. She's still holding that right arm close to her belly. I want to tell her, *Don't worry about being fat. I don't care. I can see you from the inside out; so what if you're fat, it doesn't mean a damn thing to me.* But we haven't been together in awhile, Delphina and I, and I'm feeling shy, so I don't say anything.

Delphina gazes over the rim of the black dumpster. The dumpster is so full, there is trash poking the lid up. I can smell rotted fruit. Plus, there is that stink of steam from the dishwashers. I wonder if Delphina gets tired of smelling that. I don't think Delphina is smelling anything, though, at the moment. Her thoughts are far away, "I wonder what Sherman be doing now."

"Sherman? Oh, he's probably sitting near a dumpster somewhere, having a smoke just like us."

"Sure," she says.

"Maybe he's thinking of you."

"Honey," Delphina laughs, "you lie like a rug."

"Delph, I just don't want you to be sad."

"Well, I appreciates that."

There is silence between us. Then I ask her, "How was it, anyway? Sheppard Pratt."

"They done give me electroshock."

"It help?"

"I's here, ain't I?"

"You're here," I say. I pause, then reach into my wallet. "Before I forget." I try to hand Delphina a fat roll of twenties, but she won't take them.

"I tole you fifty, girl. This roll must be a hundred easy."

"Please," I say. I try again to get her to take it.

"Oh, all righty." Delphina sighs. She's still holding her cigarette in her left hand. Her right hand, the one closest to me, does not move from her belly. Instead she rests her cigarette on the stoop and takes the money, awkwardly, with her left hand. "Now I got somethin' for you," she says. She slips the roll of twenties into the pants pocket of her uniform. Then, from the same pocket, she pulls out a Kodak print.

The picture is an old one. But I can see Delphina as she used to be. The hard living she is about to do hasn't happened yet.

"You're in your red choir robes," I say.

"I tole you I use to sing."

"You can still sing," I say.

"Oh, honey," she says. There are tears in her eyes. She lifts her cigarette off the stoop where it's been waiting for her. Gray ashes sprinkle to the ground as she tucks the Newport back in her mouth.

I hold the edges of the photograph gently between my fingers. I get the feeling it is precious to Delphina. I'll bet she doesn't have many pictures of herself. "This is great," I tell her. "But I can't take it."

"Skinny Lady, I be offended you don't."

"Okay," I say. "Thanks." In a rush of affection, I touch Delphina. I happen to touch her arm, the right arm, the one she's been holding across her plump belly.

Delphina winces, jerks back. As she jerks back, her right arm straightens enough so I can see the bruise stamped on the flesh hanging from her upper arm, big as the state of Mississippi, her birthplace. The bruise is blue and runny as cheap ink. So *that's* what she's been hiding from me. All along, I thought she was hiding her belly when, in truth, she was hiding that bruise.

"Jesus, Delph," I say.

She shrugs. "I done banged into a door."

"Was the door shaped like Clyde?"

She looks at me. She stubs out her cigarette now that she's smoked it down to nothing.

I stub out my cigarette, too. It stinks out here, and it's depressing—the steam billowing out from the dishwashers, the sickly smell of syrup, those old dumpsters. Shuddering, I say, "You've got to leave him, Delph. Take the money I gave you. Get on a bus. Just go. You've got relatives down south, right?"

"Honey," she sighs, "I leave, he jus come after me."

I don't know what to say. I look up at the sky. There is an untouched sparrow flying, free. Such a tiny bird, its wings are pumping away to beat the band, to keep it aloft on currents of air. I am glad that sparrow isn't down here.

I finally turn to Delphina.

I say, in a low voice, "We'll figure out something."

"What?" she says.

"I don't know yet. But we'll find you a place where you can be safe. I promise you that."

The minute I'm done speaking, I regret what I've said. I wanted only to comfort Delphina, but now I realize I may have overreached myself. And look at how Delphina looks at me. She takes it way serious, what I have just said. To Delphina, proud as she is, desperate as she is, I've made a covenant, sworn in blood, cross my heart and hope to die. *That* kind of promise. And when you make that kind of promise, you can't look back, you can only look foward; you've got to put out your cigarette and stand up and act like you know what you're doing.

The first thing I do when I come home from the pancake house is stand at the kitchen sink and wash my hands. Maybe I'm washing off the dirt I actually encountered, back behind the dumpsters, or maybe I'm trying to wash off what can't be washed off, which is my fear. I'm afraid for Delphina. I wish I could make Clyde go away, or Delphina's poverty, or her addiction to rum.

I'm just drying my hands on a dish towel when Will comes home. "Sorry," he says. "Camille's dad wanted to show me his CD collection and we got talking. Where were you? I called."

"Out. I went to see Delphina," I say. Then I tell him about the money I loaned her, and about the bruises. He suggests, "Why don't you call Tim

Bright? Isn't he connected with that battered women's shelter? He'll know what to do."

And so Will stands beside me, to be supportive, while I make the call. Reverend Bright recognizes my voice instantly, and I'm touched but not surprised. Before our son died, we went to church pretty much every Sunday. "Janey! How are you?"

"Good. Fine. But I could use your help."

I explain to him about Delphina and then he asks, "Do you know who's abusing her?"

"Her ex-husband. Who she's living with. Anyhow, I know you're involved with a shelter, and I wondered if we could get her in there."

"She's indigent, I take it."

"Basically, yeah. She doesn't have a whole lot of options."

"Mmmn. Because the shelter is a safe place, it's state-run and free of charge, but it's not the Ritz. There are certain rules—"

"You mean like no drugs? No drinking? She would understand that." I pause. "So where is this shelter located?"

"Downtown. They keep their whereabouts secret. There is, unfortunately, a waiting list. There's always a shortage of beds. But I'll keep an eye out for you, and let you know when something opens up."

"That would be wonderful," I say.

There is a pause between us, then Tim Bright sighs into the phone. "It's a sad business. I'm sorry for your friend. But, listen, while I've got you on the phone, I want to take a minute to talk about *you*."

"Me?"

"You coming to church Sunday?"

"Gosh," I say. I don't want to turn him down flat when he's being so helpful about Delphina. But the fact is, I'm reluctant to go to church. He knows why. Our church is small and friendly, but nothing fancy. The church itself offers a simple sanctuary. Outside there's a playground for the kids, and a graveyard. The rule is, you must be a member of the church to be buried in the graveyard. There are exceptions to this rule, on occasion, and one of these exceptions is my son.

He adds, "People are asking about you and Will. You're an important and well-loved part of our community."

A lump forms in my throat. I swallow dryly. "Thanks. I appreciate that."

"We miss you, Janey."

"I miss you all, too."

"Just *think* about coming Sunday."

"Sure," I say, "Okay. I'll talk to Will."

"God bless you and keep you," he says.

Anyone else saying it would have sounded phony. But, he makes tears come to my eyes. After I hang up the phone, it takes me a minute to collect myself, and then I dial Delphina at the pancake house. Whoever answers the phone is none too thrilled to have to go fetch Delphina in the back room washing dishes, but finally Delphina comes on, "Skinny lady? That you?"

"Yeah, listen. There's a place for you. It's a shelter. You can't drink or smoke. You have to keep up with your job. But they have beds there and offer two square meals a day, breakfast and dinner, and you'll be safe."

"Sounds real good. When we goin'?"

"That's the only hitch. They're full up at the moment. But I talked to my minister about this. He'll tell us when a bed opens up."

"Girl, he might be your minister, but you be my angel, you know that? Settin' this up."

"Well, let's don't get carried away."

"You *is*."

"In that case, do you think I should go with a gold halo, or silver?"

She starts to laugh but then she gets choked up, I can hear it in her voice, so I don't kid around anymore. "Honestly, Delphina, it's my pleasure," and I realize that it *is* my pleasure, helping her. I am smiling broadly. I am, in fact, grinning. It feels good to care about somebody else besides me for a change.

CHAPTER 6

After I hang up, Will says, "She's right, you know. You really are doing a good thing."

"You could hear us?"

"I could hear enough." He smiles. "Listen, if you're not busy rescuing somebody *else* this morning, want to come with me to the store? We're practically out of everything."

"The grocery store?" I swallow, hard.

"Yes." Will looks at me. He knows what he's asking. The last time I went to the food store—this was after I got sick but before the hospital—I was seized by a panic attack in the middle of the Campbell's soup aisle. I got dizzy deliberating over all those cans and cans of soup; I just couldn't decide what I wanted—chunky style, regular style, home style, chicken noodle, steak and vegetable, clam chowder? And so I abandoned my half-filled shopping cart and drove home.

But today I've moved beyond that old despair. I am grounded, competent, strong.

"All right," I finally say. "Why not?"

In truth, I never much liked the Giant supermarket. The aisles are cramped; the merchandise is too tightly stocked; the lines to the checkout are frustratingly long. But I remain buoyed up by my connection to Delphina and by Will's confidence in me, and so I am able to handle it just fine—the butcher shop, the wellness center with its slickly merchandized herbs and vitamins, the toilet paper aisle where you could vanish in absorbent sheets of white. I am even handling the signs that are everywhere in your face: EVERYDAY LOW PRICES, GROUND ROUND BEEF 20% OFF—handling it, that is, until I run into Antonia.

I'm alone in the fruits and vegetables when it happens. Will is off stalking ice cream in the frozen foods. If I were wise, I would meet disaster head on, greet Antonia and exchange brief pleasantries. But I'm desperate to flee. I duck my head and barrel forwards with my shopping cart. The cart balks at the abrupt motion; its bum wheel squeaks before it locks into a skid.

"Janey!" She spies me, and comes over.

"Oh, Antonia. I didn't see you."

She's wearing white pleated slacks and an expensive camel-hair jacket. Her hair is, as usual, magnificent. That pre-Raphaelite tumble of blonde.

"You here alone?" she asks me.

"Uh, alone?"

"Yes. As in by yourself."

"Right." I fumble a smile at her, "Actually, Will's around here someplace. He's scaring us up some mint chocolate chip."

"My favorite." She smiles back, revealing perfect white teeth. "Listen, I'm so glad you stopped by school yesterday."

"Oh. Me too."

"The kids adored seeing you. We didn't realize you were home from the hospital."

"Well, I am! Home, I mean. Back to my husband and daughter!"

"Actually, Janey, I've been wanting to talk to you. What fabulous luck, to catch you here."

"Yes, isn't it."

"Marianne's told me the plan, how they want to reevaluate you. And, Janey, I just wanted to say, I know how much you love teaching and so this evaluation...well, it's ridiculous. It's insulting, and I really feel for you because I know on some level that it must be a blow for you, to your pride, I mean. You have so much experience teaching, so many years...but the point is, don't worry, they'll take you back."

"Oh, why's that?"

"You're the best first-grade teacher that school's ever had."

"Next to you?"

"Oh, Gawd, puh-lease." She laughs. "I can't hold a candle to you, you know that."

I frown, thinking, *This woman is quite possibly stealing my husband. And now she pretends to like me?* I reach for the cucumbers in the bin in front of me. I'm so flustered, I start heaping cucumbers into my cart, randomly, one after another, just to have something to do. Antonia wants a cucumber, too, but her approach is the antithesis of mine: she carefully squeezes a variety of cucumbers, big and small, thin and round, until she selects a big juicy one.

I can't help thinking that this lady knows her way around a cucumber. And, well, once I start drifting along these lines, I'm in trouble. In the produce section, everything can be seen in terms of sexual innuendo, in terms of male and female anatomy. Cucumbers, tapered carrots, long green celery stalks...buxom coconuts, cantaloupes, melons. Out of repressed anger and hysteria, I start to giggle.

"What is it?" she says.

"Nothing. It's just—that's one big cucumber you got."

"Oh, did you want this one?"

"That particular cucumber?"

"Yes. I can give you this one and choose another, if you'd like."

"No, that's fine, *you* keep it. That's *your* cucumber." I pause, damp down the impulse to giggle again, then my mood turns dark. "Some things *are* mine, however, and they aren't meant for sharing. Some things *do* belong to me. And those, Antonia, you *can't* have."

She furrows her brow. Is she dense? Or, is it possible I have misinterpreted her relationship with my husband? I've no further time to ponder this, because, just now, I glimpse Will headed this way. I've got to do something, fast. I truly do not want to see my husband and this woman together. If I see them together, I will know.

"Well, gosh," I say, tossing yet more cucumbers into the cart, wildly piling them in without so much as a glance at them; they could be wilted or pickled for all I know. "This has been swell, but I really should be going. Nice talking to—"

You, I was going to say. But, now, here's Will. He has found us.

"Antonia," he says.

"Will," she says.

They both stand stiffly. They have encountered each other in perhaps the most mundane place on earth—within the sanitized confines of a food market. Under these fluorescent lights, it could be day or night, it could be winter or summer, snowing or sunny, you would never know. It is a seasonless world, or rather a world with one singular season: buying season. You can always purchase whatever it is you're looking for, whatever it is you want, unless it's the truth. Because I don't know what the truth is, what Will is feeling right now. But, I know this, he's forgotten the carton of ice cream he holds in his hands as he stares at her, three steps away; that container of mint chocolate chip is forming condensation droplets, and still he is not moving. He is not touching her; he is just standing there, the very air between them crackling with electricity.

I grow suddenly hot. My ears hum. I have fainted once before in my life, and I feel like that now. A roaring black wave looms over me, threatens to come crashing over my head. My voice thickens, "I was just telling Antonia we're in a bit of a hurry. That, you know, party we're having."

"Party?" Will says.

"Yes." I grab my husband's arm as I heave the stalled cart forwards. "Nice seeing you, Antonia."

"Yes, nice seeing you," Will says.

I wheel the cart along, leaving Antonia behind us. I don't risk a glance at Will. I give him time to arrange his expression. When I finally look at him, I discern a studiedly neutral exterior. And yet I am his wife. I notice details. I see how his jaw is clamped. I sense his profound uneasiness. I push my cart along, acting like everything's fine, but that fainting feeling clamps down on me again. Noises assault me. The piped-in Muzak, the electronic beeper of the scanners up front at the cash registers, the intercom that squawks, "Don, bakery, please." When I hear the word bakery, I grow queasy; I think of cakes and pies and coconut frosting, and I hate coconut frosting. I have to stop the cart. I know I am pale; I can feel the blood drain from my face.

"What's this about some party we're having?" Will says.

"Oh, just...I just wanted to get away."

"From Antonia?"

"Yes."

"Oh," Will says. "I'm sorry."

Sorry? I stare at him. He's not going to tell me *now*, is he? In front of the mozzarella sticks? The muenster cheese? My stomach clenches down hard. Oh, God, I think, don't tell me now.

I peer intently into the refrigerated shelves, seeking sanctuary from my life. There is grated Parmesan and sharp cheddar. Where can I escape? There is no room for me, in among the cheeses.

But then Will says, "Janey, I shouldn't've brought you here. I've rushed you. I mean, you just got home from the hospital."

"No, really, I'm fine," I say, breathing in and out once again. He didn't mention *Antonia* or *in love with someone else* or *separation* or *divorce.* The roaring in my ears subsides. I have become one of those women you see in the grocery store who is so desperate to be married, she is actually happy when her husband doesn't confront her with his infidelity. She's not asking for there to be no affair; her expectations have been tragically, pathetically, whittled way down from that: she's just happy they're not talking about it. She doesn't know if he is or is not having an affair. Even if her marriage is a sham, she wants it to go on; she will take anything life hands to her except the worst of all things, which is to be alone.

"Are you really okay?" Will asks. "Because you don't look so hot."

"No, I'm good. Honest."

"Then," he looks earnest, "do you mind me saying something?"

Uh oh. I tense up, all over again.

"Don't look so stricken." He laughs. "I'm just thinking we should maybe take back some of these cucumbers. You have like, what, over a dozen in there?"

"That many?" I say, swooning with relief. "I guess I lost count."

Will and I spend the rest of the day together. We grub weeds from the garden, then fetch Sarah from Camille's. Back home we play croquet with

Sarah—we are missing two of our wickets, but we make do—then Sarah is invited to Ruth's for dinner, and once again Will and I are alone.

When the garlic bread and everything else is ready, Will and I sit down to eat. We have spent the last half-hour boiling noodles and tossing a salad. There has been ample opportunity for us to talk. But I haven't said a word.

Will notices. He says, "You're awfully quiet."

"Am I?"

"Ever since the grocery store." He winds spaghetti onto his fork, then looks at me, "You okay?"

"Fine, sure."

"You're eating, anyway."

He's right, I realize. I am eating with appetite. I can, for the first time in weeks, taste my food. I grate more Parmesan onto my noodles, then take a giant mouthful. The parmesan cheese, the tomato sauce, the buttery pasta, I can savor every bit of it.

What a change this is, so profound as to be revolutionary. Regaining one's appetite, after losing it, strikes me as miraculous. It is like seeing the sunrise after a night spent in deep darkness and no moon, a night of such despair your soul smokes cigarette after cigarette, filling the ashtray with the lipstick-smeared stubs of all your dreams. But then, at last, the morning light creeps in over the horizon, almost imperceptibly, until what was black becomes gray and what was gray becomes all the colors you could ever want, as bright as you could ever want them. It is a very difficult thing, to make yourself eat when you are not hungry, and now I won't have to do this. I am grateful.

"You're crying," Will says.

"No." I shake my head.

It is cold this evening, very cold for April. We actually have a fire going in the fireplace. When we finish our spaghetti, we put our plates in the sink and sit on the sofa and stare into the flames. We are touching, along our arms, the length of our legs. I am feeling cozy and content until Will says, "You're sure you don't want to talk about anything?"

"Nope. Nothing. You?"

He seems startled. Is it guilt that flickers across his face?

"Me? No, nothing special. Nuhuh." For a long moment, he watches the flames. "One thing I *was* thinking..."

"What's that?"

"About church tomorrow. Let's go."

"Oh, Will."

"Too soon?"

"No, it's just...all those people."

"They're our friends."

"They pity us."

He shrugs. "Pity is tough to take, I'll give you that. On the other hand, I think it'd be good for you to get out."

"Why?"

"Because you're lonely."

"I'm not."

"Honey." He just looks at me.

"Why would you say that?"

"You haven't seen anyone lately. Haven't returned your phone calls."

"Except Delphina."

"Right, except Delphina." He pauses. "How come you can talk to her, anyway, and not anybody else?"

"I feel comfortable with her. She knows me."

"Don't your friends know you?"

"Only who I used to be." I shrug. "I've changed."

The fire needs stirring. I get up, move the fire screen aside, seize the iron tongs, and rearrange the logs. When I sit back with Will on the sofa, he pulls my head against his shoulder, to lean on him. We hold one another for the longest time and stare into that fire. We stare so hard, you would think we were looking to find, within the fluid mysteries of those leaping flames, the solution to all our problems, the end to all our grief.

"Okay, I'll do it," I say, in a low voice.

"You'll go to church?"

"Yes."

In the fire, the topmost oak log tumbles backward. Flames rocket up, blue and orange. There is a loud hiss, then *snap!* as sparks fan out in an umbrella, like fireworks falling to earth.

You can see my son's name from the church playground, especially if you're a kid sitting poised in your rolled-up dungarees at the top of the yellow slide. If you look down before you make that first forward thrust and feel the wind in your hair, you can see clearly his small rounded tombstone beyond the fence. If you squint, and if you're old enough to know how to read, you can make out his name, Max Nichols, engraved in the stone.

"You want to go with me?" I ask Will.

"No, I'll take Sarah into the sanctuary. You take your time."

And so I step alone across the grass to my son's tombstone. I am an unexceptional middle-aged woman dressed in an oatmeal sweater, flowered skirt, and black laceup boots, hiking through raggedy crabgrass. It is cool like yesterday. Only today there is no wind. The sunlight, which is the exact color of apricots, has a strange dense quality to it. This apricot light filters through the trees, and for a moment I think I can actually pluck it, like a velvetry fruit that would ripen for me on the sill and dribble sweet juices down my chin whenever I bit into it.

I didn't bring flowers, but I see that someone else has left a single dandelion, set in a jelly jar of water, on the tombstone's edge. I love that dandelion. I feel small and cold and hug myself while I stand silent in front of the son I knew for such a short while. On the raw spring grass a pinched green caterpillar inches along so slowly you wouldn't think it was moving at all. I stand for a good long moment and think of nothing much, then I turn and head inside.

It is Palm Sunday and so they give us palm fronds, a symbol of peace that the kids use without irony as swords. Sarah tickles me with hers, and Will makes a star with his, and pretty soon the service is over, and I have done it. I have sat in my pew in the sanctuary and survived my first service ever since the death of my son.

After the benediction, people approach Will and me, embrace us and offer kind words. I am touched. In the coffee room, Timothy Bright comes up to me. He reminds me of Ruth because he, too, enjoys life. He's removed his black robes; he's wearing a gray business suit. He's juggling cake in one hand, hot coffee in the other.

"Janey," he says. "Wonderful to see you. How's it going?"

"I'm, you know, functioning. Some days are better than others."

He nods.

Around us I see other members of the congregation linger nearby; they are waiting to talk to Timothy, but he continues to stand beside me.

I clear my throat. "Tim," I say, "I have all these questions. Doubts, really. About God."

"You don't know what you believe anymore."

"Yes."

He nods. He's listening.

"Why did God bother to create Max in the first place? What was the point? A miscarriage early on, I could maybe see it, but why have him live so long, all the way up to the end of the third trimester? Thirty-seven weeks." My throat constricts. "Did you know after twelve weeks the fetus can suck its thumb in utero? I saw it on NOVA. Which means my son would have been sucking his thumb, inside me. All his joints were formed, his organs. He even had hair." I am dizzy, saying this. I feel my grief will topple me.

Reverend Bright says, in the gentlest way possible, "You're asking some tough questions. And searching for answers. All I can say is, you're in good company. The disciples of Jesus asked some tough questions, too."

"Do you have questions? I mean, about your faith?"

"Of course. All the time."

"Get any answers?"

He smiles. "Sometimes when I wait, when I am silent, things become clear."

"Mmmm." My eyes fill with tears because Reverend Bright is so kind, and I am so confused. He loops his arm around me and reels me in for a hug. He isn't wearing his clerical collar or his black robes; he's just a man in a business suit who lives with the Bible and a big heart, but for the moment, in this coffee room with its half-drunk pots of lukewarm coffee, with its cake crumbs on a white doily on a silver tray, with its friendly murmur of voices, it is, briefly, enough.

"Oh, by the way, I almost forgot," he says. "I've got a place for your friend. Delphina, is it?"

"You're kidding! That's great!"

"Not till Tuesday, though. Tuesday a bed's opening up."

"Wonderful. That'll be fine," I say.

◦)◦

Outside, families drift toward their cars. I have a moment when I feel apart from everyone, disconnected. Now that they've enjoyed their cake and coffee, and Sunday school is over, fathers call their sons from the sandbox and mothers urge their daughters from the swings. A grenade explodes in my heart, and I think: how is it that they get to walk off hand in hand with their children? How dare they yell at them for getting chocolate chips smeared on their Sunday dresses? Or sand on their good shoes? They're breathing aren't they? What else matters?

And yet, I am encouraged enough by Delphina's good news to get past this moment. I am able, even, to deal with the unexpected arrival of Will's associate, Barbara Kirkbridge. She pulls into the church parking lot, her engine running. Although it is a weekend, a Sunday, she is dressed in her usual lawyerly attire, the severe jacket and skirt with linen blouse.

Will hurries over to speak to her.

When I join both of them, Barbara is hanging her elbow out her open driver's window. Will turns to me, says, "We finally got this forensics expert, and he can only meet with us today, right now. Barbara'll drive me straight down to the office. You and Sare take the van."

"Fine," I say.

Will takes a closer look at me. We were planning to spend the day together. "You okay with this?"

"Yes," I say.

"You sure?"

"Sure."

Sarah tickles me with her palm frond. She wants us to hurry home so she can play with her beanie babies. But I linger a moment and watch Will circle around Barbara's car and climb in.

Barbara, meanwhile, smiles at me from behind the steering wheel. "Sorry about this. Only one more working day till Monday. I promise to get him back to you by dinner."

"Thanks," I say. Sarah tickles me again, but I am still looking at Barbara. The sun is on my face, that apricot sun, that makes me feel anything is possible, even a human connection. "Speaking of which, would you like to come?"

"What? For dinner?"

"Yes. Tonight."

"That's kind of short notice for you, isn't it?"

"I'd like it," I say. "Honestly."

"Okay, then," she says. "It's a date."

Will stares at me from the passenger seat. I have startled him by inviting Barbara over. I haven't asked anyone to our house in a long time.

Dinner is a success, and I am happy. I'm out of practice, having company, but Barbara Kirkbridge makes it easy. Ruth has joined us, too, for crispy fried chicken, corn, and mashed potatoes. We've just begun dessert, a pound cake Ruth brought over.

"This pound cake," I munch hungrily, "is the best."

"It's just Sara Lee," Ruth says. "It's been in the freezer."

"So, don't get *too* excited," Will adds, winking at me.

"I don't care," I say. "Every mouthful is an adventure."

"It is *not!*" Sarah chimes in. She is fondly exasperated with me. "An adventure, Mom, is like when you go hiking in the woods and a grizzly bear chases you up a tree."

"Hold on," Barbara jumps in. "I think your mother is onto something. I *love* this pound cake. But then again, the closest thing I eat to homemade in *my* house is takeout pizza."

Sarah washes the last of her pound cake down with a gulp of milk from a glass so tall she needs to grip it with both hands, "Well, it *does* taste *pretty* good. How come they call it pound cake, anyway?"

"Because," Barbara laughs, "you gain a pound for every bite you eat. At least I do. My last boyfriend said I was too fat."

"You're not fat," Sarah says, and she's right.

Barbara is an attractive girl. She's not willowy, like, say, Antonia is, but she's fit and muscular; her swimming keeps her in shape. Tonight she's taken off her pinstriped jacket, and without it, she looks more feminine and less severe than usual in her powder blue blouse. Her hair, a honeyed brown, is chopped short, but layered fetchingly in a kind of feathered look. She looks cute and perky in her bronze octagonal-shaped wire-rim glasses.

"What was his name?" Sarah says.

"What?" Barbara asks.

"Your boyfriend."

"Oh. Sam."

"How come he broke up with you?"

"Sarah!" I say. "That's none of our—"

"It's okay," Barbara says. "I was too busy for him, I suppose. I really love my work, and sometimes that intrudes on time for other things."

"Like going to the movies and stuff," Sarah says.

"Exactly." Barbara nods.

Sarah gulps down the last of her milk, then burps because she drank too quickly. "Excuse me," she says, and giggles.

Barbara smiles at her, in silent conspiracy, enjoying the moment.

Suddenly Sarah turns serious again, "Miss Barbara, you don't have a *new* boyfriend?"

"Alas, no," Barbara says.

"I bet you will soon."

"Why's that?" Barbara's eyes, behind the octagonals of her glasses, sparkle.

"Oh, *anyone* would fall in love with *you!*" Sarah cries.

And Barbara laughs, "Let me take this girl home with me! Can I take her home?"

I am amused by this exchange, by the comraderie we've shared tonight. I look at Will and Ruth, wanting to share the communion of the moment, but I find I have just missed meeting their eyes. While Will reaches to pour himself a second glass of wine, Ruth seems intent on shredding her napkin.

After dinner Ruth and I do the washing up.

Barbara has gone home.

Ruth scrubs a pot while I look out the kitchen window. I can see, in the remaining pink light of day, Will and Sarah as they wheel Sarah's bicycle out onto the sidewalk. After Barbara went home, Sarah begged her father to take her out for a spin. Sarah thinks her bike is so grown-up, and it is, if you like pink and purple streamers.

I turn from the window to put away the leftover chicken. When I open the fridge, the cool air hits me. On the rack I spy an unfamiliar glass casserole dish. I lift the tinfoil to see a hamburger and cheese ensemble, half eaten. And then I realize it's Antonia Gianelli's. I grab the casserole dish and thrust it into the sink for Ruth. "Why don't we just dump the rest of this out," I tell her. "There's no room in the fridge. And, besides, nobody's gonna eat it."

"Right," Ruth says.

She scours the glass dish with a brush. I put on the kettle for some coffee, then look out the window again at my husband and daughter. Will is adjusting Sarah's seat with the wrench. His manner with Sarah is gentle; I can see this even from a distance. He says something to her, and she laughs. He has grown closer to Sarah since I went to the hospital. Has he grown closer to Antonia, too, or is it all my imagining? The moment at the cocktail party, the tense encounter at the grocery store—how much meaning do I give to them?

Ruth rinses the casserole dish then flicks off the tap. With a *thunk*, the flow of water ceases. The kitchen falls silent. I get the feeling Ruth has waited for this, a chance to catch me alone, in the silence, "Have you thought about the Island, Janey? Whether you want to go?"

"What?" I say, though I have heard her perfectly. My heart constricts. Outside, Will tosses aside his wrench to help Sarah mount her bike and start down the street. Sarah doesn't have training wheels. Since when did she take them off? My little girl.

"Janey," Ruth says, calling me back.

"Yes?" I turn and to look straight at her, blink.

"The Island," she says, as if the subject needs repeating. "This Memorial Day."

"Mmn," I say. "Well..." My voice sounds flat. "Oh, Ruth, I think it's maybe too soon."

"Sure," Ruth says. "Okay." Disappointed, she turns away. She knows it is more than likely that I conceived Max on the Island. She knows it will be difficult for me to return to the cabin, to sleep in the four-poster bed where Will and I created a life that has already ended. She also knows that if I don't go to the Island soon, I just may never go back.

"Will wants to go," I say. "I know that."

"Yes," she says.

"Why is he so keen, do you know?"

"Oh, sometimes," she is evasive, "it's good to get away. Get a fresh start."

Saying this, she starts sponging down the counter like a madman. I watch her for a moment. I frown at the casserole dish drying in the drain rack. Today has been so fine. Seeing friends at church. Having a special dinner. Why does there have to be this casserole dish in my house? A reminder.

"Ruth," I say.

She won't look at me. She won't stop wiping down the counter.

I put my hand on her arm. "Ruth."

She freezes, holds the sponge poised midair. Only reluctantly does she meet my eyes.

"What do you know?" I ask her.

"About what?"

"Will and a certain teacher."

"What?"

"Not what. Who."

"I'm sure I don't know what you mean."

"Do you know what I mean when I mention the name Antonia?"

"Gianelli?"

"Yes. How many Antonias do you know?"

Ruth studies me intently. "What you're asking me, that's for you and Will to discuss."

"But you know something."

"Whether I do or not—"

"He's talked to you."

"Yes."

"So, what has he told you, dammit?"'

But Ruth won't be pushed into a reply. "I really think you and Will should talk." She resumes her efforts with that sponge, attacking the counter until there is not one crumb left.

I stare at her back. I think I will burn a hole into her, with my staring. But, just then, the water heats to a boil in the kettle, and the whistling startles both of us. I let the kettle whine longer than I should just to irritate Ruth, to give voice to my own frustration.

Monday morning comes, and I have trouble looking Will in the eye. I am preoccupied about what he might or might not be up to.

"Here's your waffles," I tell Sarah and set the plate down in front of her.

While our daughter laces her waffles with maple syrup, Will flips through the newspaper and nibbles on some toast. I pour myself some cereal and sit down with them.

It's ironic, of course, how wonderful the cereal tastes to me. The squares of Corn Chex explode on my tongue. And the milk, sweet and rich, glides down my throat. My appetite is back to stay. But I have other concerns now. Will holds the paper directly in front of him, the sports section making a barrier between us. For this, I am grateful; I am more grateful, still, when he hurries to take Sarah off to school and leaves me alone. Now I don't have to arrange my face into an expression that approximates happiness.

At ten o'clock, I go to see Dr. Silverberg.

I find her house pretty easily. It's perched on a grassy shaded hill in an old Baltimore neighborhood, just over the bridge from the waterfalls. The house is old, painted red like a barn, and like a barn it is clumsy in shape, but friendly in that way that a barn is friendly with its smell of hay and oats and horse sweat. The house looks like it needs a lot of work, and I figure Dr. Silverberg made a smart move marrying that carpenter of hers; he can do the repairs.

I park my van in the asphalt turnaround in the backyard, as instructed. When I close my driver's door and climb outside, I see flower

WALK AMONG BIRCHES / 169

gardens tended with obvious devotion. Not much is blooming yet, but there is a wheelbarrow filled with mulch. Over by the azalea beds I see a red canoe, rounded like a beetle, resting on two sawhorses.

Inside, in the waiting room to Dr. Silverberg's office, I pretend to read a magazine. There is classical music playing. Finally Dr. Silverberg pokes her head in and says, "Janey, come in."

She gestures to the sofa for me to sit and she takes the easy chair.

I swallow dryly, and we begin. I should talk to her about Will, about my suspicions, but I am too ashamed. Suppose I'm wrong? Suppose there is nothing going on? On the other hand, what kind of wife am I, if my husband *is* having an affair?

"So how's it going?" Dr. Silverberg asks. "Being home."

"Fine," I say.

"Any problems?"

"Not, ah, no. Not really." Maybe I can talk to her about Will another time. But not today.

Dr. Silverberg watches me. "You sure you don't have something on your mind?"

"No."

"Because you look pretty anxious."

"I'm okay." I gnaw on my lip.

"Hmm," Dr. Silverberg says.

And now the office falls silent.

Finally, I venture, "I overheard Sarah say something to her Dad."

"Oh, what's that?"

"She said I wasn't myself. That I seemed sad."

"And that was news to you?"

"Not news, exactly. It's just...I thought I was able to hide it better, that's all."

"What would Will say?"

"About me?"

"Yes."

"Oh, I suppose he'd agree with Sarah."

"You mean, that you're emotionally distant."

"I wouldn't go *that* far."

"But, Janey, aren't you?"

"Well, I'm not myself. Sarah's right, I'm not. But—"

"I'd say you're stuck."

"How?"

"In the past."

"You mean, losing my brother."

"I mean losing your mom."

I give Dr. Silverberg a puzzled look.

"Because you lost her, too, didn't you? About the same time you lost him?"

"What do you mean?"

"I mean that she kept drinking. Even after the accident."

I try not to remember the car, the slick of ice, tobogganing into the woods. And the frozen lake that wasn't quite frozen, after all. Not frozen enough for Max, anyway.

"Oh, she tried to give it up. You understand."

"Mmmm," Dr. Silverberg says.

"For months, she tried. She even joined AA. But it didn't take. Or, rather, not permanently."

"Makes for a hard life," Dr. Silverberg reflects. "Hard on your mother. Hard, also, on you. In the sense that you must have felt helpless."

The word *helpless* stuns me. I shield my eyes with the flat of my hand as though the light is too bright in here, but it is not too bright in here. My throat is tight, and there is something bubbling up inside me that is so painful, I can hardly breathe.

"What is it?" Dr. Silverberg says. "You remember something."

"No."

"Come on."

"This one day. I was in sixth grade. I used to walk to school."

"Yes?"

"And when I walked home, this stranger followed me. I was wearing my polka dot dress—" I interrupt myself. Fall silent. "Look, I'm not sure I can do this. Besides, it's ancient history. I'm over it."

"Are you?"

"Yes."

"Then, why, after all these years do you remember it was polka dot?"

"Well," I smile, "it was a pretty ugly dress."

Dr. Silverberg smiles, too.

We regard each other for a long, thoughtful moment.

It is clear she's not going to urge me anymore. She wants to leave this up to me. Finally, I say, "The dress was blue. Some kind of gauzy material. When I held it up to the sunlight it shimmered....Anyhow, it was April, May. The cherry blossoms were out. School was fine; I'd had a good day. My knapsack felt light."

Dr. Silverberg nods, listens.

"I was almost to my house when this car drove up behind me. A black Impala, inching along. I got this creepy feeling, you know? And started to walk faster. When I reached my house, I glanced toward my mother's room, upstairs. The blinds were drawn."

"Not a good sign?"

"Not a good sign. But, anyhow, I had my own key, so I figured I'd let myself in. But then the Impala raced up behind me and screeched to a halt. The man thrust his head out the window.

"*Your dress*, he said.

"I looked down. My polka dot dress was rucked up past my butt. My knapsack must've snagged the hem of my dress. And so this man, this man in the black Impala, had watched me walk in my underwear all the way home."

"Oh, no," Dr. Silverberg says.

"Well, I yanked my dress back down real fast, but the man, he's got all his lewd thoughts going.

"He said, *Can I come in?*

"*No.*

"*Why not?*

"Well, by now I was trembling like crazy. I glanced up to the second floor. To those lowered blinds. *You can't*, I said. *My mom's inside.*

"So... what happened?" Dr. Silverberg asks.

"I got lucky. Another car came by. Neighbors from down the street. They waved to me as they went by, and I guess this made the man think twice. He took one last look at me, revved his engine, and peeled off."

"And your mom? Did she see or hear any of this?"

"No."

"What exactly was she doing?"

"Uh...sleeping."

"At three o'clock in the afternoon?"

"Well..."

"You mean passed out, don't you?"

"I guess."

"You went into her room?"

"Yes."

"What did you see?"

"The room was dark, but not completely. In the shafts of light I could see dust motes, cigarette stubs curled up in the ashtray, her address book draped over the phone."

"And your mother?"

"Buried deep under the blankets, but I could see her face all pasty with sweat, her damp hair. It was way too hot in there."

"Did you try and wake her?"

"Yeah. *Mom*, I said. *Mom, Mom.* I shook her arm a couple of times, but she didn't stir. I remember I gazed down at her. Then I moved to the air conditioner and switched it on. Now it wouldn't be so hot in there and she could sleep without sweating."

"Is that it?" Dr. Silverberg asks. "End of story?"

"Except for the polka dot dress. I decided I never wanted to wear it again. I rolled it up into a bundle and took it outside and shoved it deep into the trash can."

"And did you tell your mom, later, when she was sober?"

"About the man? No."

"Your father?"

"Nuhuh."

"No one?"

"Not till you," I say.

If I tell you Delphina rents rooms downtown in an old Victorian, you might imagine this quaint gingerbread kind of house. But, no, it's so ugly. The house has been sliced and diced into cheap rental units. Delphina's unit is at the top. It's Tuesday morning just before noon when I clomp up three flights of sagging stairs to get to her place, where I ring the doorbell.

There is an unexpected delay before she answers.

"Skinny Lady!" She flings open the door. "Welcome to paradise."

"Delph!" I say. I am so glad to be doing this. I can forget about Will and Antonia for awhile. "So, you ready to go?"

"I be ready directly."

"Great!" I say.

I'm smiling, but my smile fades when I realize what Delphina is wearing. She didn't exactly dress for the shelter. She's in sweatpants and a shirt with a stain on it. But this hardly seems important once I notice a far more salient fact, which is the raised welt beneath her eye.

"Aw, Delph," I say. The eye looks bad. It had to hurt; it is so swollen and purple. *Be calm*, I tell myself, *you don't want to upset her*, but I can't stand to look at her face. The best I can do is look down at my feet and then over at hers. She is wearing white canvas sneakers, the cheapo kind, where the hot glue gun has been careless, and glue shows along the seams of the rubber soles.

I feel her gaze on me, and now I have no choice but to look up at her. I watch while she raises her hand toward her eye. The skin must be tender because I notice she doesn't touch the lump; she only lets her fingers hover near it.

"It don't hurt none," she says.

"Sure," I say.

"Stop starin'. You makin' me feel like a cyclops or somethin'."

"Sorry," I say. Then, "May I?"

"Wha's that?" For a single moment only, she gives me a blank stare. I get the feeling she has forgotten who I am. I could be any white woman standing on her doorstep in the wrong part of town. Then, abruptly, she recollects herself. "Shucks, girl, come on in."

I don't expect much from her place, but even then I am disappointed.

The apartment is cramped and dark. Not much sunlight creeps its way in because of the tall brick building next door. No curtains hang in the windows. To my right, there is a bathroom, straight ahead a TV and sofa. Clyde must like watching TV because the TV is the only well-tended item in this place. It looks to be brand new. It must be a twenty-two-inch screen easy. The sofa facing the TV has fallen on hard times; it is black leather, riddled with cracks. For a bed there's a queen-size mattress on the floor. The mattress has a raggedy bedspread on it, and sheets. Near the bed is a stack of library books. I can make out some of their titles. I see some classics among them, and no trashy stuff at all; it is clearly reading material for a discerning mind, and is, furthermore, the only thing in this apartment that appears to be wholly Delphina's. To my left is the kitchen. I think I smell something burning. "You didn't leave the stove on, did you?" I ask her.

"I doan believe so, sugar. But les go check. I's fixin me a sandwich."

I follow Delphina into the kitchen. I watch her unsteady gait, and now the hair prickles on the back of my neck. My mom, when she was drinking, always got pigeon-toed. I don't know why. Delphina isn't like this. Her feet do not turn pigeon-toed. She is, however, exaggerated in her movements. Aiming for normalcy, she overcompensates. And so she's off, by a mere fraction.

And yet, I could be wrong. There's always that chance. Maybe Delphina's black eye is throbbing away, giving her a killer migraine. Maybe that's why nobody's turned on the lights in here, and it's so dark.

"Delph," I say, "you okay?"

"Fine 'n dandy."

For a moment, we stand together in the small kitchen. I see a butcher block table, a countertop, a stove. On the stove there is a skillet on the front right burner. In the skillet is a cheese sandwich, grilled and blackened. The gas burner shows no flame, is turned off safely, after all. Still, the air reeks of grease and smoke.

I say, "We should go."

She says, "Gotta get somethin' in my stomach first. Be a shame to waste this."

"Delph, it's *burned*," I say. "Why don't we buy you a McDonald's on the way, how's that?"

"Lemme at leas' have some coffee," she insists.

I'm actively surveying the kitchen now. I don't see any bottles lying around, but that doesn't mean anything. Bottles are easy to hide. "Okay, we make you some coffee. Then we go."

"I already got some, honey."

She indicates the mug on the worn Formica table. The mug stands beside a jumble of cigarette butts snailed up in an aluminum pie plate. Next to the cigarette butts is a bag of frozen peas, just sitting there. I reach for the mug, but Delphina snatches it up first. Nonetheless, I catch a whiff of the mug's contents. "That doesn't smell like coffee," I say.

"No?"

"More like rum and Coke."

"Well, there you wrong, girlfrien'. I done run out of Coke an hour ago. This be just straight rum." She chuckles. Her gold molar glints in the dark kitchen.

"Delph," I bite my lip and struggle for self-control, "you know drinking's not allowed at the shelter, right? No drugs. No alcohol."

"I know."

"So, why are you doing this? A bed just opened up, but I don't know how long they'll hold it for you. There's a waiting list a mile long. Certainly, they can't take you in...like this. You've got to sober up."

"Sober up, yeah. Les' drink to that." Delphina hefts her mug and takes a defiant gulp of her rum.

"Oh, that's just swell." I frown. "Is that what you did with the hundred dollars I gave you? Buy rum?"

Her eyes harden.

"Delph, what about all we talked about? About you moving on with your life? Breaking away from Clyde? Being independent?"

"Independent, honey! Oh, *you'se* one to talk! You got a whole army of support behind you. A husband who done love you, a daughter, and that Dr. Silverberg—"

"Stop!" I shout. "Just stop!"

"I be glad to, you get your nose outta my bidness! Clyde be back soon. Why don't you just mosey on back to your whitebread house and whitebread life!"

Stunned as I am, I can only stare at Delphina. Numbness yields to outrage, and now my ears are ringing. My stomach roils. I look at Delphina's kitchen table, at the bag of frozen peas and jumble of cigarette butts. I smell the charred grilled cheese, and I say through clenched teeth, "You won't help yourself, will you? Jesus, Delph, you're just like my mother. She drank too goddam much; she wouldn't change. And neither will you!"

I stagger for the door. I don't plan to look back, but I do. I see Delphina reaching for that package of frozen peas. It is a bag of Birds Eye. She lifts the bag of frozen peas up under her injured eye and holds it there, like an ice pack. So that's why she's got the frozen peas out.

I pound down the Victorian's three flights of stairs. My whole body is shaking. I wanted to do some good. I wanted to help Delphina. She is my soulmate. We were in the hospital together. Dammit, we *survived*. I reach for the doorknob of the Victoria's front door and then I'm suddenly so light-headed I'm afraid I might fall. I hold onto that doorknob. I am trembling. My stomach clenches and my throat gets all saliva-filled, and I think I might throw up, but blessedly I don't. I take deep breaths, in and out. On my calf, under the denim leg of my jeans, my poison ivy itches like crazy. It itches so much I have to reach down and scratch it, and of course that only makes it worse.

CHAPTER 7

Home again, the first thing I do when I curb my van is to glance across the street. But Ruth's station wagon is gone.

I hurry inside my house and call Ruth, just in case, but she's not there. I'm still shaking, and it's hard to punch the numbers on the phone, but I try Will at work. His secretary tells me he's in a deposition. She offers to interrupt him, but I say that won't be necessary. Still, I feel an urgent need to talk to someone. I decide to try Dr. Silverberg. I don't have another appointment until next week, and I know the odds are not good that she can see me, but to my surprise, she says, "I have a cancellation. Can you be here in twenty minutes?"

And so I grab my purse and drive over the falls to Dr. Silverberg's. I quick-park my van and hurry up the steps to the back door that leads to her office. On my way, I pass by a young man in an Orioles cap and lumberjack boots pushing a mower onto Dr. Silverberg's lawn. The grass is long and waving. Which means he hasn't cut it yet. He smiles at me and I give him a preoccupied hello.

Inside, Dr. Silverberg is waiting for me. She ushers me right in.

"What happened with Delphina?" she asks, as soon as we're seated. "You mentioned something on the phone, but you were talking so fast..."

"I'm sorry," I swallow. "I guess I'm a little upset."

"Tell me."

"Delphina was supposed to go with me to the shelter, only she got drunk."

"Delphina?"

"Black woman. Heavyset. Funky orange hair. I met her on the ward."

"Yes. She wasn't one of my patients, but I remember her."

"Well, anyway, the other day I went to see her and she had bruises all up her arm, and so I arranged with our minister for her to go to the shelter."

"For battered women?"

"Yes."

"Only, today, when I went to pick her up, she was a mess. She had a black eye from Clyde, her ex. I wanted to get her the hell out of there, but she was wasted. She knew if she drank, she couldn't be admitted to the shelter, but there she was, downing her rum and coke. She *screwed* herself."

"So you got in a fight."

"Yes."

"You can make up."

I shake my head. "Afraid not."

"You don't think you can repair your friendship?"

"Not after the things we said."

"Like what?"

"I told her she was drinking her life away, just like my mom. And the thing is, Dr. Silverberg, I was so unbelievably angry. I'm *still* angry. And yet, all mixed up with this anger is fear."

"Why?"

"I keep wondering if she's all right. I mean, with Clyde in the picture, who's to say?"

"You feel you should have rescued her?"

"Yes. Only I blew it."

"I doubt it," she says.

I tilt my head. "What do you mean?"

"You can't save someone who doesn't want to be saved."

"Right," I say. I stare at my therapist. I wonder suddenly who she is talking about, Delphina or me? Do I want to be saved? Or, have I pushed offers for help away, and suffered privately? And who is rescuing who, anyhow? I have assumed all along it was me rescuing Delphina, but now I'm not so sure.

"What?" Dr. Silverberg says.

"It's just...I'm thinking. About how a person has to want help."

"Yes."

"I might be guilty on that score. I haven't been exactly forthcoming with you. There's something...well, it's been on my mind. Well, actually, I've been *obsessing* about it. It's to do with Will—"

"What?" she says.

I'm about to continue when, outside, I hear the startup roar of an engine. I twist my neck to look out the window. It is Dr. Silverberg's lawn service, the young man in the Orioles cap, setting to work.

"Sorry," Dr. Silverberg says. "It'll be a little noisy, but just try to ignore it. You were saying?"

"Yes, uh..." I study my therapist. I wonder how receptive she'll be. Maybe everything in her marriage is just perfect. Maybe every night she and her husband make love, and afterwards they talk, their heads on the same pillow. Maybe when I tell her about Will she won't understand.

Dr. Silverberg tucks a strand of hair behind her ear, "You're hesitating."

"Yes."

"It must be a sensitive subject, what you want to talk about."

"Yes."

"Go ahead. Try me."

"I don't know if I can..." I bow my head, and study my hands. Maybe further into our fifty minutes I can tell her what I suspect about Will and Antonia, or next week, or next month, I don't know. We sit in silence and suddenly I shock myself, decide to come out with it after all, "I think my husband is having—"

At precisely that moment, the lawn mower thunders by, churning up the grass.

"I'm sorry. He's what?" Dr. Silverberg strains to hear.

"An affair!" I shout, and it's nearly comical because the mower has rumbled on past us, and my words resound in the room.

There is a moment of near-silence as the mower attacks the far side of the lawn. Dr. Silverberg does not appear shocked or even surprised about Will. She looks pensive. "Are you sure?"

"I didn't catch them in bed, if that's what you mean."

"This is conjecture, then?"

"No, I'm suspicious and I have good reason to be. Like my best friend

Ruth tells me something's up but she won't tell me more. She says I should talk to Will directly."

"And have you?"

"God, no!"

"Why not?"

"Because if I'm right, what's he gonna say? Sorry, but I find Antonia more attractive than you? Sorry, but I want a divorce?" I pause, and swallow. My voice is so dry it's cracked in a million places. I look at Dr. Silverberg.

"That's her name, Antonia?"

"Yes. She's a teacher at school."

"And you think Antonia and your husband are having relations?"

I nod.

"Why?"

"Because...okay, because I caught them once at this cocktail party, a strangely intimate moment. Their body language was beyond what you'd call polite. And the look in her eyes...she was...hungry."

"She's single?"

"Yes, and young and quite striking. Blonde, thin, looks great in whatever she wears. But here's the thing. I'm in the hospital and she's all of a sudden so cozy and caring. Drops by casseroles, tucks Sarah into bed, gives her backrubs....I never liked her, to tell you the truth. But Will always did. And now, the hell of it is, I can maybe see my husband's point."

"How so?"

"Antonia is...she's...at least *available*. God knows, I haven't been." It is hard for me to talk, the mower's back, threshing away, decapitating and maiming whole families of grass, parents, grandparents, entire *villages*, and I have to raise my voice and practically shout, but it's not just that. There is a lump in my throat I can't make go away. I just know I'm going to cry. I sit on the sofa with my hands interlocking. My fingers hurt, I am squeezing them so hard.

"So," Dr. Silverberg muses, "you suspect Will's unhappy."

"I *know* he's unhappy. Who wouldn't be, with me around?"

"Maybe that's the part that's true."

"What?"

"Usually with any fantasy there's an element of truth. In your case, you feel guilty that you're not your usual self with your husband. If you've been as emotionally distant from him as you fear you have, then it opens up the possibility, doesn't it? That he might seek solace elsewhere."

"That he might go after Antonia, you mean? And jump her bones."

"Well, yes. It's a possibility. But I still wouldn't assume anything. I would speak directly to Will."

"But if I'm right?"

"If you're right, well, then, together we'll need to look at the losses in your life and how you view them. I think your losses prevent you from moving forward."

"How?"

"There are consequences, in the present, from working so hard to preserve the past, from *mourning* the past so diligently that *that* becomes your life. One of those consequences, you're beginning to see, is that you could lose your husband. He may tire of not having you there."

"I'm here! I haven't gone anywhere."

"You can leave without leaving," Dr. Silverberg says softly.

I stare at her. I am hearing everything she is saying, and she is right about most of it. Maybe all of it. But, it's hard for me to accept how flawed I am, how much there is within me that needs improvement, and so I become defensive. I say, "Easy for you to find fault."

"Pardon?" she says.

"You and your perfect life. You're a hotshot psychiatrist. You have all your ducks in a row. You and your husband probably get along just swell, Mr. Hammer and Nails. You keep him so well-satisfied he wouldn't even dream of having an affair. And so you live your fairy-tale lives, you, your husband, and your—" *Children*, I was going to say, but I brake to a halt. Too late I remember Dr. Silverberg's daughter. Something wrong there. Something wrong, Sherman said.

"Me, my husband, and my what?" Dr. Silverberg asks in a careful, even voice.

"Nothing. Forget it."

"Come on. What?"

"All right." I swallow dryly. I am so thirsty all of a sudden, I could drink

182 / Carol McAfee

gallons and gallons of water. I am so sorry for bringing this up. I would do anything to take this conversation back, "I heard there's something…Sherman in the hospital said something's wrong with your daughter. Is there?"

Dr. Silverberg blinks. She is expert at cloaking her own feelings—that is, after all, part of any therapist's job—but I sense I have made a direct hit. I wish to God I hadn't hurt her. I pray she'll say, *What are you talking about? My daughter's perfectly fine. She's going off to college soon to become a doctor, following in my footsteps.* Instead, she states, rather tersely, as if she doesn't entirely trust her voice, "I don't think this would be a useful topic for us to explore right now." And then she adds, consulting the clock, "I'm really sorry, but our time is up for today. We'll talk more about this, obviously. But I would urge you to talk to Will. Get things out in the open."

"Sure, absolutely," I agree, rising from the couch. Dr. Silverberg looks bruised and hurt, especially now that I'm standing. You would never know how tall she was; I am, in fact, strangely, looming above her.

I go to the door.

She says after me, "It's unthinkable to you that my life may not be perfect? That I may have problems, too?"

My hand freezes on the doorknob.

I wait one beat, two. My heart is racing.

"I'm sorry; I have to go," I say.

I stumble blindly outside. There, I nearly collide with the mower man, who is bent over and prying clumps of wet grass from the cutting blades of his mower. Perspiration drips from his brow, at least the part I can see under the peaked orange bill of his baseball cap. The man is young enough to have nicked himself shaving this morning; he's not all that deft with a razor yet. He is wearing floppy, unlaced hiking boots.

He looks up at me and grins, and there is something about the bold thrust of his jawbone, his thick hair clipped short around his ear, and the seashell curl of the ear itself that makes my heart catch, that makes me think of myself when I was young. I'm all choked up; I can barely nod back to this man-boy. I hurry like I'm running away from something, a volcano maybe, an earthquake. As I stumble down the driveway, the sun slants on my shoulders, and I swoon to the perfumed scent of freshly cut grass.

I sit for a moment in my van, keys in the ignition. The mower roars to life again as I drive off. I mean to go straight home, but I'm dying for a cigarette. I pull in at the Royal Farm Store. Back in my van, I crumple the cellophane from the cigarettes when I glimpse, in the block of stores flanking me, a pet store. There is a sign on the door, FREE GOLDFISH.

The sign makes me think of Sarah, and how she said she'd love a pet. I don't deliberate; I don't allow myself time to talk myself out of it. I simply hurry into the pet store and emerge, some twenty minutes later, with my two new goldfish, a tank, filter, and some colored rocks.

I hit the road again, but I don't go home; I drive straight to Weybridge School. I'm early to pick Sarah up, but that's fine. After talking with Dr. Silverberg, and learning that there might be something wrong with *her* daughter, I'm anxious to see mine, and if I can't see Sarah, I at least want to be near her. I feel that same urgent need to protect her that I felt when she was an infant. My efforts were fruitless, of course, but I was in love with her and so I needed to do this: at night I would slip into her nursery and lean over her crib and watch her breathe in the moonlight. I would touch her forehead, as if I could ward off fever, sickness, and all harm by the mere strength of my devotion.

At Weybridge, it is the last class of the day. The bell will ring shortly, but I can't wait that long. I leave my van and proceed into the building. I am headed toward Sarah's classroom. I intend to poke my nose in, but I run into Charlie Moody first.

He is alone. He is walking, head down, scuffing those sneakers of his.

"Charlie," I call to him. "Where you off to?"

He stops short and gives me a sideways squint. "Principal's."

"What for?"

"Throwing erasers."

"Why, Charlie?"

"Felt like it." He notices the goldfish I hold in the cellophane bag. He pretends not to be interested, but the fact is, he's mesmerized. He can't take his eyes off those orange fins, those wriggling tails. "They yours?"

"For my daughter, Sarah. They're a surprise. I didn't want to leave them in the van in case it got too hot."

"You heard about Lucky, didn't you?"

"Oh, right. Our class mascot. Is it true, you skewered him?"

"Yeah. Lucky wasn't so lucky." Charlie snorts. "Fish are dumb."

I can hear, in Charlie's tone, so much anger I don't think we're talking about goldfish. "Charlie," I say. "I know you're going through some adjustments at home."

"My dad moved out." He shrugs. "No big deal."

"But it *is* a big deal. There must be times when your mom is busy and distracted and your dad isn't there, and it's tough."

"Nah," he says, but he is listening now.

"Sometimes when I was a little girl, oh, about your age, I was lonely."

"You were?"

"Uhuh. Sometimes my mom drank alcohol and so she was really sleepy and didn't care so much how I did in school that day, or if I made any new friends."

"I have friends!" Charlie Moody is trembling. "You telling me I don't?"

I regard him calmly. "No, Charlie. That's not what I'm saying."

But he's done talking, at least for today. He stalks on down the hall to Marianne Mullen's office, preferring the boredom and ignominy of detention to being with me. I gaze after him, and my throat constricts. I cannot, in a ten-second conversation, make Charlie Moody whole again.

I hear a commotion down the hall and, too late, I am ambushed by my own first-grade class. They're scrambling outdoors for final recess. Fifteen minutes until the bell rings, and they plan to make the most of it. Still, they slow down when they see me. I'd like to think it's me, but it's more likely the goldfish.

"Cool," they say.

And, "Hey, Mrs. Nichols, those for us?"

"Not this time," I say. "Maybe another time we can get you guys some fish. These are for my daughter."

They are happy to see me, but happier still to scamper out onto the tarmac to play hopscotch and kickball. Even Erica separates from me easily, scurrying to catch up, her tawny braid swaying.

Antonia is the last to leave. I try to avoid her, but she says, "Janey, wait here a minute, will you? While I walk them out. We need to talk."

Antonia leaves and comes back. By then I've had time to plan my escape. I ask her, "Is it school related?"

"What?"

"Why you need to talk. Because, if not, I'd rather we—"

"Yes."

"Yes?"

"It *is* school related."

"Okay, then," I say.

Antonia walks me back to the classroom. It feels strange to be here. Everything feels dear to me, in the way that everything in your house is dear to you after you come home from a long vacation. You touch your things and they feel old but somehow new. I walk over to the bookshelf, and run my fingers along the spines of the class reading books: *Henry and Mudge, The Very Busy Spider, Amelia Bedelia, Two Bad Ants.*

Behind me, Antonia says, "Whew! What a day. Thank *God* for recess!"

I turn around.

Antonia mock-collapses into Joey Green's chair, tossing back her head so her ash-blonde ringlets tumble all around her like fairies. It is truly remarkable hair, a glimmering cascade of curls so decadent, it might be straight out of the court of Louis the XVI. I wonder if Will has felt the attraction of that hair. I wonder if he has run his fingers through it.

"Have a seat," Antonia says.

"Right," I say. Unwisely perhaps, I sit down right next to her. I wonder how long I can sit here, within striking distance, blood pounding in my ears, and say nothing, do nothing. And, finally, I wonder how it is Antonia can't hear what I'm thinking, since every thought is so loud, so full of portent, like thunder. She shouldn't just sit here next to me. She should run for cover, fast.

I say, "You wanted to talk?"

"Yes." She blows air up toward her bangs, lifting the curls for a second before they fall back down. Then she confesses, "I get so tired teaching. Did you find that?"

"Oh, sure." There's still time. I should warn her. She could still get away.

"It's just that it's so constant, you know. The projects, the field trips. Yesterday we visited the county jail. One of Karen Baum's kids hurled up lunch. Big time. What a mess." Antonia shakes her head. I study her closely and realize she *does* look tired. There are dark smudges under her eyes. I almost feel sorry for her. But not quite. I am too busy radiating hostility, and yes, she realizes it now. Her eyes squint in surprise and she gets up, goes to her desk, fumbles around for something inside, and, unbelievably, produces a pack of cigarettes.

Is *everybody* smoking these days?

"I'm trying like hell to quit," she says apologetically as she tamps out a cigarette and lights up.

"I can see that."

Her brand is Marlboro. She inhales. Before she exhales, she runs to the window and throws it open. The cigarette smoke curls and unfurls outside. Since when has Antonia taken up cigarettes? Since Will? I picture her pacing the halls of her apartment, barefoot, tortured by love. Does she smoke all day, waiting for him? Before sex or after? In that case, gosh, I wouldn't want anything bad to happen to her, like lung cancer or emphysema.

She coughs, and my eyes drill into her. "Really," I say. "You're quite the role model."

"Oh, I never smoke in front of the kids," she says, offended. "What do you take me for?" She glances out the window to the playground. "Whoops. Recess is over. They're lining up." She lets her Marlboro drop to the floor where she grinds it out with the toe of her loafer, then idly nudges it beneath her desk.

She studies me. Even with that window open, even with the scent of pear blossoms sweetening the spring air and the sounds drifting in from the blacktop, the tension between us is unbearable.

"I want you to know..." she begins haltingly.

I wince, and put up my hand. She's about to confess everything. I can see it in her face. This is *not* school related, after all, "Antonia, really...I should go." I gather up Sarah's goldfish and stumble towards the door, but she stops me, seizes my arm above the elbow. I should run away;

instead I gaze stupidly at her hand, the one that's restraining me. She gives a quiverous little laugh and loosens her grip. Now I feel only the feathery pressure of her fingertips. But I cannot move.

"I wanted to tell you, back then in the Giant. You know, the supermarket?"

"Tell me what." My tone is flat, defeated. She's going to tell me, now. There's no escaping it.

"Bob and I are engaged."

"Excuse me?" She has said "Bob" and not "Will," and I am confused.

"It's not public knowledge so please keep it confidential. You know how sensitive these things are, with Bob and me both being teachers here."

"Bob?" I repeat.

"Yes. Bob Gottman."

"The science teacher?"

"Yes, that Bob Gottman."

"Who's teaching Sarah's class about rocks?"

"Yes!" Antonia smiles indulgently at me, finding me a bit dense but willing to go along. She is happy, I can see that; she is happy to talk so long as it is about Bob; her cheeks and ear lobes flush when she says his name.

"Well," I say and clear my throat. "Wow!" We both laugh. "I mean, congratulations!"

"Thanks." Antonia nods, then becomes serious. "I'm telling you all this because next year I plan to leave Weybridge and teach at Bryn Mawr. I want to teach in the upper school. I'd do a lot better with older kids."

"You're leaving?"

"Yes."

"And Bob's staying here."

"Yes."

"Does Marianne know?"

"Oh, yes. And she supports my decision. She knows I'd fare much better in an older classroom where I can concentrate. In upper school, the subject is defined. I'm teaching math by the way. The kids are in and out in forty minutes, then I get a break. The room empties out and all is, blessedly, silent. I'm not cut out to be a classroom teacher like you, Janey. The imagination required, the sense of humor you need to see you through. I just haven't got it. Hell, I can't even find time to pee." Antonia smiles at me, and her smile is, unbelievably, full of generosity and warmth. I wonder how I could've so completely misread her, and misread my husband as well. I would feel badly about this except for the relief that bubbles up inside me that I must stifle, or I'll begin to laugh giddily, madly, hysterically, like the crazy woman I'm trying not to be.

～⟨～

From the moment I leave Weybridge, and Antonia, behind, I am already in the future; I am locked in an embrace with Will, in bed, and neither of us will let go. But to get to that point I've got work to do: I need to convince Will I am not the same person who sent him off to work this morning mistrusting him. And so all evening I plan the seduction.

For dinner I bake lasagna, Will's favorite. I know for a fact the lasagna's a success, because the instant I lower the oven door, Toby comes racing over and sniffs rapturously the scent of bubbling cheeses—ricotta, mozzarella, Parmesan—the spicy aroma of tomato sauce and buttery noodles.

While the lasagna cools, I head upstairs for a quick shower. Afterwards, I apply rouge and lipstick. I dab perfume on my wrists and behind my ears.

I may have been too liberal with the perfume, because when Will, Ruth, and Sarah come to the table and we all four sit down, Sarah says, "What's that smell?"

"The lasagna?" Will says.

"No, like in a fancy underwear store."

"I have no idea," I say.

But Ruth is looking at me and smiling.

Outside, it begins to drizzle. We can gaze out our window toward the apple and birch trees, which open their leaves to the rain. The sky is gray and the rain makes a gentle patter. We feel cozy to be inside.

My lasagna is a hit. Will says it's fabulous. I think it's pretty good myself. When I reach for a second piece, everyone stares at me.

"What?" I say.

"You're eating," Will says, with wonderment. "I mean, really eating."

I munch hungrily. "I told you my appetite's back." Then, "What'd you bring for dessert, Ruth?"

"Brownies," she says.

"Great!" I say. "Bring 'em on!"

Even Sarah stares at me now.

Ruth says, "I'll bring them to the table, only if you promise to share."

"Hey," I say, grinning, "I can't help it if my taste buds are exploding at every bite. It's like the Fourth of July in there."

Sarah giggles, to imagine fireworks in my mouth. Or, maybe she's giggling for the pure joy of our family, together again, her mother well enough not only to eat, but to be teased by everyone around her. And she's pleased, too, with her new goldfish. We set up the aquarium in her room.

After dinner, Ruth hugs us all good night and leaves for her house across the street. Will goes upstairs to tuck Sarah into bed. When he comes back, I plan to make my big move. I plan to make it up to him, for my ever doubting him. He was not, it turns out, the one who strayed. It was me, in my fears and fantasies, who wandered off. Were my fantasies themselves a kind of infidelity?

The rain has stopped. I've finished washing up the plates, and I'm going crazy just sitting around waiting for Will, so I step out onto the deck for some air.

Outside, the night is damp and chill. Goosebumps prickle my arms. Everywhere there is evidence of the rain that just ended. Pools of water on the wood slats of the deck reflect, magically, the clouds wisping across the moon. Close by, a woodpecker drills a tree while a car sloshes past. Stacked to my left along the driveway, haphazardly, is our fireplace wood. The oak logs glisten with rainwater, so raw and unseasoned they look orange where the ax split them.

"Janey," Will says. He has come up behind me. I can tell from his face he is just the littlest bit curious. He wonders what his wife is doing here, illumined in the wash of light from the outdoor spotlight, inhaling the scent of damp firewood on a night too cool for lingering.

I can't admit to Will that I am waiting for him, that I was going insane with it, and so I say nothing.

"Aren't you cold?" he asks.

"Not really," I say, though I hug myself with my arms.

He stands by the railing with me, loops his arm companionably around my shoulder. Companionably, and nothing more. His is not a romantic overture; how can I change the mood?

"What?" Will says.

"It's just...can you hold me a minute?"

"Sure," he says. But he is still puzzled. His arm has been looped around my shoulder, but now he stands facing me. He takes both my hands in his, and so now we stand together but apart, like a man and a woman who have just started to dance and don't know each other very well. Just above us arch the sweeping boughs of our pine trees. Some of their branches actually brush the hair on our heads. The branches droop from the rain, and their needles look soft enough to touch, but this is misleading for they are brittle green and sharp in all kinds of weather.

Will is holding me, gingerly, as though I might break.

My throat constricts. How do I get this seduction scene going? I'm woefully out of practice. I should say something to Will to clue him in, I should lean provocatively against him, squeeze his hand, plant my hand on his crotch, even, and astonish him with a heat-seeking missile of a kiss; but I do none of these things. Instead, I inspect our pine trees. One interesting thing about evergreens is that their woody cylindrical cones actually close up tight during the rain. They only open in sunshine because that's when they shed their seeds. I let go of Will and reach for the nearest pine cone and snap it off the tree. My fingers curl possessively around the scales of the pine cone. I can't look at my husband anymore, I just can't.

But Will is watching me; his eyes won't let go. It must add up to something, all the hours we have spent together, we are not newly introduced strangers on the dance floor, after all; he knows me, he knows, now, what I want. He moves in so close I can feel his breath on the hairs of my neck. I stiffen; I hold onto that pine cone with all my might. Will pulls me to him, and kisses me, hard; my hand relaxes and the pine cone drops to the deck. I don't hear what sound the pine cone makes once it hits, or if it makes any sound at all, because by then I am making a throaty sound of my own. Blood pounds my ears, and I keep kissing Will, though I can hardly catch my breath. We kiss for so long the heat from our kissing makes white clouds of moisture in the air, under the spotlights. The heat does something else too, makes us absorb part of the damp earth, because when we turn to go inside, we bring with us into our house—on the sleeves of Will's flannel shirt, in the strands of my hair, in the pores of our skin—the achingly sweet smell of wet grass, the mothball scent of rain.

Afterwards, we lie in darkness on rumpled sheets, spent and relaxed, and watch through the window the tops of the pine trees. They sway as though dancing to music I can't hear, but for once, I don't mind. I am cuddled beside Will, my head resting against his chest, his heart.

"Janey," he strokes my cheek with his fingertip and says playfully, "we should do this more often."

"Yeah, let's get started. Get a jump on it."

"So to speak." He kisses me with great tenderness. I savor how he tastes, the salt on his lips, but we both know this kiss isn't going anywhere. We are too content.

"Janey, have you thought some more about the Island?"

"Yes."

"And?"

"Who'll take care of Toby while we're gone? And Sarah's new goldfish?"

"Her goldfish?" Will laughs. "Now you're reaching."

"No way. I'll have you know she *adores* those fish. She's already found names for them."

"What?"

"Mary Kate and Ashley."

"The Olsen twins?"

"Because she can't tell them apart."

Will's smile fades. "But, seriously, what about the Island?"

"Oh, I don't know..."

"The thing is, Janey, I have feelings about this. I *need* to get away."

From what? I should ask him, but I think I know. I think he means our son. He has returned to earth a little sooner than me, and that is why his jaw is so rigid, why he has turned back into himself, a pine cone closing up tight in the rain. I think Will means the hospital, the graveyard, the nursery, my psychiatric visits to Dr. Silverberg, the unpaid bills. He wants to get away from all that.

⇒)⇐

The next day is so blue and perfect that we take an early walk before school. Sarah pedals her bike while Will and I follow. Toby prances along with us, as though we are on parade. We must look like a real family because Ruth, who is busy gardening, brushes the dirt from her jeans and leaves her tulips behind to join us.

At the neighborhood pond, Sarah lets her bike clatter to the ground as she races to climb the cherry tree. Within seconds, she has swung a sneakered foot over a fat branch and disappeared into a world of pink. I stand underneath the tree, and I am thinking that right here, right now, I have everything I could ever want: my daughter, my husband, my best friend, pink blossoms, sky.

"Mom?" Sarah says, from above.

"Yes, honey?"

"Can we go to the Island? I like the trees there."

I look at Sarah, then at Will and Ruth. If it weren't so sublime a day, I think it would be easy. I would just say no, and that would be that. But it's sunny; it's beautiful; and I am here, standing under a cherry tree in the pink of its blooming. I take a deep breath, exhale.

"Sweetheart," I say, "I'll think about it, okay? I'll really give it some thought."

Will's face relaxes; Ruth nods; and Sarah shakes her branch in triumph, making a dozen pink blossoms rain down at my feet.

⇒)⇐

Later in the day, it's maybe mid-morning when I settle outside on the front steps with Toby. The radio says rain, but as I sip my coffee, all I'm seeing is blue sky and sun. In fact, the air is so golden and warm, the earth seems drenched in honey; gauze curtains waft in my neighbor's windows, and Toby dozes, dreaming of nothing because the day has already brought him everything he could want.

This morning has seen me energized, measuring Sarah's windows for curtain rods, cleaning out the refrigerator, but all the while my mind was on the Island. Can I face Windsor Island after my son's death? Can I bear to see the lake, the boathouse, the grandfather birch that knows too many secrets?

I am pondering the Island while I do my chores, and that is why, I suppose, I am able to decide just sitting here on the steps. Toby stirs awake, pricks his ears as a car cruises past, and just like that I think, *Why not go? It's time.*

Excited, I jump up and clap my hands for Toby, "Come on, boy!"

Inside, I toss my coffee mug in the sink and quickly punch in Will's number at the office. Busy. I hit the redial button. Still busy.

I drum my fingers on the countertop.

I want so much to tell Will my news that I am ready to move forward. I suddenly need to see my husband in person and share my optimism with him. And so, rather impulsively, I throw on a nice blouse, lock the door behind me, and fly out the door.

I park downtown, near Will's office. Even as I walk briskly toward his building, I shiver. It's getting chilly, and the skies are subtly darkening. Could that weather report be right after all?

But I don't much care about the weather. My thoughts are elsewhere. I envision canoeing on the lake, barbecuing hotdogs, hiking through fern-laden woods.

I ride the elevator to the eleventh floor, where I find Carla in reception.

"Haven't seen you in awhile, Mrs. Nichols," she says, friendly. "Go right on in."

To reach Will's office, I need to walk past the conference room and law library, plus several other attorneys' offices and secretaries' cubicles. It's very quiet. I look for Barbara Kirkbridge, but I don't see her. I don't see much of anyone. Just the isolated attorney talking on the telephone, the odd secretary printing out a brief.

I stride along the carpeted corridor and take a quick jog to the right. I can hear Will's voice even before I see him, and I suddenly wish I'd taken more care with my appearance. True, I troubled to put on a silk blouse, but I'm wearing jeans and not a dress.

My husband is busy on the phone, looking stern, even irritated. When I walk in, his face lights up. He looks suddenly, briefly, young, like he did back in high school, when we used to shoot hoops at my garage. He's saying into the phone, "Yes, I see your point." He holds up an index finger, meaning *One minute, Janey, I'll be done.*

I take the leather chair facing my husband. I like hearing his voice; I like being here. I think to myself, I should do this more often. There is a framed photograph of Sarah and me on his desk, and though the office is littered with pleadings, correspondence, and memos, the walls display Sarah's artwork far more prominently than Will's diplomas, and the door is festooned with lawyer jokes. The lawyer jokes come from clients, my favorite being *What do you call two thousand lawyers at the bottom of the ocean? Answer: A good start.*

Will's conversation draws to a close. He hangs up and comes over to me, "Hey, beautiful."

I smile and say, "I've decided to go."

"To the Island?"

"Yes."

"That's terrific!" He laughs. "We're gonna have the best time. Tell you what, lemme just clear my desk and then I'll take you out to lunch. In the meantime, there's coffee, or—" He makes a motion toward the door.

"I'll get us some," I say. "You finish up."

In the coffee room there's a vending machine with potato chips and Oreo cookies, a microwave, two pots of brewed coffee, a metal sink, and a refrigerator filled with soda. Someone has baked cinnamon and pecan sticky buns and left them out to share on a blue china plate on the counter. The buns are laced with butter-cream icing, and who can resist that? I try a small slice, then pour coffee into two thick mugs.

I'm not smiling on the outside, but on the inside I am glowing. Everything's going to work out after all. I can move on from my depression and reclaim my life. I feel like I've been treading water, so much effort, but now

I'm floating. I'm on my back and there is blue sky all around and trees, just like on Windsor Island, and it's so easy. It was so hard before, and now I'm doing the exact same thing, and it's easy. On the Island, I remember this now, you have to brush aside cobwebs draped between red pines on your way down to the weathered gray dock. If you listen, you can hear the water lapping the shore before you plunge in, and once you're in, God, it's cold. It's always so cold, the water, but you can find secret places where the sun has made a difference, pockets of warmth.

I grab our steaming mugs by their handles and retrace my steps to Will's office. Is this how happiness feels? You do everything in the world to bring it back and one blue and perfect morning there it is inside your humbled heart, a gift. It was a gift all along, even though you struggled after it. My gift is this: I am loved.

I'm able to hold on to this feeling, of being loved, for several more seconds, but the feeling becomes an illusion impossible to sustain as I walk toward Will's open office door and see Barbara Kirkbridge.

Barbara is perched in the leather chair I just vacated. She is wearing her usual skirt and heels, and her octagonal wire-rims sit securely on her nose, but she doesn't look very professional just now; her honeyed hair is in scrambled disarray and she is tipped forward, her skirt hiked up to reveal a good bit of nyloned leg. She speaks intently to Will, utterly absorbed in what she is saying to him, but she doesn't look like she is making some legal point or another, she looks *possessive* of my husband; her whole body language radiates *No trespassing*, like she is upset about something and confident enough of Will's affection to complain to him about it. For the first time ever I think of her as a sexual being rather than a business associate.

Oh, God.

The truth registers only a fraction of a second before I walk in.

Will sees me first and is able to recover slightly, but Barbara has no time at all, and I almost feel sorry for her, all social niceties stripped down to nothing but honest bone. She sputters to a halt midsentence, blinks in disbelief at me, then looks to Will in mute appeal. The look would have given her away, if she hadn't given herself away already. It is a look full of pleading, but it is also a reprimand: *Why didn't you tell me she was coming?*

She, like I am the enemy.

I don't know how long the three of us stare at each other. I do know I am the first to move. I stifle a sob somewhere deep in my chest. My hands start to quiver. I can't hold our coffees anymore, not if my life depends on it; the mugs are too heavy and the liquid's starting to slosh around because of all my trembling. I plunk down the mugs so hard the coffee slops onto Will's desk, soaking his red leather blotter and this month's glossy *ABA Journal*, dribbling off the desk onto Will's pants leg. Will leaps up, startled, and I bite my lip.

My housekeeping instincts kick in, and I cast about for something to sponge up the mess. I am frantic, as though *this* was the problem, the problem of spilled coffee. I snatch some Kleenexes from the box and start mopping away. My hands are not just shaking now; my fingers jerk, in spasm. The Kleenexes are soaked a muddy brown and still there's a puddle of coffee remaining on the desk. It's futile; I'm never going to clean this up.

"I can't..." I stammer, and then I give it up and stagger out of the office toward the bank of elevators.

"Janey!" Will calls after me.

I punch the "down" button. I'm not about to come back.

I ride the elevator down to street level and hurry down the block to the parking garage. It is hot in the garage, my lungs press down and down, fighting for air. I am practically hyperventilating by the time I locate my van. I scramble behind the wheel and gun the engine. I'm feeling wild and crazy and more than a little hostile. I startle when Will raps on my window.

I stab the button, and the glass window powers down. I smell oil, burned rubber, trapped air. And also Will's fear; I smell that, too.

"I wanted to tell you," he says.

You bastard! I think. But I don't say anything at all. My voice, when I finally do speak, is calm in the way the air is dead calm before a storm, warning you with its eerie silence that you'd better watch yourself, you'd better take care. "I'm curious, Will. How long?"

"Just once."

"Ah, just the once. Well..." I say darkly. He might be telling the truth, and then again he may not. After all, this could have been going on for some time. Since my depression. Or even before, during my pregnancy. Or even before that.

"Janey, I'm so sorry. I would do anything to spare you this. I wasn't thinking, that's all. Big mistake, clearly a mistake. It happened the night we entertained the Jefferson Pediatric people, you know, at the Chaucer Inn. You were in the hospital and I was worried about you, and—"

"Obviously not *too* worried."

"No, it wasn't like that. Just *listen*, okay? We argued, remember? Before I left the ward. And I was upset about that, and so I drank too much at the dinner. Afterwards, when everyone else left, I stayed in the restaurant sipping coffee. When I went out to the parking lot, Barbara was there."

"Oh, so it's *her* fault!"

"No. We just kind of fell into it. We checked in at the—"

"Whoa!" I hold up my hand. "You're *telling* me this? What *hotel* you went to? Why don't you give me the lowdown on the color of the bed sheets. Or how big her breasts were. Or whether she made little heh heh heh noises like a chipmunk when she came—"

"Janey, stop! Look! Let's go someplace. Let's talk."

"I don't think so." I release the brake and start backing up.

Will runs beside the van; he's not about to let me go.

"Back off, bucko. Or I'll run you down, I swear!"

Will knows I am not to be reckoned with, and so he jumps back. Good thing because I slam the van into drive and peel out of there, tires squealing. I rocket up the exit ramp and bounce over the concrete lip and onto a city street wet and slippery from a drenching downpour. The rain barely registers with me. I am driving way too fast. The light turns red on me. I stomp on the brakes, go into a skid. The tires stutter but can't grab. I pump the brakes, and the van finally shudders to a halt. You would think I would've learned my lesson, but no. The minute the light turns green, I rocket through it.

It is, impossibly, raining even harder by the time I reach home. It is a cruel rain, too, in conspiracy with the wind, the gusts aiding and abetting to create a tyrannical wild slant that goes right for my eyes as I step from the van. I shield my eyes with my hand as the rain pummels me. The grass in our yard, grown green and long, bows under the increasingly heavy pelting while our orange and violet tulips huddle together ineffectually in their unsheltered garden. What about our birds? I wonder. Can they get to our feeder? And, in all this wind, where's Toby? I can't remember if I left him inside or out.

As I bolt for the house, I'm nearly toppled by a gust of wind that shrieks in my ears and tangles my hair. Hunched against the wind, I stagger to the front porch and finally joggle my wet key in the lock to release the door. Toby is on the back deck. He is soaked. When I let him in, he is overjoyed. He leaps on me with his wet and muddy paws. "Dammit, Toby!" I scold. "You sit!"

And here I do something cruel. I don't simply urge Toby to sit, I grab a generous clump of his sable fur and squeeze, hard, yanking him down to the carpet.

Toby looks at me with huge, caramel eyes.

I have never been mean to him before, and so he doesn't understand. His eyes fill with liquid that, were he human, I would call tears. *Oh no!* I think. What have I become? A woman who unleashes her frustration at her dog because he can't speak; he can't tell everyone what a monster she is.

Contrite, I grab towels from the bathroom to dry us both. I towel off Toby first. He rests his trusting head in the crook of my arm. I bury my nose in his fur. He smells like damp straw. I probably smell, too. Hair dripping, my jeans sodden and clinging to my legs like a blue layer of skin, I coax off my kneesocks. My toes are pruny and blanched with chill, and so I try to knead warmth back into them.

I am sitting plunked down on the carpet like this, massaging my cold toes, when Ruth tromps in, dripping rain from her boots and canary slicker onto the kitchen tiles.

Normally I would be so glad to see her.

"Storm blew my power out," she says. "And I can't find my flashlight. Can I borrow yours?"

"Oh, I don't think so," I say, ominously.

Ruth tilts her head. Our eyes meet.

"No? Really? You're joking, right?" She laughs, a little nervously.

I scramble up barefoot from the carpet. Toby noses my wet blue jeans, wanting to be petted, but I ignore him.

Ruth takes her cue from watching Toby. She changes the subject. "Where's Sarah?"

"Playdate. Will's supposed to pick her up on his way home. That is, if he, in fact, comes home."

Ruth risks a direct look at me. "You mean because of the weather."

"Not the weather, no. I'm not talking about that."

Ruth doesn't say anything. She just stands there in her yellow slicker, dripping rain on my kitchen tiles. She looks cold, and I bet right about now she wished she'd never stopped by, wished she'd stopped by another neighbor's, and asked *them* for a flashlight.

I frown, "You knew, didn't you?"

"Knew what?"

I frown at her and say nothing.

She sighs, "Will did confide in me, yes."

"And you didn't tell me?"

"That's what confide means. It means you don't tell."

"Whose side are you on?"

"Don't do this, Janey. I'm your friend."

"But also Will's apparently."

"Yes, Will's too."

"Or maybe," I swallow raggedly, "you're not anybody's friend."

I am chilled clear through, my teeth chatter violently; it's just possible I may never be warm again. Outside, our apple tree flails its branches in the wind; its pink and white petals get tossed away for nothing. Just this morning the bumblebees were hovering over those apple blossoms, and the air was sweet, and the sun promised to shine.

Ruth says in an even voice, "That's not fair."

"Fair? Look it, Ruth, you can borrow our flashlight, okay? It's got fresh batteries and everything. There, under the sink. Then, do me a favor."

"Yes?" Ruth leans toward me, her face open, receptive.

My voice cracks as I deliberately rupture our friendship. "Let yourself out."

And so I leave my precious Ruth, who is like a mother to me, the only one I have left. I falter only once as I trudge up the stairs in my bare feet. I'm going to take a hot shower. After that, I don't honestly know.

PART THREE

THE ISLAND

Is it so small a thing
To have enjoy'd the sun,
To have lived light in the spring,
To have loved, to have thought, to have done?

—Matthew Arnold

CHAPTER 8

I am thinking about Sylvia Plath and bell jars lately because a bell jar, these past few weeks, has descended over me.

I feel heavy and slow, and yet I am quick to anger. The world, to me, feels like an icepick. And I, of course, am ice. Brittle, like ice, and like ice, easily shattered. The smallest tap and fissures appear, veinlike, in my mood.

For awhile there I was making inroads against my depression, climbing upwards, but lately all progress is stopped. In fact, you could say I've slipped. I'm in a free fall. Dr. Silverberg knows. How could she not? I've totally clammed up in therapy. She keeps telling me, "You need to talk, Janey. Get your feelings out. You don't talk with me. Do you with Will? Or Ruth?"

"Not even Toby," I tell her.

It seems cruelly ironic to me that, while I have become ice, the world all around me is blossoming. Winter has finally surrendered to spring. The trees have greened up; everyone's gardens are teeming with color, but gardens and color aren't for me. All I've been doing lately is plowing my way through packs of cigarettes. I just want to smoke and make everything around me turn gray and stale as the hopelessness I feel. I want to pollute the world on the outside so it matches me on the inside, where I am unbeautiful.

⁓⧽⧼⁓

Now it's a Friday in late May.

I am at Dr. Silverberg's again. I am sitting in my van, smoking, early for my appointment, when it happens: out of the blue, a hospital van pulls up.

The van is white with a red siren on top. There are two men in uniforms, light blue shirts and black trousers. One of the men wears hightop sneakers. The men climb out and open the back door of their van. There is the sound of gears engaging, and a ramp lowers.

I reach over to the ashtray and grind out my cigarette.

What's going on? I wonder. Some kind of emergency at Dr. Silverberg's? The garage door opens. Two figures appear on the driveway, a man and a child in a wheelchair. The man is pushing the wheelchair; he has a proprietary air about him, a quiet authority. I believe he is Dr. Silverberg's husband. As he maneuvers the chair down the driveway, his manner is relaxed, and I gather that this is not an emergency, but something that has transpired before. Dr. Silverberg herself emerges from the house to follow her husband and child down the drive. Once there, she is chatty with the two orderlies, who smile at something she's said.

The girl in the wheelchair is close enough now so I can see her. Her posture is rubbery, her torso buckled into the wheelchair, her wrists secured to the leather-padded arms. Her head, though propped, lolls at a sloppy angle. I can't make out her eyes; her face itself is a creamy blur, but I wonder if her tragedy stops with her body or if her mind is impaired as well? I start to hear a buzzing in my ears. I struggle to breathe, in and out.

I consider ceding my appointment, after that, but something compels me to stay. And so, only a few minutes later, after the hospital van drives off, I meet Dr. Silverberg in her office.

"It's your daughter, isn't it?" I say to her.

"Yes. Her name's Natalie."

"Natalie," I repeat. My throat is tight.

"We don't have to talk about this now," Dr. Silverberg says softly.

"No. Please. Tell me."

Dr. Silverberg smiles slightly, and goes on. "I have two children. One is my college-age son, Jason. Natalie is my twelve-year-old. Twelve being her chronological age. Developmentally she ranks equivalent to a child of six months."

"Six months? You mean, like a baby?"

"Yes. She's severely brain damaged."

"Oh." I am so stunned, the "oh" comes from someplace deep and slow motion inside me. I feel like we are both underwater, Dr. Silverberg and I. She's saying lots of words, but they're garbled. I can't make them out; it's too hard, and besides, I want so much to rise to the surface for air.

"Children with this affliction typically live fairly long lives," she goes on. "Sometimes into their thirties. Natalie may live many more years."

"I see." I'm wondering if this is a good thing or a bad thing, that Natalie will live so long. I decide it's a terrible thing. Her life is one slow dying.

Dr. Silverberg continues, "She requires round-the-clock nursing. She can't sit up unassisted, can't roll over, can't chew her own food. Because she requires so much care, she no longer lives at home, but in a pediatric hospital."

"But she was here."

"Yes. Occasionally she visits. Today her pickup was a little late. Her true home is indeed the hospital. It's where she spends the majority of her time. I bring her clean clothes twice a week and a bright new toy. She likes bold colors. She does not recognize me."

I struggle after the full import of Dr. Silverberg's words, but I am slow, slowed down, "She doesn't *recognize* you?"

"No."

"That must break your heart."

"It's easier on her, though. She doesn't cry when I leave."

"Right," I say. I want to say something else, something even, God help us, intelligent or compassionate, but I sense we have come to a place where there are no words, and I don't want to pretend there are any.

I study Dr. Silverberg. She looks as put-together, as calm and controlled as always. I suspect that she deals with her pain more gracefully than I do with mine, but I may be idealizing her. I really don't know how she is outside this office. I do know that grief is a misshapen bundle for anyone to bear; it's like you're carrying too much laundry and can't see your feet, so you keep bumping into the sharp edges of things.

We talk some more. The minutes tick by slowly. When my session is over, I get up quietly from the sofa and leave.

Outside the day continues sunny and beautiful; hot, if anything now. Inside the van, the steering wheel is scorching to touch. I roll down the windows. And then I just sit there.

A breeze comes over and finds me. I feel the sun on my neck and cheek. Birds call to one another.

A long time passes, or at least it feels that way to me. The steering wheel has cooled so I can comfortably grasp it; I can drive off now, if I want. But I stare at Dr. Silverberg's house.

How does it feel, to have a brain-damaged daughter who does not recognize you, even when you bring her cuddly toys, toys that squeak, toys so bright they dazzle your eyes? How many times can a mother's heart break?

I have assumed, up until this moment, that no one else's life could be as sad as mine. But now I wonder. I can't begin to know how Dr. Silverberg feels. It is this, finally, that makes me cry.

I'm still thinking about Dr. Silverberg and her daughter when I help my own daughter pack for her Girl Scout overnight. I keep envisioning that small child tragically slumped in her wheelchair. I want to crush Sarah close to me, and not let her go. How can I spend an entire night without her?

"Mom, I'm not going to Antarctica."

"I know."

"The campground is like ten miles from here."

"I know."

"And it's not like there are grizzly bears or tigers. The biggest thing you have to worry about is me eating too many burnt marshmallows around the campfire."

I have to laugh at this.

"There," Sarah smiles at me. "See? I'll be okay."

"Sure, you will. You're my grown-up girl." I fold her into my arms in yet another hug, and she indulges me.

Together we load her sleeping bag, duffel, and ground cloth into the van.

"Besides," she adds, tossing in her pillow, "without me here, you and Daddy can talk."

I stare at her.

"You're only fighting because of me."

"Oh, no, sweetheart. We're not fighting, are we? I mean—"

"Well, you're not talking much."

"That's true," I say.

"So, you must be fighting. Probably because I did something wrong."

"You mustn't think that. Honestly, it's between us—your Dad and me. Issues between us."

"Like what?"

"Oh, adult things."

"Can you fix them?"

"Well," I hesitate. What's Sarah really asking? She just wants to go to sleep happy tonight in her sleeping bag next to her friends, with the smell of woodsmoke curling into the trees under the stars. She wants to drift off knowing she is loved, that she has a family. In all truthfulness, I don't know if what's broken between Will and me can be fixed. Or, perhaps more to the point, the things broken inside of me.

These past few weeks, I've been a little shaky, that's for sure. My thinking has grown increasingly warped. How warped I didn't realize until Will found me out. One week ago, he discovered the extra prescription in my wallet. He was frantic for cash, the pizza guy was at the door, and I told him to go ahead, see what I had. That's when Will fingered through my billfold to uncover a twenty and a five and two ones, along with an unfilled prescription, a white neatly creased paper that fluttered to the floor, that, when Will, curious, opened it and read it, understood it to prescribe twenty milligrams daily of Prozac. The prescription was not scribbled by Dr. Silverberg, but by my internist, Dr. Hoffman. Dr. Hoffman doesn't know anything about Dr. Silverberg. He doesn't know I am already getting all the Prozac I need. He doesn't know I was contemplating, with varying degrees of seriousness, a clandestine visit to a different pharmacy than the one we usually go to, to have his prescription filled. I had not acted on this yet, and I was waffling on the issue, but I had the impulse to stockpile my antidepressants. "Jesus, Janey!" Will said, after he paid the pizza guy and slammed the door. "What have you been thinking of?"

"I don't know," I told him, and this was the truth.

"You have me worried. I'm going to talk to Dr. Silverberg."

"Fine," I said.

"For now I'm going to rip this up."

"Good," I said. And I was relieved when Will tore the extra prescription into bite-size pieces and dumped them in the trash.

But even now I can so vividly picture my green and cream Prozac capsules waiting upstairs in the medicine chest. What allure do they hold for me? How can I even consider taking more than my alloted dose? Sylvia Plath left out milk and cookies for her two small children sleeping upstairs, and then she turned on the gas; she said the hell with it. Is this ever excusable? How much pain does a person need to be in? What about the ones left behind, their lives convulsed with sorrow? And so I remind myself of Sarah. Because I mustn't forget, not even for one instant, that if I leave this earth, I leave her behind, this girl of mine who climbs trees to get closer to God, this girl of mine not quite nine years old whose auburn ponytail, tied back with a frayed red rubber band, bobs with every long-legged step she takes?

"Sare," I say, "I'll do my best to patch things up, okay? I'll try with all my might."

"Okay," she says.

⇒)⇐

And I do try. I try that very evening when Will comes home from work. I'm in the middle of fixing dinner for just the two of us; in fact, I'm still working on dessert, when he surprises me. The shortcake is baking in the oven and I'm hulling the strawberries at the counter, but I wipe my hands on a dishtowel to greet him at the door, "Hey, you're home early. It's only five."

"I'm going to Virginia, remember?"

"Tonight? But it's Friday."

"The conference? Castlerock insurance? My second-biggest client?"

"Oh, right."

"They're hosting their annual golf tournament. They expect me to be as good a golfer as I am a lawyer. Fat chance. I'm so rusty, I'll be lucky if I can dig my golf clubs out of the cobwebs in the garage. So hey—" Will looks at me directly for the first time. "Where's Sarah?"

"Girl Scouts."

"Oh. The overnight. So, wait a second. That means you'll be here alone, Janey."

"I'll be fine. Besides, Ruth's just across the street." I pause. I want to say this just right. "But I'm sorry you won't be here. I was fixing us a special dinner. Linen napkins. Candlelight."

"Really?" He is dumbfounded but trying to hide it. Why am I being so nice to him? We have not been particularly nice to each other lately.

I tell him, "Sarah and I were talking. She's worried about us."

"Oh...so you went to all this trouble. I can smell something baking in the oven."

"Shortcake."

"Wow." He glances at his wristwatch. "I'm real sorry I can't stay. Matter of fact, I should probably get packing."

"Wait!" I say. "Can you at least sit with me a few minutes?"

"Well..."

"Try some shortcake?"

"Okay, sure," he says.

Just then, the timer dings, and I remove the steaming shortcake from the oven. The shortcake is golden brown and looks delicious. I tumble on fresh strawberries and squirt on the whipped cream. But, the shortcake is too hot, and it melts the whipped cream. Not only that, but Will is in such a hurry, he wolfs down a giant hunk of shortcake, and it scalds his throat so badly he leaps up from the table to guzzle water straight from the kitchen faucet.

Still, I try to salvage our time together. I've promised Sarah, after all. Will sits back down at the table. He hasn't left for Virginia yet. He is still here. I reach for his hand, take a deep breath and say as soulfully as I can, "I want you to know I forgive you."

"Forgive?" His tone—edgy, defensive—is not what I was hoping for.

"Yes," I say.

"You're talking about Barbara."

"Of course."

"Barbara," he wags his fork at me, the fork ludicrously top-heavy with its speared strawberry, "was a mistake."

"A mistake, Will?" My voice walks a tightrope as I try to balance my anger with my urge to be conciliatory. "No. A mistake is when you forget to put a stamp on the envelope when you mail it."

"Okay. Lapse. How's that? A serious lapse in judgment. One I have abjectly apologized for. But, hey, while we're on the subject, you're not perfect, either."

"Oh, I know, honey. Don't I know it." I nod in agreement. I am in control of my anger again. I want this to work, between us, and to do that, I need to be more sympathetic. My husband's had a tough day, after all. He may be home from the office—his suitcoat draped on the chair behind him, his tie loosened—but he's still at work. He's about to make the long trek to Virginia.

I watch while he chews a mouthful of strawberries. I meant the strawberries to be a celebration, something I did for my husband, to nurture him. But his expression is joyless. He says, "Just don't go around annointing me, okay?"

"*Annointing?*"

"With forgiveness. Like you're some saint. Because I've had to forgive you too, you know."

"For what?" My cheeks flush.

"Oh, lots of things." He shoves his plate aside; the mounded strawberries topple off the shortcake. One rolls to the edge of the table, plops onto the rug. It would be funny, that rolling strawberry, under other circumstances, but isn't now.

My plans for a lovely evening are spoiled, that's for sure. I only hope now that Will can leave on his trip without a major rift between us. I wanted to tell him about Dr. Silverberg and poor Natalie. How grateful I feel to have our Sarah, healthy and bright. But I will not get a chance to tell him now. "Will, let's just...maybe we should just drop the subject. I'll fetch your golf clubs from the—"

"Let me finish, dammit! Don't cut me off."

"I wasn't—"

"While you were sick, I was hurting too, you know. But I took care of Sarah and held down my job. I didn't abandon my responsib—"

"Oh, unlike me?"

"You *were* in the hospital."

"Jesus, Will!" If he wants to argue, I won't stop him, because, now, I can't even stop myself. "You think I *liked* it there? You think it was the Four Seasons? Room service? Tennis? A little massage?"

"I'm not just talking about the hospital. But *after.* You haven't exactly been yourself. And meanwhile I'm shouldering all the—"

"Not Sarah! You can't say—"

"You're taking care of Sarah, again, granted, but not like you used to. You're still distracted, Janey. You don't *initiate* anything. You're like a shadow of who you were, dragging yourself through the day. Weekends you don't even get out of bed."

"That was one Saturday! One bad day after I found out about you and Barbara."

"You know, I miss our son just as much as you, Janey. Only I didn't fall apart. I went to the funeral and then I kept on going."

"What? And I didn't?"

"You checked out. You know how hard it was for me to juggle everything? My job? Sarah? All my courtroom trials? Your timing couldn't have been worse—"

"I'm frightfully sorry for the inconvenience."

"Look, you didn't choose to get depressed, I know that. But it seems to me you could choose to get better. This was hard on all of us. Not just you. Me and Sarah and Ruth. But you don't see that. You're so self-absorbed. You just care about *your* hurt, *your* pain."

"God, that is such a crock! As if you never think of *yourself.* What were you thinking of when you were with Barbara, huh? Don't tell me you did that for me. Or Sarah."

"You don't understand."

"What?"

"You keep blaming me. But, Janey, I went away for one night. *One night* I strayed. You, on the other hand, keep toying with those pills in your head."

"What?"

"Oh, come on. I found that extra prescription in your wallet, remember? What, you think I'm stupid? You think I don't know about you and your little suicide fantasy?"

"Hey, now this is below the belt, Will. Stop."

"Stop? No. You wanted to talk. Let's talk."

"Stop right now!"

"You make some kind of pharmaceutical exit and you'll be leaving us, Janey, not just one night, but permanently. The only thing is, you won't be here to see it. So, you tell yourself it's okay. It's okay if Sarah and I hobble through the rest of our lives. It's okay if we're in pain because our pain doesn't really count. Our pain isn't like your pain. We don't feel as much or as deeply as the great Janey Nichols, connoisseur of grief..."

Connoisseur of grief. His words penetrate, and drill right through my skin, a psychic tatoo that I know even now will be permanent. I turn cold, even though I am seething. I am so chilled my teeth chatter. "Damn you!" I say, in a flat voice, my fury so evident it needs no emphasis. I scrape back my chair from the table and stand up. I don't know where I'm going, but I've got to get away, fast.

"That's right, Janey, crawl back into your shell," Will yells at my retreating back. "That's what you're good at."

I don't get very far, just to the living room where I fling myself onto the sofa. I am all sprawled out, and then I hear Will. I quickly straighten up, and there I sit, rigid as an ironing board until he pounds past me up the stairs to fetch his suitcase.

I shouldn't follow him up the stairs, but this is just what I do.

Maybe I want to get closer to my husband, or maybe I want us to fight some more, draw more blood. I don't know.

While I am furious with Will, at the very same time, I don't want him to leave me. I stand at the doorway to our bedroom. My fists are clenched. I watch my husband travel back and forth from the bed to his dresser, tossing socks and underwear into his suitcase.

He takes one look at me, then glances quickly away.

I think he must be feeling like me, so angry he is afraid to trust himself to be near me, but also wanting us to make up before he goes.

I want to go to him; I don't want to go to him. The best I can do, in a kind of compromise, is enter the room. I walk to the window and look out.

Through the window I see the day has changed. Rank humidity has rendered the air sticky and cloying; I can tell this by the way nothing moves, nothing breathes. I reflect on what Will said to me, downstairs. I know that much of what he said, while uttered in the heat of his anger, is true. I have cared only about myself these past months. Self-absorbed, utterly lacking in compassion, neglectful to those dearest to me—my litany of failures makes me vibrate with shame. I hear Will open the closet; I keep my back to him, but I know he is fetching his suitcoat now, and ties. My eyes fall on our birch tree, melancholy and elegant, its jagged leaves a dull yellow-green, its male catkins drooping pendulously. I am thinking how much I despise myself. I am thinking I cannot bear this, how awful I have been, but then it happens; I am rescued by a minor miracle. While I am idly contemplating our birch tree, I see the most beautiful bird. The bird must be a male, for he is glorious, his body a stunning yellow, such yellow I have never seen before, ever. It pierces my heart that such beauty should exist, and me so unworthy to see it, so close by, just outside there, beyond the glass of our window. The bird flits over to a branch of the birch and starts nibbling seeds. It's only a bird, I tell myself, but perhaps it is also a sign. I turn away from the window to face my husband, ready to try once again.

I am timid, at first. I don't want to renew our argument. I want to keep things neutral, keep things light. I say, "Will, there's the coolest bird in our birch tree. Bright yellow. Come see."

"No thanks," he says.

"Please," I say.

"I'm already late," he says.

"I'll just look it up in our bird book," I say, and head for our bookshelf over on Will's side of the bed, away from him. This way I am close to him but nonthreatening. "Maybe it's some kind of rare bird or something." I keep on chatting, to keep us safe; if we are talking, we must be communicating, right? I unshelve our bird book and position myself cross-legged on the bed, near the garment bag Will has draped over the bedspread beside his open suitcase. He grabs two dress shirts from the closet and, as he hooks them by their hangers inside his garment bag, says to me, "Since when are you into bird watching?"

"Oh, I'm not really," I tentatively smile.

He frowns.

I believe I have one last chance. I pray I'll say something just right, something that will give us a foundation for peace, but what comes out is simply, "This bird's incredible, Will. Maybe it's still there. Why don't you take a look?"

"Look, I don't give a shit about some bird. You got it? It could be the find of the century. The missing link between dinosaurs and birds, I don't care. I gotta go. I'll call you." And with that, he fiercely zippers his garment bag and thuds downstairs.

The front door slams.

I sit in silence for a long minute. I'm still cross-legged on the bed when I hurl the bird book across the room. It hits the wall and then drops to the carpet, its paperback spine cracked open, its pages flipping madly until they settle. You would think I might have some luck here. But no, I'm never lucky at the slots: the machine never stops at three cherries for me. Likewise, this book does not stop on the page I want. The page that stares up at me doesn't show the yellow bird I've been searching for: this bird is brown and gray, a ruffed grouse.

I am sure Will is gone, truly gone, and yet I can't help believing that he may turn his car around before he goes too far and he may come back. So I wait. But after awhile my foot falls asleep as I sit there on the bed. I retrieve the bird book from the floor, slot it neatly back on the shelf, and go downstairs.

In the kitchen there is only a mess to greet me. Strawberries bleed on the cutting board while the sharp knife lies there quietly but with passive menace, reminding me of a shark's fin seen circling in the water. There is also flour, salt, a box of Bisquick. I wasn't hungry when Will was eating, but I am hungry now. Ravenous, in fact. I don't care if the whipped cream is thin and watery, the strawberries runny. I plunk myself down at the table and plunge forkful after forkful of shortcake into the yawning emptiness that is me. I stop only when my stomach starts to ache. I push back from my chair.

When the phone rings, I ignore it. I feel too bloated to get up. But then I'm suddenly hopeful it's Will, and so, on the fifth ring, just before the answering machine is about to click on, I lunge for the receiver.

As soon as I realize it's not Will but Reverend Bright, I want to hang up. Get off. Disconnect. I'm not up to polite conversation.

I am just about to tell Reverend Bright this, or rather, I am about to fabricate some excuse to get me off the phone when I hear him say, "... your friend Delphina?"

"Yes?"

"I don't mean to alarm you, but she's in the Emergency Room down here at Sinai."

"Oh," I say. "Clyde?"

"Yes."

I close my eyes. I pinch the bridge of my nose, where the pain begins. I have never met Clyde, but I know he is a big man. I see him coming at Delphina...inside my eyelids it is red with black spots. I am faint. I open my eyes again, and Clyde disappears.

"I was here in the hospital making a visit when they brought her in. The police are involved. They brought in a woman from the shelter who spoke to me. I thought I recognized Delphina from someplace, the name, and then I remembered you, so—"

"How...is she?"

"Roughed up pretty good. Head trauma. She lost consciousness for awhile. They're concerned about swelling, a possible subdural hematoma, but it's looking less likely. They sewed up the gash in her forehead, and they're keeping a good watch on her."

"Is she...in much pain?"

"Well, besides her head injury, her arm's got a compound fracture, and her lip was split."

"Oh, Jesus. Compound fracture?"

"Apparently he threw her down the stairs."

"Mmmm..." I bite my lip. I hear a buzzing in my ears.

"The good news is, Janey, she's in stable condition. No other internal injuries. Like stomach or kidney—"

"Well, that's...that's something, then." The initial buzzing in my ears is becoming something other: a roar. My skin prickles with goosebumps.

I tuck the receiver under my ear and go to the kitchen tap to splash water on my face.

"Janey?" Reverend Bright says.

"Yes, I'm here."

"You okay?"

"Sure, fine." The tap thunks off. I remain at the sink. I take the phone in my hand again; I am, in fact, gripping the receiver.

There is silence on the phone between us. In the kitchen around me it is silent, too. No Sarah. No Will. I wish they were with me now.

"Listen," Reverend Bright adds. "I know Delphina let you down. You tried to help her, and....But the thing is, she won't talk to anyone. Not the counsellor from the shelter. Not the police. Doctors. Nurses. The one person she asked for is you."

In the hospital everything is white. White halls, white walls, and the white fear inside me that flares up the moment I step through the entrance doors of the ER.

You would think "emergency" would connote speed, but I can tell at a glance that the families in the waiting room have been kept there for hours. I wonder how long Delphina had to wait.

I give my name to the nurse at the counter. I just pray she'll stay with me, but she ushers me into Delphina's room and departs.

Delphina's eyes are closed, and maybe this is a good thing, since her room is truly frightening. Big, scary machines are everywhere you look with monitors beeping, and of course, the white-sheeted gurney with its IV trailing from her arm. Mostly Delphina looks like one big bruise, and I find this painful to behold. Her head, all that wild orange hair of hers, is lost in the white of her bandages. Does she sense my presence? Her eyes flutter open. "Hey," I say, "I brought you some flowers." I offer her the bouquet I purchased in the gift shop.

"No flowers." She tries to smile, but her busted lip makes this difficult. The lip is swollen and cracked, with blood filling in the crack. "I ain't dead yet."

"I'll just put these here, then." I lay the flowers down on her bedside table, next to a pitcher of water and a plastic cup with a straw. I'm trying to maintain my cool, but my hands are shaking.

"No flowers," I say. "So how about a Snickers bar? Got that from the gift shop, too."

"Can't hold nothing down."

"Right," I say. "I'll just put your Snickers here, then, by the flowers. Maybe you'll get hungry later."

She studies me.

"So..." I rub my hands together. "Can I get you anything? A magazine, perhaps? Can I turn on your TV? Oh, there *is* no TV in here. Well..."

Delphina says nothing. She is still studying me.

"I know. You thirsty? How about I pour you a fresh cup of water?"

"Don't need none," she says.

"Please! Let me do *something* for you."

"Okay, I'll take me a sip."

I bring the cup over to her. I bend the plastic elbow straw and adjust it to fit her swollen purpled lip. She can barely take a sip. She is so helpless. She reminds me of my Sarah, when Sarah has one of her throwing-up bugs. Except that Delphina isn't a child. She's a giant of a woman.

"You know," I say to her, "I can tell you really *are* hurting when you turn down a Snickers bar."

Done with sipping through her straw, she relaxes back against her pillows. I keep wanting to talk, to fill the room with words, with nonsense even, it doesn't matter, but Delphina seems content with the silence. A moment goes by, then she says to me, in a lopsided way, on account of that balloon lip of hers, "I missed you, girl."

"I missed you, too," I say.

And after that I just sit beside her on a chair by the bed and I put my hand on the bed, close to her but not touching. I don't know if I can touch her fingers that stick out from the cast, not without hurting her, and the other hand is over by her side, hampered by the IV. So we don't touch at all. We both just stay like that, her lying there, and me sitting here, and we don't say anything, and it's all right; we can listen to the nurses' footsteps, the murmur of voices outside the room, and every moment I am sitting here and she is lying there, we are safe.

$$\backsim)\frown$$

They have Delphina on some kind of painkiller because she drifts off. She's just coming to again when Officer Hayes appears.

Officer Hayes is a black man, stocky, medium height. When he strides in, he removes his cap to reveal a band of sweat ringing his forehead. His hair is short.

The officer carries a clipboard. He rips off the top sheet and hands it to Delphina. He doesn't so much as blink at her condition. He doesn't say I'm sorry, and there is no glint of compassion, as far as I can see, in his eyes. He could be from Motor Vehicles, and she could be standing in line to get her license, except for his gun, which rides on his hip in a black holster. He says, "Lady, if you want to lodge a complaint, you need to fill out this form."

"Complaint?" she says. "No, Officer, I just fell. Clumsy, I guess."

I look at Delphina. She won't swear out a complaint against Clyde because she doesn't want to make him any angrier than he already is.

But I want her to think about this. I try to buy her some time. I say to the officer, "How's she supposed to fill out a form, anyway, with a broken arm?"

"She can dictate it to you."

"And what exactly does she need to say?"

"Describe the incident in detail. Then get her signature at the bottom to certify under penalty of perjury that the foregoing is true and correct..."

I stare at Officer Hayes. He is so detached, he makes me angry. Is there a person in there? I want to give a knock on the door of his soul, see if anyone answers.

He proceeds, "Once I have possession of the complaint, I'll take it from there. Put it before the commissioner. Get an arrest warrant and go pick the perp up."

"Perp?"

"Perpetrator."

"His name," I say, "is Clyde."

"Clyde," Officer Hayes repeats.

"Yes. And this woman here, who's in such pain, her name is Delphina."

"Ma'am." Officer Hayes manages a nod.

He and I stare at one another.

Long seconds pass. Even Delphina, in her current condition, can't miss the uneasiness between us.

I keep staring at Officer Hayes, and then something happens. The minute I decide to truly dislike him, suddenly, I don't. Tonight is Friday. Friday night must be the worst night of all for cops. Social Security checks arrive on Friday, paychecks get cashed, and the bars are flowing with booze. How many Friday nights has Officer Hayes seen? How many dozens of battered girlfriends, lovers, wives?

I find that my voice changes, and something about Officer Hayes's voice changes, too. "Can you tell us," I say, "what will happen to Clyde?"

"He's got some jail time coming, that's for sure. He's already VOP for a prior assault."

"Sorry?" I say.

"Violation of Probation. Guilty of second degree assault against a police officer. Happened six months ago."

From the bed, Delphina nods weakly.

Officer Hayes flips through his clipboard. "Yeah. Here it is. Defendant got drunk and disorderly in Moody's Bar, started trashing the place. When an officer of the law intervened, defendant assaulted him with his fists."

"I'm still a little confused," I say. "What's this violation of probation got to do with Delphina?"

"Means we can pick up the perpetrator and hold him in Baltimore City Jail."

"How long?" Delphina croaks.

"What?"

"Is you fixin' to hold him."

"Until his trial date, unless he makes bail. But he won't. He'd need to post, say twenty-five grand in cash. He have that kind of money, ma'am?"

"Lord'a mercy, not a chance," Delphina says.

"Well, then," Officer Hayes says. "You ready to dictate your complaint?"
Delphina sighs, turns away.

She intends to look at that white wall in front of her until Officer Hayes gets the hint and leaves, but I can't let her do that.

"Delphina," I say. "Do you understand? He can't come after you. He'll be behind bars."

"What about that there home detention, he have that before."

"Home detention?" Officer Hayes scoffs. "No way, ma'am. This perp will remain locked up but good."

"All right," I say. "So, Delph, will you do it?"

I think Delphina is going to tell me no, and that she is maybe even going to tell me to mind my own business. She moves her head, which must set off a world of hurt because she sucks her breath in and squeezes shut her eyes. When she opens them again, she says, "Whata' we waitin' for? I ain't getting no younger."

Officer Hayes leaves us alone. I drag my chair closer to Delphina on the bed. She's getting tired now. Her voice is low and gravelly and I have to pay careful attention to understand her. I scribble notes.

It is hard to listen to the horrors she describes, but I tell myself I can do this for her. She did a lot for me, back in the mental ward.

Delphina is talking and I am writing. We are, in fact, finishing up when the nurse interrupts us. "The doctor will be by shortly," she announces, and she briskly begins attending to Delphina, taking her pulse and temperature, jotting something or other in her chart.

We think she is through now, and she will leave us, and we can get back to our complaint, but she turns to Delphina, "You do realize, don't you, that we can't keep you overnight. Pending your final neurocheck by the doctor, of course."

"What?" I say, incredulous. "You're discharging her? Tonight?"

"I'm sorry," the nurse says.

"But, hold on a second," I say, trying to sound calm, even though my heart is hammering in outrage. "What about the gash in her forehead? All the stitches? Her broken arm? Don't they count?"

"Not with Medicaid," the nurse says.

"Well, what *would* count?"

"Oh, honey, you don't want to know," the nurse says darkly. I get the impression I really don't. If Delphina, with all her injuries, doesn't rate admittance, I don't want to think how seriously damaged you need to be to stay overnight in this place.

Delphina is looking so pitiful there in the bed. I know the nurse is only doing her job, but I want her to just plain leave Delphina alone. Instead she turns directly to Delphina to ask, "Do you have someplace to go?"

Delphina blinks. She has clearly not thought this out. And how could she? She's been battered to a state of unconsciousness, then rushed here in a hospital ambulance. She has waited her turn behind countless others down on their luck. She's been visited by an orthopedic surgeon to set her arm, and had her forehead stitched up by the plastic surgeon; she is now just finally able to lie against the pillows and not be touched.

"For instance, any relatives?" the nurse presses.

"My sister," Delphina says.

"Great. Where does she live so I can contact her?"

"Mississippi," Delphina says.

I have to smile. Delphina is well enough to mess with the nurse, and this makes me, briefly, happy. Delphina and I exchange looks.

"That won't quite do," the nurse says. "Anyone closer?"

"No." Delphina won't look at me now.

"Friends?"

"Nobody I wouldn't be no burden to." Delphina refuses to look at me. She won't appeal to me for sanctuary. She's too proud. Instead, she says, "I's fixin to check myself into the shelter, somethun like that."

"The shelter," the nurse repeats. She jots that down in her chart. "All right. We'll arrange it—"

"Just one second," I say.

The nurse looks at me. Delphina looks at me.

I am standing here, surprised I spoke up at all. It was a mistake. I should have kept my mouth shut. I stare at the hospital floor. When I finally look up, I look straight at Delphina. Her eyes shine, and I don't think it's the pain medication. I open my mouth. I want to invite her to our house, then and there, but my head is all buzzy and the room opens up hot as an oven. Sweat beads on my forehead even as my skin turns clammy.

God help me, I need to get out of here. "Excuse me," I say in a hollow voice. "I need some air."

"Fine." the nurse stands aside for me. "I see the doctor's here, anyway, for a neurocheck..."

But I hardly hear what the nurse is saying. I step outside the room. Here I am met with a surprise. "Ruth," I say. "How'd you know to—"

"Reverend Sharp. He thought you could use the company."

"I can," I say.

I don't know if I lean toward Ruth or if my legs buckle a little, but in any case, she's there to steady me with a hug. "That bad, huh?" she says.

"Oh, she's pretty bad off, all right," I say.

"You're looking a little peaked yourself. Let's go to the cafeteria. We'll talk."

⊰⊱

The cafeteria is closed, save for the tables and chairs that remain available for use. What we've got instead is vending machine heaven. Ruth buys tea and chocolate fudge Pop-Tarts while I get the mystery beverage labelled "Coffee."

We find seats and Ruth says, "So you wanted to ask Delphina home with you."

"Yes."

"But something held you back."

"Yes."

Ruth dunks her tea bag in her cup of hot water. "Maybe you still don't forgive her."

I nod, swallow. "Maybe not."

"And Will? Do you forgive him?"

I look down, away.

"He misses you, Janey. Being with you, I mean."

"Not tonight," I say. "I think he was plenty happy to leave for Virginia."

"Do you really think that?"

"No, I guess not." I sip at my coffee. I am anxious, anyway, from all that's been happening; the caffeine is probably the last thing I need, and yet its warmth comforts me.

"She seduced him, you know," Ruth says. "Not the other way around."

I stare at Ruth, and tilt my head. It is a cheap vending machine coffee cup I hold in my hands, and yet I hold the cup like a baby chick, just like that, between my hands, as though it were precious, and had a tiny heartbeat. "Sorry?" I say.

"Maybe this is a good time to bring this up," Ruth says. "Maybe not. But I thought you should know."

I look around the cafeteria and try to get my bearings. Does this matter? Does it matter if Barbara Kirkbridge pursued my husband, and not the other way around?

Ruth is waiting to see if I want to go on with this. She is patient. She lifts her tea bag from its cup, and winds the tea bag around her plastic spoon to squeeze the water out.

"Why, uh, why are you telling me this now?"

"Honestly?"

"Yes."

"I didn't think you were ready to listen."

"And now?"

Ruth smiles. "You appear to be listening just fine."

I swallow. It's hard to talk about this. So hard. I say, "So you think Barbara pursued *him*."

"I'm certain of it."

"Why?" I pause, frown. "And why the past tense, anyway? How do we even know the affair is over?"

"Because it was never an affair in the first place."

"What *was* it, then?"

"Something that happened once. A regrettable...error."

I look at Ruth, wait.

"You understand, this is all based on what Will has told me. He himself never blamed Barbara." Ruth pauses. "The night it happened was the night Will took his clients to dinner at the Chaucer Inn."

I grimace. That was the night Will and I had that argument. The night he left me in anger, his footsteps echoing down the hospital corridor. I could have run after him, but I didn't.

"Are you okay?" Ruth says.

"Yes," I say. "Go on."

"Well, the dinner went on quite a while. Finally, the clients went home. Will stayed on, alone at the table, sipping coffee. He'd had wine with dinner and he wanted to give it some time. When he got up to leave, there was Barbara waiting for him out there in the parking lot. He was just getting into his car; she came over and hopped in."

"Friendly."

"Oh, and it gets friendlier. He said he really needed to be going, and that's when she told him she had a crush on him, that she had for some time. She started kissing him."

The word *kissing* goes on and on in my head. After the word *kissing* there are no more words. My mind throws up a wall. "Ruth," I finally say, "he still could have said no."

"Yes," she says. "He could have."

"You condone what he did."

"Not condone. *Understand.* He was lonely. He made a mistake. Haven't *you* ever made a mistake?"

❦

I leave Ruth and tell her I need a minute.

I go outside the ER. If I'm looking for fresh air, I've come to the wrong place. The night is suffocatingly close; every smell that comes off that sidewalk just hangs in the air—oil and grease from the asphalt turnaround, bubble gum left to melt, the scuff marks of people's shoes, their disappointed dreams. Even so, I tap out a cigarette and light up. I have become one of those misfits you look at and shake your head, wondering what kind of crazy they are. *Smoking,* in air too humid to breathe. But now I know. The next time I see somebody smoking on a night way too hot for anything but complaining, I'll know they're maybe smoking because it's all they can think to do, to keep from falling apart.

Even while I am grateful for a friend like Ruth, who cares deeply about me, I am reeling from what she has shared. I try not to picture Will and Barbara there in the hotel room, the passion inside that room, the loneliness sitting in the corner, in the empty drawer where the Gideon Bible would be kept. I try not to think of them together, and of course that is all I *can* think of—his sounds, her sounds, her sounds that would be different from mine. How did the sheets feel, rough or smooth? Did they play the radio? Was their coupling frenzied or slow and meandering? When he climaxed, did he close his eyes? Did he think of me at all? Or, was I banished from the room, kept away by the DO NOT DISTURB tag hanging from the door?

I pace in front of the hospital, then stop to take a deep drag on my cigarette, exhale. And what about Delphina? I am thinking about her, too. Impossible to forget what she said in her police report—how Clyde slammed her into the wall so hard, her head gouged a hole in the plaster, how it felt to be throttled, his massive hands squeezing off her air supply, her momentary illusion of safety when he quit hitting her only to yank her by the roots of her hair to hurl her down the stairs, where her skull bounced bm bm bm and her whole body went tumbling, out of control, with nothing to stop her until she reached the landing. Just like there was nothing to stop us, my brother and my mother and I when we hit that ice slick and tobogganed through woods by the frozen lake until we hit that grandfather birch. BAM.

Delphina...Delphina...I think.

I start to cry. The thing of it is, I don't know why. I am sad, for me and Will, for Delphina, but there's also rage mixed up in there, because I am still unable to forgive either of them.

In a minute or two I wipe away my tears, toss my cigarette to the sidewalk, and grind it out, then go inside to invite Delphina home.

CHAPTER 9

My heart's not in this, and Delphina knows it. Sedated as she is, she interprets my mood.

Well, she always was smart.

"You wanna tell me, Skinny Lady?"

"What?"

"What's eatin' you."

I shake my head.

It's after midnight, and Delphina's been discharged. We're sitting in my van in front of the hospital. We're waiting for Ruth to fetch her car. When Ruth finds us, we'll caravan home.

"You won't rap with me, at least gimme a smoke."

I frown at her. "You shouldn't be smoking."

"I shouldn't be wearing no bandages round my head and my arm stuck in a cast, neither, but here I is."

"Okay, okay," I say.

I light Delphina's cigarette and stick it in her mouth. I am careful to avoid the purpled swell in her lip, but that is all. I give the gesture not an ounce of tenderness, and Delphina notices. "Come on, girl. Say it."

"What?"

"My body's in a heap o' pain, and it be all my fault. I shoulda left Clyde. I left him, this wouldn't be happenin'."

"Well," I say. I bite my lip. I am thinking *Please. Not now. Just let it go.*

But she can't. Maybe her mind is swirling from the painkillers they gave her and that's why she lacks good sense, or maybe she really wants to get to the bottom of this. "Fess up, girl. I *knows* what you thinkin'."

I try not to respond, one last effort to hold back the words, but they are waiting at the door. I open it and they come tumbling out, "Why'd you have to get drunk, Delph? The day I came to take you to the shelter."

"It be too hard not to."

"All you had to do was stay sober."

She stares at me. "You jus' don' understand."

"Understand what?"

"The black hole."

"What black hole?"

"You be sucked down into. You be trapped."

I shake my head. "You know," I say, "Delph, you're right. I don't understand. Why you don't run like hell from a bastard like that, who hurts you, who might even goddam kill you one day if he gets drunk enough or mad enough or maybe because he just feels like it. Well, I just don't have a clue." I am trembling as I say this. I've lit up my own cigarette by now, but the cigarette's not helping calm my nerves one bit. I yank open the car ashtray and stub out my cigarette.

I am looking out the windshield, and, suddenly, I don't know why, I get that feeling in the pit of my stomach, the same exact feeling as on the day the man followed me home from school. I peer into the shadows that surround the hospital. A couple goes through the entrance doors, the woman huge with child, the man solicitous and worried. That is all. I glance into my rearview mirror, and see the sweep of headlights in the dark, tense. I recognize the car and release my pent-up breath. It's just Ruth. Her car pulls up behind us. We're ready to go.

I shove the van into drive, but I still don't leave the curb.

"You buckled up?" I ask Delphina.

"Hell," she says, "we be in a accident, I get banged up some, I figure it be an improvement."

"Put your seatbelt on. I mean it."

The drive home is not long. We don't talk. Ruth follows in her car. The roads are quiet. Well, it's late.

Finally, we pull up in front of my house.

"This where you live, Skinny Lady?" Delphina asks. Clearly she's trying to make up between us. "This be real nice."

"Thanks," I say. I switch off the engine. "Here, I'll come around and help you out." In my rearview mirror, I see Ruth drive by in her station wagon. She parks by her house.

I climb from the van. I have cranked open my door and I am just thrusting it closed when I hear a sound I shouldn't. It is of another car, cruising fast. Ours is a private street, not much traffic. Who else could it be at this hour?

A Mustang careens into view. Rusted chassis. No hubcaps. My stomach gets that clamped down feeling and I know now what I knew by instinct all along; we were followed from the hospital. It is Clyde.

In all our discussions, we assumed the police would have no trouble apprehending him. But here he is. He's in such a hurry, he barely screeches to a halt before he hurls open his driver's door and leaps out. His radio's blasting a rap song that pounds its beat so thunderously the Mustang shimmies and vibrates.

Ka thump...boom...boom. Ka thump...Ka thump...

I have never seen Clyde before in person, and what goes through my mind is, *dangerous*. Muscled and bulky, he is not just big, he is colossal; his rage sizzles in the already hot greasy air. And that's not all. He is high on something. It is not merely intoxication. Something about his eyes. Your eyes don't get that way from just alcohol.

Our neighborhood is dark, but there are street lamps. I can see he is bare-handed. But then he is so powerful, his body itself is a weapon. He conquers the asphalt in three strides. I have just the van between him and me and it does not seem like nearly enough.

"Where my old lady?" he hollers to me, and then he spots her, cowering, inside the dark interior of the van.

"Lock up!" I warn her. "Put the buttons down!"

She just manages to lock the van when Clyde seizes the door handle and yanks on it, growling in frustration because the door won't budge.

I suck the stale night air into my lungs. I am quivering, my whole body, but I make my voice steady, "You don't want to do this," I tell Clyde. "Why don't you...Just. Go. Away."

For a moment, I think, incredibly, that he is going to take my advice. He turns back toward his Mustang, which still pulsates with the heavy bass from his sound system, the concussive vibrations low and rumbling and visceral, and so powerful I can feel the *Ka thump...boom...boom. Ka thump...Ka thump...*pounding into the black asphalt, clear across the street, and up through my shoes, through my legs, right into me.

Clyde doesn't get into his Mustang and drive off. He reaches into the trunk for something, and when he turns around again, I see the crowbar.

When I think crowbar I think *steel*. I think *heavy*. But you'd never know this judging by Clyde. He hefts the crowbar light and easy; it's a beach ball to him, a plaything.

Even in my panic, I spy Ruth across the street sizing up the situation. I pray she'll have the presence of mind to slip into her house and phone the police.

The bass thumps in the Mustang.

I holler, hoarsely, "Clyde! Let's think about this!"

But all he does is laugh.

He strides across the street, pivots, and with one magnificent swing, unleashes the crowbar at the van window. Cobweb fractures radiate out from the central blow, but the window holds. Growling, he bludgeons the window again, the contact so violent his shoulders judder. This time the glass shatters in a hail of broken teeth upon the ground. He flips the button, hurls open the door, and wrenches Delphina from the van. He locks her neck in the commanding embrace of his sweaty bicep. All I can see of her expression is her mouth, which twists in pain.

"Please!" I cry. "Let go of her!"

"This ain't none of your bidness!" Scowling, he drags Delphina toward the Mustang. Glass crunches and sparkles under the streetlamps. Delphina goes limp in his arms. She does not fight him.

I stand there on the sidewalk. All of this, everything, is her fault; Delphina's right, I do think that. She has willingly enslaved herself to Clyde. She has let him dominate her with all the force and subtlety of a natural disaster. Why in God's name would she do this? I don't understand. Choosing Clyde is suicide.

And yet, and yet.

Haven't I contemplated suicide myself these past weeks? The urge to do myself in and take the easy way out.

I claim not to understand Delphina. But this is not true. I understand her *exactly*, and that's why I can't forgive her.

The black hole.

What black hole?

You be sucked down into. You be trapped....

She told me about the black hole, and I pretended not to understand. But I do.

He's hauled her over to the Mustang. He's getting ready to shovel her into the car. If I'm going to help, it has to be now.

Clyde has the height and weight advantage. And all those drugs whirling in his bloodstream. All I have going for me is surprise. Adrenaline pumps through my veins, and a frenzied clarity takes hold. I don't care if Clyde is bigger than me; I am too full of fury. My ears are ringing. Heat pops behind my eyes. I launch myself at him in a flying tackle.

He does not flatten me. I am lucky, that way. But he shrugs me off, quite easily, then flourishes that crowbar, cranking it up high above his shoulders. His eyes pinwheel from the drugs. He's about to smash that crowbar down, unpack all that gravity and steel on me. I see it coming. But I am not fast enough to dodge the blow. I suppose I am fortunate that he misses my skull and collarbone and connects only with the meat of my thigh. Even so, the pain is monumental.

I clutch my leg, keening in agony. My thigh is a bonfire of white heat, flames that shoot down the length of me, into my toes. I stagger forward on the street, struggle for balance. I grit my teeth, and fight to remain conscious. My vision swims in and out.

But the worst part is not physical. Clyde has rattled me down to my soul. Oh, I was scared of him before, but not like this. My terror gallops way beyond fear. To regression. To paralysis. My insides are watery. The whole world is Clyde and me. Clyde is thunder and lightning. He is hurricane, volcano, flood, and fire, and I am nothing.

I want to whimper, to plead with him, "Not again! Please don't hit me again!"

I will do anything he wants if he just promises to not hurt me.

And here, now, I realize for a split second what it feels like to be Delphina.

Nauseated and dazed, I feel my knees buckle. I am submitting to a blow that hasn't even happened yet. This is what Clyde has done to me. I glance up, and here it comes. But, no, the crowbar misses me, slams onto the asphalt. In my instant of freedom, I know I should run. Get away. It would be so easy. But I can't leave Delphina. Instead, I hurl myself toward the crowbar, throw my weight at it, and tackle it. Clyde, caught offguard, fumbles the crowbar.

Now I've got the crowbar. I possess it.

From the Mustang the rap song pulsates; my own brain pulsates; *Ka thump...boom...boom. Ka thump....Ka thump...*

Recovered, now, from his astonishment, Clyde lumbers toward me. I know I have only one chance. *Ka thump....* I gather together all my anger at all the losses I have ever suffered, and I gather all my love, too, and I grip that crowbar like a baseball bat and power it up and away. I connect solidly, *boom*, the thudding force of impact vibrating up my arms and into my shoulders as the crowbar snags his groin. At first he is, merely, shocked. His mouth opens and closes silently, like one of Sarah's goldfish. Then the pain finds him. He heaves his lungs in search of air, and, clutching his balls, doubles over to retch on the street. I raise the crowbar again. There is a savage thing that beats inside me. The music is still pulsing. I am pulsing in rhythm with it. *Ka thump...*and I heft the crowbar and aim to crack his skull. Payback time.

One of the hardest things I've ever done is to sigh and lower that crowbar. Clyde's not about to attack anybody, not now; he is defenseless. And so I stand there, shuddering, my muscles in spasm, my injured thigh complaining ferociously, as two police cruisers rocket down the street. Ruth must have dialed 911, because here they are, wailing away, *wee-aw, wee-aw, wee-aw,* their sirens loud enough to drown out even that Mustang's rap song. Doors fly open, three officers in blue drop to a crouch and level their firearms at Clyde. I hear the click of their safetys being removed, and I am glad.

The rest happens in a blur. I hear commands, directed at Clyde. I see Clyde slammed up and spreadeagled against his Mustang, Clyde searched for weapons. Clyde is just starting to resist again, his groin recovered by now, when they snap handcuffs on him and prod him into the dark night of the cruiser.

I look toward Delphina. Under the arc of the streetlamps, I can't tell if she's crying or not. I hobble across the street toward her. I don't really have anything to say, I just wouldn't mind sitting beside her.

And that is when time stops, for me. All around us there is a cacophony of noise. A third police cruiser races up, siren blaring; car doors slam open and closed; police walkie-talkies squawk, but within me there is a mothy cocoon of silence. I put my arm around Delphina, so I can include her in the silence, too.

≈)⊂≈

About an hour later, we're in my house. A police car is parked across the street with an officer inside keeping watch over us, more a courtesy than anything else since Clyde is truly in custody. But Delphina and I appreciate it. Delphina, in fact, felt relaxed enough, or worn out enough, to drop off to sleep on my sofa. I cover her with a blanket and let her be.

≈)⊂≈

I'm just about to head upstairs myself when I hear footsteps on the porch. The lock clicks in the door, the door opens, and Will steps in.

"I got news for you," I tell him. "This isn't Virginia. You must've made a heck of a wrong turn."

"No, I made the right turn for once," he says. "I turned back."

He opens his arms and I move into them, and for a moment, we lean together like old trees.

Afterward

At our cabin on Windsor Island, Ruth and I make s'mores and carry them into the living room where Will and Sarah are sprawled out on the braided rug playing *Monopoly* near the wood-burning stove. It is Memorial Day weekend, but cold enough up here in the Adirondacks to warrant a fire.

At sunset, after Will is badly trounced by a gleeful Sarah, he tosses two more oak logs into the belly of the cast-iron stove, stands up to brush sawdust from his jeans, and turns to me and asks me if I want to take a walk. I tell him I do.

We bring along the flashlight. We're starting off in plenty of daylight, but you never know; some woods are darker than others. We don't need the flashlight yet, though. I swing it along in my hand as we stride along the path. We can still see everything we need to with the naked eye—the pine cones, deer droppings, roots, moss, the tendency of the trail, a curve to the left, a curve to the right, a gradual or steep incline. It is a sweet pleasure, this walk at sunset. The air so refreshing and cool, but the sepia light begins to gray, and colors fade, just enough so I can tell it would be very hard to hike these woods in the total dark. You would grow frantic with the sound of your own breathing. You would stumble with no moon.

The final stretch of woods ends at the boathouse. We walk the causeway to the boathouse dock. Will takes my hand, and our sneakers bounce along the wood planks. The planks give a little under our weight, sloshing water, but that is the only sound we hear. We stop at the edge of the dock and sit. The lake spreads out before us. The horizon is layers and layers of ruffled pink, like pink carnations laid down to rest on their sides. From here I can see our cabin. I can see the green shadows in the cove where this morning Sarah and I caught a sizeable tree root, but no fish.

The mood of the lake changes hourly. Earlier today, there was a rainstorm and the wind kicked up. The waves were roiling with turbulence, white-capped and frothy, but now the lake is so still. It is like glass. I have never seen the lake quite like this. The trees are mirrored perfectly, if backwards, in the water. The clouds, too. They are full-bodied and cumulus, as white as Queen Anne's Lace. A bird flies by and I can follow its progress; in the air, or on the water, it is the same. Even the boathouse, which looks like a green barn, can look upon itself and see its twin.

In the pink of the sunset, we hear first the drone of an airplane, then a motorboat. The noise disturbs the stillness, but only momentarily. When the lake settles back into itself again, we continue to sit beside each other; our shoulders and thighs do not even touch, but it is the closest we have been in weeks.

Since the incident with Clyde, and all that happened with Delphina, we've been quiet with each other, the way you are quiet when you have not too few but too many things to say.

"Delphina wrote you a postcard, I see," Will says.

"It came on the mailboat."

"What's it say?"

"It's postmarked Petal, Mississippi. That's her hometown. She says she's feeling pretty good. She's singing in the choir again. At church. Says she's looking for a job."

"That's good."

"Yes," I nod.

We are silent for a moment.

Then Will asks, "What did it feel like, anyway?"

I look at him. "What did what feel like?"

"To go up against Clyde."

We are a million miles away from the thumping beat of Clyde's Mustang. My thigh is no longer black and blue, just yellow and gray now, a little tender. But I remember. "It was scary. I've never been so scared. When he hit me with that crowbar, something inside me shifted. I realized I had lost my son, but I had other things, and I could lose them too if I wasn't careful."

He asks, in a low voice, "What about Barbara?"

"You mean, are we gonna fight about her?" I shake my head. "Not anymore."

I gaze out over the water. The whole scene is so beautiful, really, I don't know why this particular stand of birches calls to me. But I notice the trees on the opposite shore, edging the cove. They arch out over the lake with such grace, such green elegance, they disguise the fact that this is, after all, a competition for sunlight, which gives them life.

I look at Will. He hasn't said anything for awhile. He is still staring out over the water, but he is no longer seeing the lake or the trees; he has gone deep within himself. He says, "It's not too late, you know. To have another."

I squeeze his hand. "Oh, I don't think so."

"Me neither."

"I'm not bitter. It's just—"

"—something we're not going to have." He nods. "But remember all we *do* have."

We sit in silence for a minute. "This is comfortable," I say. I lean back into my husband's arms, and before I know it, I'm yawning.

"Tired?"

"Yes."

"Let's head back to the cabin," he says, but I put my finger to his lips; I have heard something. Together we listen, tilt our heads, barely breathing, as the sound of the loon finds us.

It is a forlorn cry, touched with hysteria, and yet this evening we are glad to hear it. It is the kind of thing you're afraid one day you'll have to hear a recording of because loons will be extinct, and that would be a shame because a loon's tremolo over still water is music.

They say that loons search for each other that way, singing their love songs; they aren't so very different from us. Will and I listen until the loon glides past, still without a mate. Then Will stands up and reaches out his hand to me, and I take it.

ABOUT THE AUTHOR

Carol McAfee has published a mystery, *The Climbing Tree*, and a young adult book, *Who's the Kid around Here?* She lives in Baltimore, Maryland, with her husband and two daughters.